# MAGIC, MIRTH & MAYHEM

by

## Susie Swenson

Cove and
Lantern Books

## Titles by Susie Swenson:

### Havenwood Cove Series
*In Reading Order*

**Magic, Mirth & Mayhem**


**Coming Soon**
Secrets, Spells & Shadows

# Dedication

To Deanna —
Thank you for your insight, help, and endless encouragement while I wrote this book. Love, Mom

In Memory of my mother, Marijo Swenson, who introduced me to fantasy late in life and started me on my current road. Wish you were here to see this book.

### Special Acknowledgment

To my dear friend Pam, who wears many hats. Official titles include: Lorekeeper's Shadow, Assistant to the Keeper of the Realm, and, on many days, Techno-Fae of the Inner Circle. Your attention to detail and steady support kept me on track (and mostly sane).

# Contents

# Chapter One

May 20 - Mornings, Mishaps & the Myth of Ordinary

"Happy big 4-0 to me," Seraphina Blackthorn muttered as she scanned her final divorce papers with mixed emotions. Freedom lay in those documents—a clean slate to start anew, but it also marked the death of a dream. Fifteen years with Evan Stanford—love of her life turned snake in the grass—and nothing to show for it. "Not a damn thing."

She squared her shoulders even as her nails beat a rhythm on the table. Love had shattered the moment she found him "celebrating" their anniversary with his young admin. She'd left her home, her job, her marriage, and his powerful family had made sure her career lay in ruins.

Sera stuffed the paperwork back into the envelope. Evan's betrayal still stung, but it was his baby—his new son, born just last week to the mistress who stole her life—that twisted the knife. Anger. Sadness. Regret. It all churned. Even if she admitted the marriage had been dying long before the affair.

"Breathe," she ordered herself, shoving a golden-red strand of hair behind her ear. She clutched the heart-shaped crystal at her neck. Its warmth calmed and grounded her. "What a fool I was."

She slapped the table with the envelope before tossing it away from her. It slid into a vase of roses, lilies, and sunflowers. A cheerful *Happy Birthday* balloon poked out from the blooms. The gift from her mother provided a cheery splash of color, but its sweet scent couldn't mask the townhouse's musty air of neglect.

Compared to the mansion she'd shared with Evan, the cramped townhouse reminded her just how far she'd fallen. She inhaled deeply. "Not fallen—freed," she said aloud as she squared her shoulders and thumped the table with her knuckles. "I have my life back. But now what?" Accounting was all she knew, but the thought of working for another big firm left her feeling cold. Maybe she'd start her own CPA business—or leave numbers behind and try something new.

Elbows planted on the table, chin resting on her interlaced fingers, she blew out a breath and considered her options. The townhouse came fully furnished, as she'd taken very little from her marriage. No sense in accumulating stuff until she found a permanent place to settle.

A screeching sound, like an owl with laryngitis, interrupted her thoughts and broke the silence. Her head whipped around to the front door. "Stupid doorbell needs replacing," she muttered, "along with the refrigerator and stove—all on their last legs."

Crossing the room, she peeked through the peephole. A man wearing a delivery driver uniform stood on the tiny porch, holding an enormous bouquet of purple blooms. A smile tugged at her lips. More flowers for her birthday? She opened the door, a welcoming smile in place. "Good morning," she said, eyeing the bouquet with pleasure.

"Delivery for Seraphina Blackthorn," the driver announced, his soft voice carrying the hint of a musical accent nearly drowned out by the whooshing sound of a bus braking behind him. He bowed his head slightly, touching the brim of his hat with two fingers in an informal greeting.

"That's me." The scent of peppermint made her draw a deep breath. Her heart clenched as it reminded her of her father, who'd loved to suck on the red and white candies. He'd always shared his stash with her, even though her mother disapproved.

Tears stung her eyes. She swiped a finger beneath her eyes. In front of her, the driver's form shimmered faintly, as though there were two of them. "Sorry. You remind me of someone."

The driver's eyes flickered with something she couldn't quite name—recognition? Familiarity? She blinked, and the strange feeling vanished.

"Then these should cheer you." He extended the bouquet with a smile and another head bow.

Sera stepped out onto the tiny square porch to accept the heavy crystal vase, wrapping both hands around it. Her eyes widened with pleasure. "Wow. These are beautiful," she said, studying the vibrant purple blooms with glowing blue centers. Their scent hit her like a wave—heady and intoxicating. She laughed softly. "Like catnip to a cat," she imagined aloud, as she'd never owned one.

He tipped his head, indicating her necklace. "The flowers match your *aestralite* crystal," he offered, his voice deepening.

Sera touched the purple and blue crystal, comforted by its warmth. "I've never heard of that stone. I thought this was either Alexandrite or Aqua Aura."

"*Aestralite* of the Celestial Gate," he affirmed. "A very rare stone," he added with a smile.

She tilted her head to one side. "Hmm, okay. Whatever it is, it's ... it's special to me."

"More than you know," he murmured, his tone heavy with meaning.

Sera frowned, but before she could respond, he pulled a wrapped package from inside his jacket and held it out. She switched the vase to one arm and held out her hand. Their fingers touched as he passed her the wrapped parcel—soft brown paper tied with black twine. "A gift," he murmured, eyes too shadowed to read. "Old truths wrapped in silence ... gifts once lost, now returned. Let memory bloom, and the new take root."

A shimmer in the air followed by the snap of static electricity startled her. She gasped as a pulse shot up her arm, spreading through her body in a searing wave that flushed her skin. The words lodged deep—not just in her bones, but in her chest, her mind, her memory. They echoed in her skull like a song she'd forgotten the lyrics to but somehow still knew by heart. She froze, the cadence of his voice threading through her—strangely familiar, hauntingly intimate. She swayed slightly, disoriented, as though something important hovered just out of reach. Something she should know. Or remember.

The warmth from their contact wasn't unpleasant. It was familiar, like stepping into sunlight after being in the shadows. She shook her head to clear her mind. A strangled laugh escaped as she pulled her hand free, the package clutched tightly in her grasp. Her fingers twitched as if reaching for something unseen. "Wow, the air must be really dry or something." None of it made sense—her reaction, the heat, the ache in her chest.

Her smile faded when she noticed the haunted look in the driver's deep green eyes, as though he carried a heavy burden that had suddenly become too much to bear. His eyes flickered with something unreadable, watchful, waiting.

"Or something," he offered with a sad smile before drawing himself to his full height. His casual demeanor shifted, replaced by something sharper, more resolute. His gaze deepened and held hers with unnerving intensity. "Seraphina Blackthorn." His casual air vanished. "It is time to remember."

Sera clutched the gift to her chest. The command rippled through her, chilling her spine. "What? Remember what?" Her voice was barely a whisper. She cleared her throat. "Who are—"

*"Remember."* The word struck like a bell tolling in the distance. With another bow, the delivery driver tipped his hat, turned on his heel, and hurried down the steps, whistling a lilting, almost whimsical tune that was at odds with his formal, old-school behavior.

"Okay." She frowned. "That was weird. Nice but quirky old guy." She tried to put him out of her mind, but confusion gnawed at her as she stepped back inside and closed the door. The familiar tune stuck in her mind. Something about the jaunty tone resonated within her, almost a sense of déjà vu. "That tune," she murmured. "I know it, but from where?" She shrugged as the melody wrapped around her like mist and the words swam to life in her mind.

*When the stars light up the night,*
*dreams will take their flight,*
*in the moon's garden,*
*we'll be together soon.*

She closed her eyes as more verses, along with the tune, played in her head. Suddenly, she remembered. Her father used to sing that simple song to her! Another memory surfaced of her sitting on her father's lap while unwrapping her peppermint treats. Sera whirled around and stepped back outside.

She scanned the street for the driver, but there was no sign of him. Her breath caught. Something about him tugged at a memory she couldn't quite place—too familiar to be a stranger, yet impossible to name. She pressed the door closed and leaned her forehead against it as if the wood might steady her. Her chest ached with an old longing, the kind stirred by forgotten songs and half-remembered faces. Whatever her heart wanted, it was impossible.

Turning, she held the vase up and studied the bouquet. Who sent it? Frowning, she searched for a card but didn't find one. "Not from Mom, as I already received flowers from her, and The Cheating Bastard wouldn't remember that today was my birthday. Okay, very strange." Reflected in the cut-glass vase, her crystal glowed and fractured like a turning kaleidoscope. A shimmer of memory tugged at the edges of her mind: her as a child skipping down a forest path. She swung a basket filled with flowers, just like the ones in her arms.

*Hurry,* she called out to a shadowy figure. Sera's brows drew together as she tried to recall more, but the memory slipped away, leaving her chest tight with unease.

She shook her head to clear away the fanciful notion. "Enough. Back to reality. You have plans to make." She put the strange encounter with the driver and the unsettling return of a childhood memory behind her as she sniffed the flowers. Once again, she jerked her head back as the overly sweet scent went to her head.

"Wow." She cautiously sniffed again and felt slightly drunk on the heady scent.

She set the vase on a small table displaying her birthday cards. Today should be a celebration—forty years old, single, free. A new beginning. Yet, unease coiled in her chest. The flowers, the package, the song. They didn't feel like coincidences. Something was happening.

She wandered into the poorly lit living room; her gaze fell on the ripple-patterned crocheted afghan draped over the sagging couch. Her grandmother had given it to her when she was ten. Decades later, it still looked as new as the day she'd received it. A couple of crocheted pillows, along with a lap throw she'd just finished, added her own personal touch to the otherwise dreary room.

Plopping down onto the couch, avoiding the spot with the broken spring, Sera set the wrapped package on the worn coffee table and leaned forward to study it. She was eager to open it, yet strangely reluctant. Her encounter with the driver left her with a vague sense of unease.

"Maybe there's a card inside." Sera ran the pads of her fingers across the wrapping—which wasn't paper after all, but a giant leaf? Or softened bark? With trembling fingers, she untied the twine and slowly peeled away the wrapping. She gasped with pleasure. A journal gleamed in the dim light; its golden-brown leather cover was etched with intricate Celtic designs.

A luminous moonstone sat in the center of an embossed Tree of Life. Six glowing gemstones: emerald, amber, sapphire, amethyst, ruby and opal each pulsed faintly with an otherworldly energy and surrounded the tree. Sera picked up the journal with both hands and blinked as a faint vibration ran up her arms. "Wow," she breathed as she stroked the cover, tracing the intricate patterns.

The journal felt alive, and the moonstone reminded her of a moon peeping out between the tree branches. She touched it, surprised that it felt warm, as did each of the gleaming, polished gems. The stones and design gave the journal a magical, almost ethereal feel.

Her gaze followed the curling tree roots that intertwined in complex, vine-like patterns that anchored the entire design. The Celtic knots framing the cover gave the journal a protective and ancient appearance, as if it held secrets waiting to be unlocked. The overall effect was one of elegance and mystique.

Closing her eyes, she brought the journal to her face and inhaled the scent of ancient parchment and rain-drenched earth—magic and nature intertwined. As though waking from a dream, she opened her eyes and shook her head. "Okay, that is pure fantasy," she murmured. In her mind, she heard her mother admonishing her to be sensible and not foolish.

Sera frowned as she studied the unexpected gift. She tilted her head to one side. Was it her imagination, or was the journal larger than when she'd first picked it up? She juggled it in her hands. It also felt heavier. Instead of a small, diary-sized book, it now appeared to be the size of a family Bible.

Spooked, she dropped the leather book back onto its wrapping and stared, mouth agape.

Not her imagination. It *was* larger. Leaning forward, she tried to re-wrap it, but there wasn't enough wrapping to even cover half the front. "Not possible," she whispered, scooting back on the couch. The ancient-looking journal hummed faintly, as though alive and begging her to open its cover.

Her hands flew to her throat. Her heart skipped a beat, and she shivered. "How is this possible? Objects do not grow and change size! Or act alive." Rubbing her arms to rid herself of the chill, she murmured, "not real." She pinched herself.

"Ow! Okay, I'm awake." Her attention shifted to the small table near the door where she'd placed the vase of flowers. "Am I drugged? Hallucinating?" Was it the flowers? She shook her head to clear her mind. "No more sniffing those until I find out!"

Warm air blasted into the room and swirled around her. The gust flipped the cover of the journal open. Startled, she glanced up toward the ceiling, toward the vent. Weird. The furnace had quit weeks ago. Shrugging it off as just another malfunction in her life of imperfections, she rested her palms on the table and read the single line of script flowing across the page in gold ink that shimmered faintly:

*Do you accept?*

Sera blinked once. Twice. "No way," she breathed. Surely the words hadn't just magically appeared as if written by an unseen hand? She shook her head. "Ridiculous," she scoffed as she tipped her head to one side as she considered the question. "Accept what?"

Her voice wasn't much more than a whisper as her gaze darted to the page that held three images: a golden quill, an ornate key, and a small, pale blue envelope. Though wary, curiosity had her leaning closer to make sense of the odd gift. After all, if this was some sort of weird, drug-induced dream, it couldn't hurt her. Could it?

She focused once more on the three words that pulsed and shimmered on the page as though waiting for her answer. Reaching out, she touched the quill and gasped when she felt the downy softness of feathers. The key felt cool. Hard. So real, she swore she could pluck it from the page. The script on the envelope was too small for her to make out, so she carefully picked up the journal as though it were as fragile as a bird's nest.

Squinting, Sera still couldn't bring the handwritten lettering into focus. She sighed. One drawback to hitting the big 4-0 was the need for reading glasses, and she'd left hers on the dining room table. "Too bad I can't just snap my fingers and have them appear!"

She snapped her fingers as she stood to fetch them, when a faint sound drew her gaze back to the coffee table. Her jaw dropped when she spotted her reading glasses. She glanced from one table to the other. "I swear I left them over there." She'd needed them to read over her divorce paperwork.

"Wow, I'm being totally forgetful today. Must have dropped them here when I went to answer the door." Shrugging it off, she snatched them and put them on. Peering at the tiny graphic of the envelope, she read:

*To Seraphina Blackthorn*
*Newly Divorced Granddaughter*
*Guardian of the Moondragon*

"Woah!" Sera reached out and slammed the journal closed, the sound sharp and unnaturally loud in the room's silence. "Is this a joke? Some kind of trick?" Who knew her divorce was final? Evan, of course, but this gag, or whatever it was, was far beyond his scope of imagination. Leaning forward, she gingerly opened the cover once more and focused on the last line. "What is the Guardian of the Moondragon? Sounds like a role-playing game."

She snatched her cellphone from the table, intending to call the florist and demand answers, and just as quickly, she lowered the phone. Without a card, she didn't know where the flowers had come from. And the man who'd delivered it ... he didn't feel like a typical delivery guy. No logo on his uniform or hat. And no delivery van either.

*The driver. The flowers. The journal*—none of this made sense. And the look in his eyes when they'd held hers had seemed very personal. How could someone be a stranger and yet feel so ... familiar?

"Get a grip, Sera. It's just a weird birthday present," she told the room at large, but her instincts screamed it was more than that. Her gaze shifted to the bouquet. The blooms appeared to give off an ethereal glow. She shook her head, blinking hard. Must be a trick of the light spilling in from the bent window blinds.

Unnerved, she stood and paced from one end of the tiny room, across the dining area, into the kitchen, and back. She wanted to brush it off—brush all of it off—as a prank, but there was a nagging pull in her chest, a feeling she couldn't ignore that unsettled her. She strode into the thumb-sized kitchen to fix a soothing cup of tea. Maybe some caffeine would counteract the strange, lingering mental fuzziness she attributed to the flowers.

For a moment, she rested her palms on the counter and took several deep breaths. Her reflection in the toaster's brushed steel looked older, paler—more tired than she remembered. Not broken, but not quite whole either. Shaking off the past, she filled the electric teakettle, grimacing as the pipes banged in protest. She prayed the fuse wouldn't blow when she plugged it in. The fridge shuddered to life and let out a grinding growl.

Sera set the pot down with a bang. "Nope, no tea." The electric kettle and fridge could not be on at the same time, and her stovetop only worked now and again, as did the oven. Frustrated with a large dose of mad building inside her, Sera jabbed her finger into the fridge door.

"Knock." *Jab.* "It." *Jab.* "Off." *Jab-jab.* "I do not need you to burn out another motor. Work for another week! That's all I ask. Play nice, and I'll soon be out of here." She gave the appliance a small kick for good measure.

To her shock, the fridge fell silent. Just like that. Her breath caught. No hum, no grinding, no electrical stutter—just instant obedience. That. Was. Not. Normal. Grasping her crystal heart-shaped pendant in one hand, she stepped back and stared at her still-tingling finger that pulsed with heat, as though she'd burned it. Instinctively, she pressed her palm against the fridge, half-expecting—what? Yanking her hand away, she whispered, "Never mind. Don't want to know."

Quickly, she plugged in the kettle, casting a wary glance at the fridge as though expecting it to roar back to life. When the water boiled without incident, she scooped a spoonful of Earl Grey Lavender into the teapot, the citrusy-sweet scent familiar, comforting, as though memory itself had a fragrance.

When the kettle whistled, she poured the boiling water into her porcelain teapot, the one covered with enchanting and dancing fairies. The whimsical tea set usually made her smile. It was one of her prized possessions she'd taken with her when she moved out of Evan's home, but today, even the familiar ritual of brewing tea couldn't steady her nerves as nagging thoughts of the strange delivery driver tugged at the edge of her mind.

Once again, the tune he'd whistled played in her head, a reminder of her father. "Coincidence," she muttered. "The dead don't return to life."

After the tea leaves had steeped, Sera poured the rich, golden-brown liquid into her teacup. The scent of lavender and bergamot should've calmed her. Instead, it felt like wrapping herself in a favorite sweater that no longer fit—familiar, but wrong somehow. Her gaze kept straying across the room to the journal where it waited, innocuous yet unshakably present, as though waiting for Sera's next move. Sera paced the room. She couldn't get the three words out of her head.

*Do you accept?*

"Accept what? The question pulsed like a riddle, its answer just out of reach. She threaded her fingers through her hair. "Can't refer to the journal or flowers as I obviously already accepted those."

The question hung in the air like a puzzle, and no matter how hard she tried to dismiss it, something deep inside her whispered that this was more than just an unusual birthday present. The journal felt ... alive. She could feel its energy radiating clear across the room. But more than that, it felt as though it belonged to her; a long-lost treasure newly returned. Which was ridiculous, as she'd never set eyes upon it before.

*Old truths wrapped in silence ... gifts once lost, now returned. Let memory bloom, and the new take root.*

"Old truths ... gifts once lost, let memory bloom ..." she recited.

"What did all that mean?" she asked the empty room. Her tea forgotten, she continued to pace, her gaze flicking back to the journal where it waited. But for what? The question, *do you accept,* echoed in her mind, pulling her closer with each step. Returning to the couch, she sat and reluctantly pulled the journal onto her lap and opened it. The gold-inked words on the first page still shimmered, asking the same question: *Do you accept?*

Once again, she traced the quill with a trembling fingertip and again felt a strange vibration deep in her very soul. Her breath caught in her throat, and she snatched her fingers away. A mix of awe and trepidation tightened her chest. This wasn't just an *old journal*—it was infused with purpose.

"Come on, Sera. Now you're being fanciful." Yet, deep down, she knew it to be so.

Before her eyes, the words faded, and new text flowed across the page as if written by the same invisible hand. Sera gulped, her hands flying to her face as she stared in disbelief.

No. Not disbelief. Recognition. Deep inside her, beneath the layers of logic and numbers, she had always known she was meant for more. That the world had secrets no one else could see. The ink shimmered, and her pulse thumped in sync with the flickering gold letters. A voice not quite her own whispered inside her mind: *Remember.* Her fingers sought and found her crystal as she read:

*Seraphina Blackthorn, you are a hereditary witch, gifted with a lineage woven with magic. You are in line as the seventh Guardian of the Moondragon, a title passed down through generations, with each Guardian sworn to protect and uphold the balance between realms. This legacy is as old as our family itself, a binding call that marks us as both protectors and keepers of ancient magic. The tapestry of our world is woven with threads of magic and the hues of countless dawns and dusks. A light, bright and steadfast, marks the legacy of our lineage. This light, so delicate yet strong, is now entrusted to your care, as it once was to mine and to those who walked the path before us.*

Sera's eyes widened as she reread the words: *You are a hereditary witch.* She chewed her lower lip, rejecting the declaration. "A witch?" Her voice rose with disbelief as she stared at the journal's shimmering words. Her laugh was sharp and hollow. "I'm a divorced forty-year-old woman living in a townhouse, not some mystical being guarding a castle. Witches belong in fairytales."

Yet what if it were true? A witch? Her? She laughed, a dry, incredulous sound that filled the silent room. "Okay, this was definitely a joke." She'd lived her whole life grounded in reality, in numbers, logic, and the comfort of proven facts. Witches were characters in stories, in fantasies, not ... family. She'd locked her imagination away the day she started college, trading daydreams for deadlines and make believe for financial statements.

The words *ancient magic* jumped out at her. She shook her head in denial. She said them aloud, as though tasting the foreign words. A faint thrill ran through her, mingling with a surge of skepticism. Her practical side rebelled—she was Seraphina Blackthorn, an ex-accountant from Boston, not some spell-casting, mystical protector. And yet, another part of her, long buried and almost forgotten, responded to the words as if they were an answer to questions she hadn't known existed deep within her.

"I should toss this book in the garbage and get on with planning the rest of my life." She groaned. "What life?" Drawn almost against her will, she traced a golden sentence and, holding her breath, she continued to read.

*I, Elowen Blackthorn, bear the title Guardian of the Moondragon—a role held with pride, humility, and an unbreakable resolve to protect the magic within our veins. This journal is more than mere pages; it is a vessel for our ancestors' magic, their triumphs, fears, sorrows, and joys. But above all, it holds their dreams, woven into this sacred book to guide, protect, and empower you, the next Guardian.*

*Today, I pass to you the title of Guardian of the Moondragon, a birthright and sacred responsibility. You, my granddaughter, are more than worthy. Your courage cannot be taught, and your spirit is as fierce as our family's love. Each stone on the cover, borne by the Guardians before you, holds their strength and wisdom. May these stones be a well of strength in times of need and a reminder of the indomitable spirit that dwells within you.*

*This power is meant to be wielded with honor, compassion, and the knowledge that you are never alone. Shadows move within our world, and I fear they will break free. The time approaches for the true Guardian to stand, or all will be lost.*

As the words pulsed on the page, the air in her lungs left with an audible whoosh. Sera's heart thudded in response. What shadows? Breathing shallowly, she continued to read.

*My heart aches for the burden you bear, but I know you alone are capable. You are our only hope, and my pride in you is boundless.*

*Remember, once accepted, this legacy cannot be undone. It is a vow, a bond, tying you to the protection of our realm and to the Guardians who came before.*

The final line shimmered, golden and steady: *Do you, Seraphina Blackthorn, accept the title of Guardian of the Moondragon, with all the honor, power, and sacrifice it entails?*

Sera leaned back and chewed her lower lip. "Guardian of the Moondragon? What does this even mean?" she whispered as she reread the words, half-hoping they'd change. But they remained, golden and shimmering, waiting for her to accept a reality she couldn't quite grasp.

The question shimmered before her, as unyielding as fate.

Sera's breath caught. Her gaze jumped from one word to another.

*Legacy? Shadows? Sacrifice?*

*Grandmother?* She fingered the afghan beneath her. She'd grown up believing she had no other living family except her mother.

Needing a moment to think and absorb everything, she set the journal back on the table. The words on the page stirred something deep within her. Logic told her to laugh it off, wait for someone to own up to the best prank of the year, yet a long-buried part of her— a part that used to dream—ached to believe. She ran her fingers over the smooth page, feeling the weight of the words sinking in. Was this real? Could it be? She closed one hand around her crystal. It pulsed, throbbing in sync with her heartbeat—low and insistent, like it *wanted something from her*. Like the journal was somehow alive.

*Accept your birthright, your legacy.* She tapped her front teeth with one nail as the words popped into and out of her mind.

*Shadows threaten our world ... True Guardian to step forward ...*

Sera swallowed hard, her hands trembling as she closed the cover, studied the leather design, and admired the stones nestled on its surface. Leaning forward, she touched each one, gasping as they glowed faintly, their warmth radiating a soft hum that sent a thrill up her arm, leaving her feeling breathless.

"Witches? Magic? Legacies?" Sera muttered. "Nope. Not real."

Yet, as she opened the journal again and the shimmering words refused to fade, her doubts wavered. Accepting this would mean accepting all of it: magic, realms, quests—things from fantasy fiction. But what if it were true? She had always craved more— more than spreadsheets and safe choices. Once, she'd dreamed of being the hero in her own fairytale, before her mother's sharp words chased those dreams into silence.

Some part of her, long buried under practicality and logic, still wanted to believe. She pressed her palms against her knees, her mind spinning, her gaze held by the shimmering words: *Guardian of the Moondragon.* It was absurd, impossible. There was nothing special about her. In fact, her life had crumbled—from a prestigious VP position to an out-of-work divorcee. How could she be some heroine or Guardian of ancient worlds? Yet there it was, a formal, elegant document, as legally binding as her divorce decree.

The page opposite shivered. Her eyes widened and her jaw dropped when the golden quill rose from the page, its sharpened tip glowing faintly as it etched the final question, unyielding and eternal.

*Do you accept?*

The room seemed to hold its breath. Sera swallowed hard, her pulse hammering in her ears as she sat back and drew her knees to her chest. The weight of the words settled over her as a feeling of destiny took hold. The ending lines echoed in her mind, unshakable:

*Once accepted, the legacy cannot be undone. Do you accept?*
*Sera didn't move. Not yet. But something inside her already had.*

# Chapter Two

May 20 - Through the Looking Glass and into Trouble

The quill hovered, defying gravity, defying reason. "This isn't happening," Sera whispered, hugging her knees to her chest, her fists clenched as though to stop herself from reaching out to see if the quill was real or a figment of her imagination. The golden quill hung poised over the journal.

Magic wasn't real.

Yet the quill floated above the journal, tapping the air insistently, demanding her answer. Her acceptance.

"I'm going crazy." Her head dropped to her knees, and she tried to cling to logic. *This is just a vivid dream.* Magic belonged in fantasies, not in her cramped, ordinary living room. Scrambling off the couch, she fled to the bathroom, her breath hitching as she splashed cold water on her face.

"Just a dream," she repeatedly told her reflection in a voice not quite steady. But the pale woman staring back—bright green eyes wide with panic framed by a mane of wild, golden-red curls that tumbled around her face and shoulders—looked all too real. "Me, a witch? Absurd," she stated. Numbers and facts were her reality, not spells and magic.

Staring into her confused eyes, her reflection rippled and swirled, transitioning into something impossibly vivid—a golden beach stretching to the horizon. She felt the cool spray of saltwater on her skin, heard the cries of gulls in her ears and laughter from a child running into the ocean, a blaze of gold and ember curls streaming behind her and her father lifting her high to avoid being knocked down by the waves. Before she could process the memory, another followed, this one of her, slightly older, walking along a forest path with her father.

The memory tasted bitter as it reminded her of all she'd lost when her father had died. It was as though her memories had also died with him. A fresh wave of grief rose. Had she grieved for him? How could she have when she didn't remember him beyond peppermint candy and a silly song? Her grief felt sharp and raw and not just for the father she'd forgotten, or her grandmother, but everything, including magic—if it truly was real.

Palms flat on the sink, Sera leaned forward. "How did I forget this?" she whispered, tears pricking her eyes. Another glance in the mirror revealed a cheerful Victorian house painted a buttery yellow. Wildflowers danced in the breeze, their scent mingling with the sharp tang of the ocean. And then she saw her—Nonie Wenna. Her grandmother, standing in the doorway, her golden-red hair glinting in the sunlight.

The images in the mirror were too vivid to be imagined, too real. The odd driver's voice telling her—no, commanding her—to remember echoed in her mind.

Sera touched her lips with trembling fingers. "I do. I remember," she whispered as her gaze drank in the sight of her grandmother wearing a flowing tunic and a floppy hat crowned with wildflowers. Her emerald-green eyes shimmered, deep and knowing, as if they carried the weight of a thousand secrets.

Sera reached up to touch a strand of her own hair, perfectly matching the older woman's. The image in the mirror shimmered and glowed, and Sera swore she felt the warm rays of sunlight bathing her face, even as clouds stirred overhead.

Each memory slammed into her like a wave—salt-laced, stinging, unstoppable. "Why didn't I remember all of this until now?" she asked, her voice thick with tears. Sera's fists clenched, the sharp sting of her nails digging into her flesh, grounding her. Anger warred with grief—anger at the loss of her childhood memories. The mist in the mirror twisted and curled as if reflecting her emotions.

"I just don't understand what is happening." She lifted her hand, but hesitated, afraid to touch it. "Am I doing this?" Sera whispered hoarsely, her voice faltering. A chill scraped down her spine when she recalled how her reading glasses appeared on the table, and the way the refrigerator silenced. Had she done those things? She shook her head. "Me? A witch? That's fairytale nonsense ... right?"

A voice whispered in her mind, "You've always been more, Sera. This is real—as real as the magic in our blood."

Sera tipped her chin up, determined to end this fantasy. Or whatever it was. "I am Seraphina Blackthorn—"

Her grandmother's image appeared once more. This time, her lined face filled the mirror as though she stood on the other side of a window, her green eyes intense and unwavering. "*You are Elowen*

*Blackthorn's granddaughter, seventh in a long line of Guardians. It was always meant to be you. The seventh. The strongest. And the last—the only one who can stop what's coming.*

Sera's knees buckled. "Stop what?" she whispered.

*"The destruction of Havenwood Cove and all within,"* her grandmother said gravely, her voice faltering, as though she could barely speak the words.

Chilled, Sera rubbed her stomach to ease the hollow ache her grandmother's words brought. "How is this possible? It can't be real."

*"As real as you, my dear child. Your gift lies in your ability to see what is not there. Veil sight. See the truth."*

Her grandmother's image wavered, then sharpened, her bright hair now tucked beneath a shawl woven with colors of the moon and stars. *"Listen closely, my child. There isn't much time. A portal to another world lies hidden somewhere within Havenwood Cove,"* her grandmother said, her voice grave. *"The oldest tales whisper of a love so powerful it sealed the portal, of a sacrifice so great it bound the magic to this place forever. It must remain sealed at all costs."*

Shadows flitted across the image like smoke, forming monstrous shapes. Her grandmother's green eyes darkened with fear. *"I must go, child. Trust yourself. You've always had the gift."* Her face shimmered.

"Nonie, don't go!" Sera slapped her palm against the glass as the mirror flared silver. Light blinded her—then only her pale, tear-streaked face stared back. Her grandmother's words pressed against her chest like claws. She staggered, crashing into the door, gripping the knob as if it could anchor her to reality.

*A portal. A legend. A great love. A greater sacrifice.*

And her? The seventh and strongest Guardian? She shook her head in denial. This was insanity. And yet ... her heart pounded in agreement, like some forgotten part of her had been waiting for this truth to surface.

Feeling disoriented, as though a rug had been yanked out from under her, Sera stumbled out of the bathroom. Across the room, the golden quill continued to hover over the journal, its gleaming point tapping insistently against the page.

"This just can't be real," she whispered, leaning against the doorjamb. A portal between Earth and another world? Chaos and evil? She glanced over her shoulder into the bathroom and saw that the mirror was just a mirror. Yet moments before, it had revealed so much.

Another memory surfaced: herself as a child floating feathers for a ghost-like cat to catch and wishing for one of her grandmother's freshly baked cookies. And it appeared in her hand. She smiled faintly as she also recalled the scolding she'd received, not from her grandmother, but from her mother.

The sudden influx of memories became too much. She pressed her fingers against her temple and rubbed the growing ache gathering. Was that truly a memory, or a dream? Pulling her hands down, she stared at her fingers and wiggled them. Nothing happened. Stepping back into the bathroom, she snatched a tube of mascara off the counter and tossed it onto the rug. She held out her hand, palm down.

"To me," she commanded firmly—and gasped as the mascara flew up into her outstretched palm. Breathing hard, she could not deny that magic was real. The proof lay in her palm, and in the living room, as the quill awaited her answer to three simple words:

*Do you accept?*

"Wow! Nonie is right. I. Am. A. Witch!" She savored each word. A thrill surged through her, but her chest tightened with fear. If that was true, did that also mean she was the seventh Guardian, responsible for protecting a portal that led to another world? If she accepted one, didn't she have to accept the other? She recalled her grandmother's plea not to waste time and go to Havenwood Cove.

"How can I just race off to some unknown place to save a world? I'm one person." Her voice rose, tinged with a bit of hysteria. She clutched the crystal at her throat, its warmth a steady throb—like a borrowed heartbeat, undeniable and alive.

She glanced into the living room, where the quill hovered silently over the journal. Waiting. Sera wanted to run to her bed and hide under the covers, like a child, but she shook her head. "I will not run," she said firmly. Doing nothing wasn't an option. Ignoring this ... this legacy felt more dangerous than confronting it.

Without taking her eyes off the journal, she crossed the room and sat gingerly on the edge of the couch. Though she dreaded talking to her mother about magic, she had no choice if she wanted answers. Maryann Blackthorn had little use for dreams or dreamers.

Facts, not fiction. Hard work and results, not dreams or intangibles. As a child, her mother had drilled those words into her.

Drawing a deep breath, she pulled her resolve around her like a cloak and hit the speed dial button on her phone.

"Mom," she said when Maryann answered, sounding distracted.

"Sera. This isn't a good time. I'm working. I'll call you tonight for your birthday. We can chat then."

"Sorry to interrupt, mom, but I need to talk to you. Now." Sera heard her mother whispering to someone.

"All right," she sighed with disapproval. "What's wrong? Your divorce?"

Sera grimaced at the disapproval in her mom's tone. Maryann thought Evan walked on water and that his being unfaithful was her failing. Not his. "No, the divorce is final."

"Well, good. You'll find another—"

"Mom," she interrupted. "Is Elowen Blackthorn, my grandmother, still alive?" Her voice was steady, but her hand tightened around the phone.

The silence on the other end stretched, sharp and telling. "We'll talk later, Sera. I need to—"

Sera pinched the bridge of her nose. "Answer me, Mom." Sera cut her off, her tone leaving no room for evasion.

"How would I know?" Maryann said, her voice tight. "I haven't seen her since your father died." In the background, Sera heard the rapid tap of nails on a desk.

She pressed on. "My grandmother needs me, Mom." Sera's voice softened, the certainty in her words surprising even herself. "She says I'm the Guardian of the Moondragon. That I'm the only one who can protect it and save the town."

"Sera, stop this nonsense," Maryann's voice hardened. "You don't belong in Havenwood Cove. It isn't safe for you."

"Why isn't it safe? What aren't you telling me?" Sera's grip on the phone tightened as the driver's words rang in her mind.

Old truths wrapped in silence.

Sera stared at her hand. *Gifts once lost, now returned.*

The truth hit her. Somehow, her gifts had been taken away or removed. And that strange old man, with his strange words, had restored them.

"Sera! I'm talking to you! Are you there?"

"Yes, Mom." For the first time in her life, Sera defied her mother. "You knew about Nonie. About me being a witch, about all of this. And you never said a word. Why?"

"It was for the best. You made yourself a good life, had a good man—"

Sera laughed bitterly. "A man who cheated on me, had a child with that woman, and his family destroyed my career. Tell me what was so good!"

"You'll get another job, find another man. Come home. Plenty of jobs here, and I know a few eligible men ..."

Her mother's voice faded to static. In her mind's eye, Sera saw the dark shadows in the mirror and the look of fear in her grandmother's eyes before her image faded. She dropped the phone onto the couch beside her, her gaze drawn to the quill. Her hand trembled as she reached for it. It flew to her hand. Wrapping her fingers around it, warmth spread through her palm, steady and certain. The journal's weight pressed against her resolve, urging her forward.

"I'm sorry, Mom," she whispered, her voice trembling, "I have to go to Havenwood Cove. She needs me. They all do."

Taking a deep breath, Sera steadied her hand and penned,

*Yes. I Accept.*

*Seraphina Blackthorn, May 20, 2024.*

The quill dissolved, and light flared from her crystal, tendrils of energy weaving around her wrist. When the light dimmed, a bracelet of seven gemstones circled her wrist, pulsing gently. At its center, her aestralite glowed, warm and steady.

Breathless, Sera stared at the stones set in silver. Magic surged through her veins, grounding her yet making her feel as though she stood on the edge of something vast and unknown. "I've just become ... the seventh Guardian," she whispered.

The journal closed with quiet authority. The Tree of Life seemed to shift, its intricate Celtic knots glinting faintly, alive with energy. Where gemstones had once rested, faint symbols now glittered—subtle but significant, as if the book itself had awakened.

Sera leaned back. This wasn't just a book. It was a key—one that unlocked the legacy her grandmother had passed down to her, a legacy she could not ignore. "I've spent years being what everyone else wanted—a dutiful daughter, a perfect wife, a flawless professional. Maybe it's time to be something else. Someone else. It's time to be me."

She touched the aestralite, now surrounded by the six other stones. The familiar warmth grounded her; its presence unnervingly intimate. The stones seemed alive, their energies distinct yet harmonious, like seven voices singing in perfect unison. Her crystal at the center pulsed in time with her heartbeat, comforting her even as her mind spun with questions.

The cover opened once again, revealing the square envelope and the ornate silver key that moments ago had been mere images on the page. They were now as real as the quill had been and waited for her to claim them. Her fingers hovered over the two objects— no, they weren't just objects—they were invitations. Or perhaps warnings.

Whatever lay ahead—the key and what the thick envelope contained—would open the door, but to what? Power? Danger? Or something she couldn't imagine yet?

Sera held the key and envelope in her hands, their weight heavy with purpose. An icy dread coiled in her chest, yet a thrill of excitement pulsed alongside it. Whatever lay ahead—danger, power, or truths she couldn't yet fathom—she would face it. Clutching the key, she whispered, "I'm going to find out." Her bracelet's steady pulse echoed the rhythm of her growing resolve.

# Chapter Three

May 21 - Baggage, Beginnings & a Hint of Magic

Sera handed Pam her favorite herbal tea, then joined her at the table. The two women, sisters of the heart, sat in companionable silence. "Thanks for coming over, Pam. I appreciate you taking the time. Hopefully, you didn't have to cancel any appointments." Pam Ashwick owned a New Age shop where she specialized in healing, herbology, and energy work.

Pam waved a hand in the air. "Anything for my sister. You sounded upset last night, so of course I came. You look exhausted."

Sera didn't mention she'd been up most of the night packing. And practicing magic by calling things to her and proving to herself over and over that, yeah, she was a witch.

"Another delay with the divorce?" Pam narrowed her hazel eyes, the flecks of gold and green flashing. "Still say you should have let me hex him!"

Sera giggled, the sound edged with nerves. "You know you wouldn't have. Bad karma and all that."

Sighing, Pam sipped her tea. "So true. What about the divorce?"

"It's final and I'm ready to move on. In fact," she paused and set her cup down. "That's exactly what I'm doing. It's a bit scary" And wasn't that the truth! Magical journals? Witches? Becoming some sort of guardian? It didn't seem real. She eyed the journal on the table, then the bracelet around her wrist with the gemstones that had been on the front of the magical journal. A thread of determination and excitement mingled with nerves.

"Where there's a will, there's a way and I've finally found both," she said, as she leaned forward and rested her forearms on the table. "Pam, I'm going home," she announced.

Pam's brow shot up. "To California?"

"No. To Havenwood Cove, a tiny town on the coast where I was born."

"Havenwood—?" Shock rolled through her voice as she jumped to her feet, the bangles on her wrist jangling. She gaped at Sera.

"Yes. I was born there. Mom and I left after my father died of cancer." Sera sucked in a deep breath. "I have family, Pam. My dad's family. A grandmother. Maybe now I can learn about him."

"Oh, Ser—" Pam's voice broke off as she paced. Tall and willowy, she wore her habitual white cotton top tucked into an earth-toned tunic, her dark chestnut hair pulled up into a messy bun. Pouches dangled from a wide belt, bangles lined her wrists, and rows of necklaces added fall colors to her outfit.

Sera picked up the letter her grandmother had left her—the full-sized pages were once in that tiny, magical envelope in the journal. The letter gave her a connection to a woman she hadn't seen since the age of ten.

Sera blew out a breath, sending a wayward strand of hair out of her face as she studied her friend's shocked expression. "Are you happy for me?" She couldn't help the glimmer of uncertainty that found its way into her voice.

"Of course I am, Ser. You just surprised me. No one said—I mean, you've never told me your grandmother lived in a magical town."

"Wait—what?" Sera blinked. "I never said it was magical."

Pam hesitated. "I just meant ... quaint. Seaside towns always feel enchanted." She took a deep breath and hurriedly added, "Wow. When you said you had news, I thought it was about your divorce or that creep Evan."

Tipping her head, Sera studied Pam, noting the way she rubbed her thumb and forefinger together—a nervous tell. Normally, the woman, a couple of years her senior, wore composure like a second skin, but now, she looked not just shocked, but stunned.

"This is the perfect answer for me," Sera said softly. "I'm going to take over my grandmother's yarn shop for the summer and that will give me time to figure out what I want to do with my life. And best of all, Havenwood Cove is close enough that you can come visit or I can come back for the day—if I can leave the shop."

All business, Pam returned to her chair and tucked her legs in her sensible calf-high boots to one side. She folded her hands on the table, her gaze intent. "How did you find out? Your mother?"

A laugh escaped. "Yeah, um no. You know she won't talk about the past—our past. Not even when I asked her about Nonie Wenna yesterday. All she did was tell me not to go." Sera shrugged. "As she can't give me a good reason not to go, I'm going."

Sera clasped her fingers together, bit her lower lip, and debated saying more. But this was her best friend. Her words came out slowly and hesitantly. "Pam. There's more."

Leaning back in her chair, Pam narrowed her eyes. "I think I'm afraid to ask."

Nose scrunched, fingers twisting together, Sera drew in a deep breath. "You'll think I'm nuts. Crazy. Certifiably crazy," she added.

"Ser, you're as grounded and steady as they come."

*Not anymore*, Sera said to herself. "Okay, but let me ask you a question first. You're a witch. Can you do … *witchy* things?"

A wary look entered Pam's eyes. "Like what?"

"Move things. Call things to you. See visions. Stuff like that."

Drawing herself up, Pam sent Sera a quizzical look. "You know my talents are with healing and herbs and energy work, and I dabble in Tarot and Runes."

Sera nodded and pushed the journal toward Pam. "What do you think of this?"

Pam's hand hovered over the journal—and then jerked back like she'd touched a live wire. She sucked in a breath and shook her fingers as if trying to fling off invisible sparks. "Great Goddess! I can't touch this! Where did you get this? It's—" Her eyes locked onto Sera's, wide with something close to fear. "It's full of power."

Sera nodded. She didn't need Pam's confirmation of what she knew to be true, but welcomed it. "It's the Blackthorn journal that belonged to my grandmother. It now belongs to me. And that's not all, Pam. I'm a witch."

"Sera—"

Sera held up a hand, palm out. "I know how it sounds. But according to my grandmother, the family legacy—whatever that really means—has passed to me. I'm the seventh Guardian of the Moondragon." She drew in a breath, then flicked her finger. The journal slid across the table as if it recognized her.

She laid her palm on the cover, feeling its pulse beneath her skin. "This is why I'm going to Havenwood Cove," she whispered. "Not just because I want to. Because I have to. I'm supposed to save it."

Pam jumped to her feet. "I-don't—this can't—no." Her hand slashed the air. She took several steps back. "Just. No." With one last stricken look at Sera with her hand resting on a journal that radiated power, she turned and ran.

The echo of the front door slamming held Sera frozen in her seat, her hand still on the journal, her heart pounding. "What just happened?"

###

With her mind still in turmoil from Pam's unexpected reaction and a deep ache in her heart, Sera finished loading her beloved Mini Cooper convertible. She'd reach out to Pam later. Or in a few days. Right now, the rejection was raw, an open wound that needed healing, so she concentrated on the task at hand.

The blue car, a doll's toy compared to the life she'd been dragging behind her, promised freedom and a new life. She swung two suitcases into the trunk. Boxes filled the backseat. Everything she owned fit into her tiny car. Like magic, the space accommodated whatever she added.

"I'm going home." The words brought equal measures of joy and trepidation. Her grandmother needed her, and, more importantly, trusted her with her shop, even if it came with a frightening quest. She thought of both her mother and Pam's reactions. Why would her going to Havenwood Cove evoke negative responses? Sighing, she closed the trunk and paused.

She wasn't sure where "home" had ever been. But despite the gaps in memory, Havenwood Cove felt like a beginning. The question was: What was she returning to? The fear of the unknown was both thrilling and terrifying.

Returning to her living room, her gaze fell on the afghan draped over the back of the couch. She picked it up, smoothing the soft, ripple-patterned yarn as more forgotten memories rose unbidden. "You've been with me through everything, haven't you, Nonie?" she whispered. The Afghan smelled faintly of vanilla and lavender, a scent she now remembered and associated with her grandmother.

She unfolded the letter from the journal, still amazed it had once fit inside that tiny envelope, and read:

*My Dearest Granddaughter,*

*I've been called away on urgent business. I've turned over the Yarns of Wonder, my yarn shop, to you. You'll find*
*all the paperwork in order and more details on the next page.*

"Yeah, providing I can figure out how to run the shop." She silently read more of her grandmother's letter.

*Maude, my house, is yours while you are in Havenwood Cove.*
*Molly is my caretaker, and she'll see to your needs as well.*
*Don't delay, Sera. I need you.*

Sera hugged the letter to her chest, the words pulling at something deep inside her. "Nonie Wenna," she murmured, her voice cracking. "Why now? You were so close all these years and you never let me know you were alive. Why?"

Her phone pinged.

Sera tucked the letter back into the envelope and slid it back into the journal, hoping it wouldn't get reabsorbed as she planned to reread it tonight. Sera picked up her phone and swiped the message icon. Incoming from Pam.

Holding her breath, she opened the message.

Pam: *Sorry I freaked out. That journal has serious power. Guess it caught me off guard. Just know it's ... more than just a journal. Trust your instincts. And go where it leads you. That's all I can say. We'll talk more later.*

"All she could say?" What did that mean? Pam was not one to dance around things. So why not just tell her the truth? Pam's message felt more like a warning dressed as encouragement. "It may have caught you off guard. But what about me?" She eyed Pam's closing words. "Yeah, we'll talk more. But right now, I need to get moving."

On the table, the journal glowed faintly, as if it agreed. After sending Pam a thumbs up, she gathered the last of her belongings. After stowing them in the front seat of the car, she returned for one last check of the place she'd called home but wasn't.

Inside, she stopped short. The flowers by the front door were gone. The vase held a faint blue glow, like a memory. A chill ran down her spine. "Well, that's not creepy at all," she muttered as she backed away.

"Goodbye," she whispered, her voice trembling. This place had been both her prison and her refuge, but as she locked the door behind her, she felt something shift inside her—a tether breaking, a weight lifting. She was finally free to move forward to rediscover who she was.

Inside the car, the moonstone on the journal glowed faintly, as if urging her to hurry. "You just can't help yourself, can you?" she said aloud, her voice a mix of sarcasm and awe. "Fine," she said, a little louder than she intended. "We're going. Don't get bossy."

Drawing a deep breath, she started the car and opened the garage door. She gripped the wheel, her thoughts spiraling. "Magic? Witches? Guardianships? What if I'm not enough?" Her grandmother's voice echoed in her mind: *"You're ready, Sera, even if you don't feel it."*

"That's the trouble, Nonie. Ready for what?" The car's engine purred smoothly, its rhythm as steady as her mounting doubt. Exhaling, she shook her head as she adjusted the rearview mirror. Her own reflection stared back, a mix of determination and uncertainty.

She patted the dashboard. "Okay, Cricket, wee'rrreee off to see the wizard," she sang beneath her breath. On the passenger seat, the journal now looked like any other normal book or diary.

"Best keep it that way," she muttered as her mind absorbed and accepted all that had happened. "Magic is real." Speaking the words aloud made it feel not just real, but acceptable. It also thrilled and unsettled her in equal measure.

She shook her head, forcing her focus back to the road ahead. Whatever strangeness had taken over her life, it was taking her to Havenwood Cove. She just hoped the town came with a manual. Or at least a decent therapist. She jabbed a finger in the air. "No, a witch doctor," she said, chuckling. If her laughter held a tinge of hysteria, well, who could blame her?

Her new job title? Guardian of the Moondragon.

Her first assignment? Save Havenwood Cove—a town she hadn't set foot in since childhood—from an ancient portal she didn't know existed.

Her survival odds? Debatable.

"This is fine," Sera muttered. "Completely fine."

Still, the offer of a job and a place to stay had come at the perfect time. Fate? Or something else, because it was clear it was more than happenstance at work. She just wished she knew more about the Guardianship. Nothing in her grandmother's letter or the journal explained what the job of Guardian of the Moondragon entailed beyond saving Havenwood Cove. Saving it from what? Or who?

*There is a legend, a story of love and sacrifice. Learn its secrets and truths.*

That was all her grandmother had penned in her letter. As Sera had no answers, she concentrated on what she knew. The most terrifying realization wasn't the magic—it was that she'd spent her whole life blind to it. How much of her past had been a lie—or worse, erased?

*Old truths wrapped in silence ... gifts once lost, now returned. Let memory bloom, and the new take root.* The delivery driver's words echoed in her mind, as vivid as the spark that snapped between them when their hands brushed.

Truths silenced ... Her past? Given the return of her memories, it made sense that someone had erased her mind ten years ago. The question was, why?

Gifts once lost ... That was easy. Magical abilities and what her grandmother called veil sight. Her grandmother's voice from the mirror shimmered in her mind. *Your gift lies in seeing what is not there. See the truth.*

Sera suddenly recalled how, as a child, she'd seen ghostly cats. Blue and pink cats. Were those magical abilities? What her grandmother called veil sight? Or just her creative imagination? What about what she'd seen in the mirror? Had those visions and images been real? She sighed.

Memory bloom—new take root. She nodded. She was on her way to Havenwood Cove. That qualified as the new taking root. Those simple words were a spell, undoing whatever had been done to her.

Who was the driver and what connection did he have with her or her grandmother? He'd reminded her of her father, but her memories of him were faint. She vaguely remembered his funeral. Unless that was a lie, a false memory planted before her mother took her to California.

Her fingers tightened on the steering wheel. Why had her mother kept her past from her? Kept granddaughter from grandmother? Question after question bombarded her mind. "Shut it down," she ordered herself. There were no answers. Yet. In returning to her birthplace, she'd surely learn the truth.

Boston faded into the rearview mirror. Ahead, Havenwood Cove promised something she hadn't felt in years—possibilities. Her heart pounded in sync with the rhythmic hum of the engine as mile markers flew by.

"Pretend this is just a nice, relaxing, scenic drive," she told herself to quiet the fear of the unknown. She rested her arm on the open window, the wind flowing through her outstretched fingers. But she couldn't delude herself. Yesterday had started off as an ordinary and mundane morning and morphed into a breathtaking fantasy. An unfamiliar surge of energy buzzed through her. A mystical journal and enchanted ritual words had burst the dam of a hidden reservoir within her, releasing a torrent of magical energy that electrified her every sense.

She held up her left arm. Sunlight from the window lit up the stones circling her wrist, their glow sparking a quiet excitement in her. Somewhere in all the passing years, she'd lost herself. This trip was the first step in rediscovering who she was and who she wanted to become.

Glancing at her GPS, she noted she had ten miles to go to reach Havenwood Cove. Thirty-six miles had separated her from her grandmother. Sera didn't understand why the woman had kept her distance. She let out a huff of air. Maybe it wasn't for her to understand but to accept and hold onto the now.

A breeze tugged at the silk scarf around her head. Grinning, she ripped it off and let the wind tangle her hair. For the first time in years, she felt free. A black motorcycle roared past, its engine echoing like a primal beast. The raw surge of sound matched the wild energy thrumming through her.

*Guardian of the Moondragon ... protect it with honor and courage.* The words flashed in her mind—a riddle she couldn't yet solve. She reached for the journal on the seat beside her, seeking comfort. "Oh, Nonie," she whispered. "What kind of spell have you cast on my life?" With no answers yet, she focused on the road.

Dappled sunlight filtered through tall stands of eastern white pines with their straight trunks and feathery needles, creating a green tunnel that shadowed the road. The crisp scent of needles filled the air. Breathing deeply, a current of anticipation surged through her, the air alive with possibility and tinged with excitement.

She let the doubts drift away, carried off by the wind tugging at her hair. This was a new beginning, and she wasn't looking back. After years of conforming and being in control of herself all the time, this new freedom to be herself was electrifying, like a wild dance pulsating through her very being. She shook her shoulders and forced herself to relax.

She glanced at the navigation screen. Her eyes went wide. "Yikes. Two miles to go." Licking her lips, suddenly nervous, she forced herself to focus on the scenery, not her trepidation. *Forty and free*, she reminded herself. Her heart sang with possibility.

Through the intricate weave of pine branches, the sea glinted in flashes of cerulean blue. The cool, fresh breeze sent shivers down her spine and carried the sharp, tangy scent of salt. As she tasted the brine on her lips, memories of living by the ocean surfaced. How or why she'd forgotten no longer mattered. Just that she felt as though she were coming home.

To her left, white pines and hemlocks with their dark green needles formed a continuous wall of nature with houses interspersed here and there. She spotted a majestic red oak and a few sugar maples, their leaves whispering secrets in the wind. The shimmering sign appeared as if conjured from thin air: Havenwood Cove—one mile.

She licked her lips. One mile. Just one mile until she stepped into whatever fate her grandmother had set in motion. Maybe she should turn around. Maybe she still had a choice.

But when her eyes flicked to the sign again, the wind whispered through the trees, carrying words she didn't quite hear—but felt all the same. Beside her, the journal pulsed softly, its moonstone glowing faintly as if to say, *almost there.*

She didn't have all the answers—crikey, she didn't know all the questions, but one thing she knew: This wasn't just a destination. It was a homecoming to something she'd lost, something she was finally ready to reclaim.

She eased up on the gas pedal and held her breath as the car decelerated. Afraid to blink in case she missed it, she sighed in relief when, like a secretive oasis, a road emerged. Leaving the highway behind, she drove into a dark tunnel created by two formidable rows of trees on each side of the gravel road that gave the illusion of a solemn regiment standing guard over the land.

The trees pressed in tight on either side of the road, their branches arching overhead like clasped fingers. The deeper she drove, the darker the road became, even though the sky had been clear moments before. A sudden gust of wind shook the leaves, whispering in a language she almost understood. For just a moment, the world felt too still, as though it held its breath.

Then, just as suddenly, the tension in the air broke. The wind shifted, the light returned, and the road rose, following a slight incline. She patted the dashboard. "You can do it, Cricket," she said. She'd had the car longer than her marriage and had refused to get rid of it for something more befitting her status. Besides, Evan hated the car and had refused to ride in it, which made it her rebel car.

A strange energy, thick and buzzing like a thousand angry bees, crackled in the air beneath the towering trees, making her skin tingle. Strands of her golden-red hair lifted, swaying in the unseen pull of a static charge, forming a halo around her head. The stones on her bracelet glowed violently in response, nearly blinding her.

Glancing up, she searched overhead for the power lines but found none. "Strange," she muttered, puzzled by the enigmatic sensation. "No, *magical*," she breathed as bright flashes of color lit the air like tiny fireworks, pulsing with joyous energy as though welcoming her home. The journal on the passenger seat flared briefly, the moonstone at its center glowing. Sera reached for it, her fingers brushing the cover as a faint vibration thrummed through her hand.

Leaving the dim, cool shade of the thick trees, Sera blinked rapidly as the bright sunlight hit the windshield, momentarily blinding her. The trees to her right thinned, revealing a picturesque harbor. The salty smell of the sea mixed with the scent of pine from the trees. Ahead, the playful yaps and excited barks of several dogs, along with the joyous shrieks and peals of children's laughter, shattered the tranquil spell, jolting her back to the bustling reality of Havenwood Cove.

A girl with a sparkling tiara perched on top of her head waved madly. The house behind her, a multi-storied Cape Cod-style home, bore the sign: Mystic Shores Realty. Sera grinned and waved back and watched as the child mounted her bike and took off down the road.

She passed the Cove Market, its open windows spilling the scent of warm bread into the breeze. A chuckle escaped when she spotted the girl on her bike joining two boys. The trio raced off down a path, their laughter trailing behind them on the breeze.

Tantalizing aromas wafted from the Crispy Crust Diner, making her stomach growl. She hadn't thought about food since breakfast.

Just past the businesses, the road split. A sign pointed right toward the fishery, wharves, and Seaside Haven Inn, but Sera continued straight, eyes drawn to the stand of trees to her left. The thick canopy swallowed the light, golden motes flickering within like floating embers.

Something darted between two trunks. A flicker of movement.

"Don't be silly," she muttered. "The highway's just a few hundred feet away." Still, the woods felt ... watchful. Returning her focus to the road, she gasped and slammed on the brakes, gravel crunching beneath the wheels. The shoulder belt tightened as she jerked forward. Gripping the steering wheel, she gawked at the fantastical sight ahead—two massive trees twisted into whimsical treehouses, straight out of a fantasy movie.

Thick green canopies formed their roofs. Tiny motes of golden light danced among the branches, vanishing and reappearing like fireflies. Her bracelet pulsed gently, the glow of the stones matching the rhythm of her heartbeat.

The tree branches wove together to form a grand arched bridge over the gated road. Spiraling staircases wound around the massive trunks. The multi-level treehouses with windows and small doorways gave the appearance of a towering village in the trees, stitched by magic.

Enchanted by the charming architectural details and magical atmosphere, Sera lowered her gaze and grinned. The base of each treehouse reminded her of a hobbit house with the way the twisted and gnarled roots formed two tiny homes, complete with round doors and small circles of glass that allowed light to enter.

"Adorable!" Sheer delight filled her voice. "Wow," she breathed, her voice full of wonder. Adding the view of cliffs and harbor to her right and the forest to her left, she felt like she'd driven into a secluded and magical woodland location. Her eyebrows shot up. Pam had used the word magical regarding Havenwood Cove but had quickly amended herself by saying all seaside towns were quaint. Mystical. "Hmm, something to follow up on," Sera decided.

A tall, wooden gate stretched between the trees, barring entry to the town. "Now what?" It seemed wrong to honk her horn and disrupt the tranquil beauty. Just then, the door of one hobbit home swung open. Sera tried not to stare, but she wasn't quite sure what to make of the figure that emerged.

Barely three feet tall and impossibly thin, he wore a patchwork vest and lime-green pants tucked into battered boots. The dull jingle of dozens of antique-looking keys at his waist added a musical clanging sound. He reminded her of a garden gnome, though more crusty than cute.

"Don' got all day, ya kno'," the short figure shouted, his deep voice rumbling like distant thunder. His eyes beneath his feather-topped hat gleamed like polished amber.

Her brows shot upward as she'd expected him to have a higher-pitched voice. "Holy cow," she mumbled. A grumpy gnome! He clapped his hands sharply, and her car suddenly jolted forward. She squealed in surprise as the car continued to move, even with her foot firmly on the brake pedal.

"Magical *and* impatient!" Adrenaline shot through her veins, her heart pounding in her chest, a mix of fear and exhilaration. She leaned forward, gripping the steering wheel. Her stomach tightened as the air buzzed with an unseen energy. The gate loomed ahead like a silent sentinel. Whatever lay beyond—it was the unknown. One deep breath. One heartbeat. And with the gate yawning wide, Sera drove into the waiting magic.

# **Chapter Four**

May 21 - No Turning Back Now ... Not That I'd Know How

The car stopped, and the gatekeeper—she wasn't sure what to call him—stomped to her side of the car and peered up at her. He crossed his twig-thin arms across a narrow chest. A wide-brimmed hat sat upon his wild, bushy tangle of hair, and his slightly bulbous nose reminded her of garden gnomes she'd always found appealing, though cute was not a term she'd apply to this man.

"Welcome home, Seraphina Blackthorn, Guardian of the Moondragon," the little man declared, sweeping his hat from his head with a flourish. "I be Bramblewick Nettlefoot, but folks call me Bram." His deep bow nearly swept the ground.

Sera leaned out the window to get a better look, only for him to spring back up with surprising speed, jamming the hat onto his head. She drew her brows together. "How do you know who I am—or that I'm the Guardian?" she asked, her voice tinged with disbelief.

Thick, bushy brows nearly hid bright, moss-green eyes that twinkled with mischief. "*The Mother* knew ya as soon as ya arrived." He waved toward the thick stand of trees. "An, ya have the look of yer gran."

"Uh, oh, thank you. Can you point me—"

Bram, with hands planted on his hips, nodded knowingly. "Bound for Maude, ya be. The road be not just stone, sand, an' dust, but filled with magic, memory an' trust. Keep yer heart open, yer mind clear, an' ol' Maude will care for ya." He ended his speech with a firm nod, letting her know he was serious.

Her grandmother had named her house Maude—odd but endearing. She wished her grandmother were there; she longed to reconnect with the woman who'd been such a big part of her first ten years.

"How do I get there? Nonie didn't give me the address." Her GPS on her phone had gotten her to Havenwood Cove, and the map her grandmother included of the town just had the house name on a point of land.

Bram laughed, the sound a deep rumble in his chest. "Maude, she needs no address. She *be* the address!" He sent her a knowing look and pointed one finger toward the harbor. "No roads here, jest journeys. Vista Cliff Road be more than just a route to reach ol' Maude."

Sera sighed. His speech was certainly ... different. "Okay, I take Vista Cliff Road. Then what?" she asked as Bram turned toward the gate fashioned from tree branches. With a wave of his hand, the gate parted and slowly withdrew *into* the tree trunks on either side of the road.

Eyes wide with wonder and shock, Sera's jaw dropped. She craned her neck, searching for hidden mechanisms or openings in the twisted trunks. There were none. The tree was reabsorbing the gate! "Holy hell," she muttered. "What have I gotten myself into?" she muttered, a shiver of apprehension running down her spine. Her stomach churned with nervous energy, like a thousand butterflies taking flight.

Bram pointed. "Jest follow the Rootwall to the far point. Take ya right to Maude. She overlooks the cliff."

A breeze picked up from nowhere, swirling dried leaves in a tight spiral at Bram's feet. The trees groaned—a long, indistinct groan like an old house settling—and the air grew strangely dense, almost sticky.

Bram tipped his head, eyes narrowing at the treetops. "Hmm."

"What is it?" Sera asked, glancing around warily.

"Ah, nothin' that need worry you," he said too quickly. Then, muttering, "The shield's twitchin' again. Not right. Not this soon."

Still watching the forest, she focused back on Bram. "Shield? What?"

Bram jerked as though he'd forgotten her. He smiled wide, showing surprisingly perfect teeth. "Just the woods bein' moody. Off with ya, Guardian. Maude be waitin'." With that, he stepped back into his hobbit-like treehouse.

Feeling nervous, Sera eased the car through the gate that no longer existed. "Concentrate on the road," she muttered. Still, the refrain of "follow the yellow brick road" played in her mind, and she giggled. "Just hope there are no wicked Witches along the way."

She gripped the steering wheel so tight her knuckles turned white and her shoulders were stiff. It would all make sense once she reached her grandmother's lovely Victorian, the peaceful, yellow house she'd seen in the mirror. Beside her, the pages in the journal fluttered, as though eager to return home. "Me too," she agreed. "I need time to process all that has happened."

Bram and the magical trees faded behind her, and she drove past an open space that held dozens of parked cars. Everywhere she looked, she saw people riding bikes or driving a golf-type cart. Or walking.

The road split. Seaside Haven Inn, The Fish Shack, the wharves and harbor veered off to the right, and Vista Cliff Road lay straight ahead. Past the split, the land to the right fell away, leaving her driving along a tall cliff with the harbor far below. Rippling waters cradled fishing boats that bobbed with the rhythmic swells, and gulls dotted the sky—picture postcard perfect. "Beautiful," she breathed.

Waist-high gnarled trunks bordered the cliff, their tangled branches forming a natural fence that framed the stunning vista. "Must be what he referred to as the Rootwall which seemed a fitting name as it looked as though thick roots sprouted up from the ground to form a fence that followed every twist, turn, and curve of the road. Vibrant greenery and delicate spring blooms added an air of quiet magic. Driving slowly, she relaxed. "This is normal," she said— until three people on bikes zipped past. No pedals. No motors. Faster than her car. The road must slope, she reasoned, but her curiosity lingered as they veered into a neighborhood of whimsical homes.

The mixture of sizes, colors, and roof shapes charmed her, especially the thatched roofs like English cottages. One very crooked house made her grin, adding to the town's quirky charm. Colorful gardens shimmered with light, and the smooth road added to the town's mystical tranquility. It felt almost like a movie set— too perfect—with children playing in yards and neighbors tending gardens. Many waved as she passed.

*A journey.* Bram was right. Sera felt captivated by the blending of the natural splendor of the cliffs and the enchanting charm of the community. Sera inhaled the sharp scent of the sea carried into her car by a stiff breeze off the ocean.

As she took in the peaceful scenery, her thoughts drifted to the cold, sterile life she'd left behind, and her divorce felt like a lifetime ago. Was this magical town the fresh start she desperately needed?

Never could she have imagined that a day that had started with the end of one chapter of her life would lead to the revelation of a new one filled with magic, Guardians, and a portal to another world. Nor that it fell to her to save this town? "Surreal." The word slipped out. "How can I make sense of this? It's impossible!"

A ray of light struck her bracelet. Glittering colors danced across the dash. Besides her, the journal hummed, a slightly discordant noise. Sera threw up her hands. "Okay, I get it. Magic. I'm surrounded by magic. No need to chastise me. Guess I best get used to this."

The road curved away from the harbor, and she continued at a leisurely pace as she appeared to be the only car on the road. She soaked in the view of white-capped waves rushing to pound against the rocks below the cliff. For the first time in perhaps years, she felt truly at peace. All her misgivings fell away, replaced by the warmth of a long-overdue homecoming. Her grandmother was right—this was what she needed.

Without warning, a boy on a bike zipped down a slight hill onto the road in front of her car, heading for the edge of the cliff at a fast clip. "Oh no!" Sera screamed as she slammed on her brakes. She jerked forward hard, the shoulder harness tightening. Her heart leaped into her throat, and she shook with horror when the child hit the fence.

Heart pounding, Sera threw open the car door and sprinted to the front of her car. Her breath hitched as she skidded to a stop. The hedge of roots, greenery, and flowers were now sprawled across the road—writhed and twisted, its roots growing impossibly fast to form a protective barrier. "Oh no," she whispered as she crouched down to scan the tangled greenery in panic. Had the boy gone over the edge? A chill raced down her spine. But then she spotted a single sneaker poking out of the root-like branches.

Relief washed over her, followed by shock as the branches parted, revealing a dark-haired boy, laughing as though he'd just been on a carnival ride. She recognized the boy as one she'd seen earlier with his friends on their bikes by the market. Sitting back on her heels, she stared, mouth agape, as the child emerged unharmed from beneath the greenery.

"Holy—" she whispered, her gaze on the roots which were slowly releasing its hold on the child. "How?"

*A living fence? Like the treehouses and the gate?*

"Nate! Nate!"

The shrill shriek startled Sera. She glanced to her left. The blond-haired girl with her tiara askew slipped and slid down the short hill. She landed on her bottom, jumped to her feet, and shoved her hands on her hips, mimicking any furious mother. "You're gonna be in so much trouble! What were you thinking?"

A sandy-haired boy with gray-green eyes whooped and yelled as he ran toward the dark-haired boy getting to his feet. "Wow! Nate! That was crazy!" The boy's voice held awe. "Did it hurt?"

Nate, with a slight swagger in his step, rejoined his biking pals. "Nah, told you it wouldn't. It tickled me. Want to try—"

"That was stupid, Nate," the girl yelled. She glanced over her shoulders as if suddenly afraid. She lowered her voice to a whisper. "What if *she* comes?"

Both boys suddenly looked fearful, and Sera wondered if they were afraid of the boy's mother. Still reeling from the fright the child had given her, she fell back against the hood of her car for support. Before she could fully process what she'd seen, the air shifted. A soft hum, like a distant melody, filled the air, and the faint scent of sage and thyme drifted past. The hedge rippled with anticipation. Then, as if stepping from the very fabric of the earth, a woman appeared.

"Nate Clarkson." The commanding voice carried the sting of a whip. All three children froze. "Oh no, Nate," the girl moaned. "Now you've done it!"

Sera's jaw dropped. "What in the—" She stared. Where had the woman come from? Thin air? Out of the road itself? She blinked once. Twice. Still there. How ...?

"Impossible!" she breathed as a soft, melodic hum filled the air, like wind whispering through ancient trees. The woman's robe was stitched with leaves and vines, her silvery hair glowing like moonlight, her glacial-blue eyes kind yet ancient.

Nate swallowed convulsively. He hunched his shoulders and scuffed the road with the toe of his sneaker, kicking up small bits of gravel.

Each child bowed, signifying the woman's importance. *Okay, maybe a goddess,* Sera amended, holding her breath, unsure what she should do. To her surprise, the woman kneeled in front of Nate and lifted his chin with slender fingers, her every movement calm and loving.

"Nate, do you understand what you've done?" she asked, her voice calm as a breeze through treetops, yet firm. "The Rootwall is there to protect you. It is not a plaything."

"I'm sorry, Lady Lillian. I couldn't resist. It would never harm me."

Lady Lillian placed a gentle hand on his shoulder. "That is so. The Rootwall is alive and serves to protect Havenwood Cove and all who reside within."

Nate grimaced. "But she's lonely. And bored. I felt her excitement when she caught me."

"Also true," Lady Lillian chuckled. "But visit her next time. Touch her gently, tell her your heart—don't waste her energy with stunts like this."

Nate cocked his head to one side, eyes wide. "I can talk to her? Will she talk back?"

Smiling, Lady Lillian placed a hand over Nate's heart. "You'll hear her here," Lady Lillian said. "Magic is a gift, but it has rules. Respect them. One day, if you are wise, you may find your own path. Until then, promise to be more mindful."

Nate heaved out a deep breath. "Okay, Lady Lillian. I promise. I'll try really hard," he said, his voice earnest.

Lady Lillian stood and indicated Sera. "Your actions also frightened Seraphina Blackthorn."

Wrinkling his nose, Nate stood straight, hands clasped behind him as he eyed Sera. "Um, sorry for scaring you, ma'am."

Startled, Sera's eyes widened, but she managed to smile reassuringly at the child. "I'm just glad you weren't hurt."

Nate opened his mouth, but a raised brow from Lady Lillian stopped him. "Off with you three," she commanded.

The children didn't need to be told twice. All three scrambled back up the low hill, Nate hauling his bike that now lay in the roadway, uncovered by branches and leaves.

"Welcome home, Guardian of the Moondragon." Lady Lillian offered a bow.

Startled by the bow, Sera straightened, folding her arms as she eyed the mesmerizing woman. Everyone knowing her role when she'd barely accepted it was ... unsettling.

"I suppose *The Mother* told you I'd arrived in Havenwood Cove as well? Does everyone know?" To say it was disconcerting was an understatement. She hated feeling as though she were one step behind, and right now, she was totally confused and lost.

Lady Lillian nodded. "Of course. She watches over all her children. Including you." She smiled, her clear blue eyes sparkling with amusement. "I apologize for any fright I may have inadvertently caused."

"Startled." She put a hand to her throat. "You startled me. Where did you come from? How did you just appear?" She snapped her fingers. "Like that?"

Lady Lillian laughed softly. Gently. "So many questions, little sister." She lifted the intricately carved wooden staff topped with a deep purple crystal that emitted a soft, enchanting glow. Sera felt an answering hum vibrating from her own wrist. She lifted her hand and gasped as her heart-stone glowed in response. "They're the same," she whispered, her gaze darting from one stone to the other. Wonder mingled with confusion.

Lady Lillian nodded. "Yes. Both are gifts from the forest, carrying its wisdom. One day, your stone will sing with the same power." She raised a hand to stop Sera's questions. The silver cuff on her arm flashed, its feathered etching seeming to shift, ready to take flight.

"The Mother speaks to us in ways we cannot always understand. She chose you, Seraphina Blackthorn, for a reason. Your answers will come in time, but the path ahead will not be easy. Trust yourself, little sister."

She inclined her head as she waved her staff toward the tangled roots on the road. Sera watched as the fence returned to its normal size and position at the edge of the cliff. "Wow, it really is alive. She turned back. "Lady Lillian, what do you mean this is my—"

Sera gaped. Lady Lillian was gone—no footprints, no retreating figure. Stumbling back to her car, she sat, heart pounding, sweat chilled. Who was this goddess of a woman? And *The Mother*? Bram and Lillian spoke of her as if she were a god.

With her head aching and thoughts spinning, Sera stared at the living fence one last time before putting the car back in gear. She desperately needed to reach her grandmother's house—needed some time to sort things out in her head, figure out her next move, and find out who could tell her more about this Guardian business.

With the cliff plunging to her right, the Rootwall stretched on, peaceful now, as if nothing had happened. Sera tightened her grip on the wheel. "Trust yourself," she repeated Lady Lillian's words under her breath, as if saying them might make them true. Her heart still pounded from adrenaline, but a tiny flicker of warmth spread through her chest—hope, maybe, or the first fragile thread of belonging.

The journal fluttered on the seat beside her, pages rustling as if urging her forward. "Yeah, I know," she muttered. "I'm going." She glanced at the map clipped to the passenger visor and changed her mind. Instead of going to the house first, she'd check out the yarn shop. That should be normal enough! She exhaled, pulling back onto the road.

# Chapter Five

May 21 - Of Fae Bargains & Whispered Fates

Sera slowed at the sign for A Street, just behind her grandmother's yarn shop. She studied what she could see of the main section of the town. A long expanse of green stretched up between two long lines of buildings. Colorful storefronts and vibrant flowers lined the bustling main street. People moved leisurely. She tipped her head back and sniffed. The rich aroma of freshly brewed coffee blended with the salty tang of the sea.

The town looked picture-perfect, framed by the open sea on one side and a thick wall of forest on the other. Her heart raced, and a tingling warmth spread from her chest to her fingertips, as if she were being embraced by the magic of Havenwood Cove itself.

She tapped her fingernails on the steering wheel. The desire to check out the yarn shop vied with her need to reach her grandmother's house. She pondered what she knew of Havenwood Cove as the sound of seagulls echoed in the distance. Along with her grandmother's letter and the antique silver key, Nonie had included a map of Havenwood Cove, which revealed a tiny, quaint town nestled by the shimmering waters of a tranquil bay.

It was odd that the town didn't have any large franchises, just privately owned businesses and small specialty shops. Sera also found the limitations of cars in Havenwood Cove peculiar. Shop owners and employees had designated parking spaces behind their buildings. With a few exceptions, tourists and visitors used the main parking lot behind the gatehouse and either walked or rented bicycles or carts.

"Okay, let's do it. A quick stop." She drove a short distance up A Street and parked behind the yarn shop. From behind, the shop looked quite large—a two- or three-story structure. Sera followed the path, the white gravel crunching beneath her feet as pink, blue, and purple blooms hugged the building's side. She reached down, running the pads of her fingers over the velvety softness of one bloom.

To her surprise, a soft tingle shot through her fingertips. Startled, she frowned. All the flowers had subtly shifted, their colorful heads now facing her as though drawn to her touch. "Strange," she muttered, turning away. An uneasy feeling lingered. She felt almost as though the flowers were watching her. Reaching

Main Street, Sera stopped in her tracks. And lost her heart in a single breath.

Main Street was a magical wonderland: a theme park without rides. Each quaint and colorful building stood alone. Not a single boxy row of businesses in sight. The cool, fresh breeze felt welcoming, as did the soothing heartbeat of the ocean.

Benches and tables dotted the cobblestone walkway, inviting visitors to linger between the colorful shops. A wide swath of green, spring grass dotted with tiny purple and golden flowers ran up the center of the street, rolled out like a welcome mat. Fountains bloomed like flowers from one end to the other.

And in front of every shop, planters of every shape spilled bursts of color. People hustled from one shop to another, calling out greetings. Music blasted from what looked to be a pub or tavern.

Reaching the front of her grandmother's shop, Sera gasped in delight. The shop stole her breath away. The two-story Victorian stood like a painting brought to life, its pastel blue facade framed with coral and cream accents. Intricate scrollwork adorned the eaves, and large bay windows glinted in the sunlight, showcasing bursts of vibrant yarns and handmade garments within. A wave of warmth rolled over her, as if the building itself welcomed her home.

A unique, antique brass doorknob shaped like a spindle added to the charm, and the large display windows on either side of the door invited visitors to step inside and explore the shop's offerings.

Loud laughter from behind drew her attention. Three men sat on a bench, their dogs lounging at their feet. One—a bald, broad man—gestured wildly as he talked. She was close enough to hear the other two men arguing with him, but it sounded good-natured. Three old coots, she decided with a silent laugh.

The black Labrador lifted its head and spotted her. The dog crawled out from beneath the bench and ran to her, tail whipping from side to side. Sera held out her hand and laughed when the dog jumped and planted its paws on her shoulders. A long, pink tongue lashed out to lick her chin. "Oh, you're a big love," she cried.

"Mariner! Down, you foolish mutt!" His owner, a grizzled-faced man with red hair going white, rushed over. "Sorry, ma'am. He's a friendly beast but has no manners whatsoever."

"He's handsome, aren't you, fella?" Sera had the dog's rump wiggling in delight as she stroked and scratched and petted. *I'm getting a dog*, she promised herself, especially when a bulldog and black and tan cocker spaniel rushed over.

"Oh my." She plopped onto her butt, laughing as all three dogs clamored for attention. "Now this is a friendly welcome." If the residents were as friendly as the dogs, she'd enjoy her time in Havenwood Cove.

"Name is Tommy," Mariner's owner said. "You visiting?" He thrust out a hand to help her up.

She shrugged as Tommy's companions ambled over to join them. "Sorta. Going to be running my grandmother's yarn shop for the summer." She indicated the shop behind her.

"Ah, you're Ea—"

"Elowen's granddaughter," a tall, impeccably dressed man with snow-white hair interrupted. "Henry's the name, and that well-mannered spaniel is Lady." He slapped the third man on the back. "This bald, old chap is George, and his dog, Salty. Both are incorrigible."

She narrowed her eyes at the three men. What had Tommy been about to say that his friend cut him off? She tipped her head to the side and regarded the third man, recognizing him as the loud, boisterous one she'd first noticed. Mentally shrugging, Sera grinned. She liked the three personable men and their friendly manners and even friendlier dogs. "Yes, Elowen is my grandmother. I'm Sera," she said. "Your dogs are beautiful, although Salty is a bit—drooly." She laughed.

Henry spoke. "Welcome to Havenwood. You need anything, the three of us are usually around most days."

Tommy nodded vigorously and raised his bushy eyebrows. "Anytime you want to hear about the ghost ships in the harbor, join us. Seen them myself."

Sera smiled, amused by the idea of ghost ships. "I'll have to take you up on that," she replied, curious about the town's stories.

George cuffed Tommy playfully. "No one wants to hear your tall tales, you old fool."

Tommy huffed. "Who you callin' a fool?" he demanded.

Rolling his eyes, Henry pointed toward the yarn shop. "Looks like you have a customer." He led the men back to the bench, where the three of them once again set about engaging in their loud discussions. The dogs ran ahead and reclaimed their spots, which told Sera she'd indeed see this group often.

Shaking her head at her first taste of what this small town offered, as well as feeling relief to find normal humans, she turned back to her grandmother's yarn shop and spotted a tall, blonde woman inches from the door painted a vibrant coral color. She had her forehead pressed against the glass insert, trying to peer inside. A strange rhythmic clicking filled the air, sharp and deliberate, like a ticking clock.

She hurried toward the woman. "Hi, sorry, the shop isn't open at the moment," Sera called out.

The woman in her mid-thirties whirled around, her violet-gray eyes darting nervously before landing on Sera. "You're Seraphina? Eamon Blackthorn's daughter?" Her voice wavered slightly as her fingers continued to worry the black beads dotted with red as though they were a rosary.

Sera's welcoming smile faltered as the woman's words struck like a thunderclap. "You know my father?"

*Eamon*—the name resonated, unlocking a door in her mind, reminding her of how much she'd forgotten, or had stolen from her. She hadn't heard that name spoken aloud since she was a young girl. The name brought forth an image of her father's face, his warm eyes, and a deep, reassuring laugh—both so vivid they made her chest tighten with both wonder and pain. How could she have forgotten something so vital?

Why had her mother never spoken of him? Cancer had taken him from her, but so had her mother's bitterness.

The woman's hands moved to the beads, slipping them through her fingers: black with streaks of crimson that gleamed like blood under the sunlight. The sound they made—soft, deliberate, hypnotic—seemed to carry an unspoken weight.

"I was five last time I saw you, but who else could it be? You have his eyes." She looked away quickly, her fingers moving faster along the beads. She cleared her throat. "Can we go inside? I need some yarn," she said, her smile growing tighter. "And maybe ... I could tell you a little about him. He was well-known here. People still talk about him."

Sera hesitated, torn between the offer of answers and the overwhelming need to process her memories alone. Finally, she nodded and stepped onto the first step leading to the front door. "I don't remember you. What's your na—"

The words died in her throat when a shadow moved above them, darkening the porch. Sera's brow furrowed as she tilted her head back to glance up just in time to see a body falling from the roof. Both women shrieked.

Sera stumbled back, her feet tripping over themselves. She fell onto her backside; the impact reverberated through her bones. Her heart pounded fiercely in her chest, the rapid beats a thunderous rhythm in her ears. She glanced around to be sure the woman was okay, but she was already gone. Who could blame her?

Sera blinked rapidly at the man hanging upside down from the roof overhang in front of the yarn shop's door—a very much alive man with silvery-green eyes shining with pure glee. "What in the world?"

He wore a pointed elf cap, had elongated elf ears, and wore a wide ear-to-ear grin. Her gaze traveled up, taking in his Christmas-red tunic and matching pants complete with black boots with curled toes. He looked like a life-sized Elf on the Shelf. As she watched with mouth agape, the elf swayed gently in the breeze and radiated a sense of mischief and mayhem, as though he possessed the power to create chaos with a single glance.

The sound of loud laughter startled her. She glanced over her shoulder to see Harry, George, and Tommy slapping their knees.

Tommy shouted, "Good one, Fin—better hope Sam doesn't catch you this time!" Laughter rippled through the crowd as others called out, eager to watch the spectacle. Embarrassed, Sera hopped to her feet and rubbed her backside as she glared at the cobblestone path. "Gonna have some bruises," she muttered. Her gaze darted back to the man dressed as an elf hanging upside down, his legs gripping the edge of the roof. She pressed her fingers to her lips and shook her head in disbelief.

"Oh my stars," she muttered.

"I prefer Holy Wands & Willows myself," he said with a mischievous grin. He snapped his fingers, showering her in a fine cloud of gold glitter. "A magical moment, don't you agree?"

Sera waved the sparkles away from her face. "Nice trick. Now please, come down." It was very unnerving to have a man, or elf, or whatever he was hanging upside down in front of her.

"You might be right—getting a cramp," he cried. Sera's heart lurched as he straightened one leg, then the other, dropping a few inches. She darted up two steps, arms outstretched to catch him, but he playfully evaded her grasp.

"Priceless, my dear lady. Just priceless." His laughter, a joyful symphony that mingled with the commentary among the crowd gathering behind Sera, made her feel silly.

"Um ..." She pressed a hand to her head, panic creeping up her spine and confusion swirling like a storm. This was insane—yet he only swung lazily, as if this were normal. No one else seemed surprised, or even afraid for this man's safety. Unease twisted in her stomach. Their laughter reminded her just how much of an outsider she was.

Havenwood Cove wasn't just chaotic; it was surreal. The streets buzzed with laughter, drinks sparkled with floating embers, and an elf dangled from her roof. It wasn't normal. But it wasn't frightening either. A strange, reluctant thrill tingled at the edges of her nerves.

Sera feared this move wasn't the fresh start she'd envisioned. Uncertainty loomed like a shadow over her decision. As there was no way to focus on logic—an elf hanging in midair was not logically possible—she focused on facts. Frustration sharpened her focus, determination set her jaw, even as a reluctant curiosity had her asking, "Who are you, and why are you hanging from my roof?" Her voice ended in a squeak as both her heart and stomach seemed to be jammed in the back of her throat.

"Finley Greenwood at your service, but you can call me Fin." He waved one hand with a flourish, and a business card appeared between his fingers. He floated it down to her.

Sera snagged it.

Finley Greenwood

Elf on the Shelf

For Rent

*"OMG, for real?"*

Fin, his humor restored, nodded vigorously, causing the roof to creak. Sera's heart jumped in fear. "How are you—you even—" she began. She blinked rapidly as her mind sought to make sense of each encounter since her arrival. *Nonie, you have some explaining to do.*

"Uh, perhaps you could come down so we can talk?" She did not need an elf to go splat at her feet!

Fin spread his arms wide, all traces of seriousness gone. "Fear not, dear lady! I specialize in the fine art of mayhem." He wagged his eyebrows. "In the market for a prank? First one's free."

Sera's mouth opened and closed, unable to form words for a moment. "No," she finally managed, feeling a bit overwhelmed. Was it just yesterday that she'd received her final divorce papers and was contemplating her future? Now she was a witch dealing with elves, gnomes, portals, and an unclear role as a Guardian. How had her life flipped so completely?

She took a deep breath, her hands still trembling, and spoke more firmly. "No, thank you. Just, please, come down. I need to ..." At that moment, she wasn't sure what she needed. Oh wait, after all that she'd seen today, a nice glass of wine might settle her nerves. No, make that a shot or two of whiskey straight!

Fin ignored her, swinging lazily as he dangled his arms. "Tell you what—free welcome-home prank, just for you." With a wiggle of his fingers, his hands turned a vibrant shade of purple. He grinned. "Imagine this on a cranky customer. Harmless, but oh so satisfying."

For a brief, absurd second, Sera imagined turning Evan's skin purple after one of his snide remarks. The thought made her smile— almost. Sera smacked her forehead. "Not in Kansas anymore, Dorothy," she mumbled as the weight of her predicament settled onto her shoulders.

Fin tapped his lips. "Who is Dorothy, and why would she think she was in Kansas?" he asked, his head cocked to one side and brows drawn tight.

Sera slapped her forehead. "Ugh, never mind. Why are you here?"

Fin turned serious. "Just my way of welcoming you home, Seraphina Blackthorn, Guardian of the Moondragon," he offered, his voice loud enough to be heard by all. He lowered his voice, his grin gone. "Will you save our tiny, little town from tyranny and destruction? Will you fight our monsters, Sera darling?"

Sera swallowed hard. Everyone seemed to know her role better than she did. Tyranny? Monsters? What had she signed up for? She pressed her fist into her stomach to calm the nervous flutters. "What do you mean? What am I saving this town from?" Hugging herself tightly, she leaned forward, her gaze searching Fin's.

Fin's eyes closed as though he was in pain. Sera held her breath as she waited for his reply. His eyes, when opened, were unfocused, as though he were seeing something only he could see.

Fin's arms crossed, his fingers curled like he was holding something too fragile to release. "From death and destruction," he whispered. "Darkness gathers beyond the portal. If the seal fails, they will come, and all will be lost."

A chill prickled her arms. "Who, Fin? Who will come?"

His throat bobbed with a hard swallow, his eyes flickering—not with fear, but with longing.

"Someone ... everyone," he corrected hastily, his voice smooth. His hands unclenched, falling back to his sides, but Sera swore she'd caught something raw before he buried it. Fin glanced at his hands, flexing his fingers like something unseen ached. When he spoke again, his voice was low, almost reverent.

"I've said too much." Then softer—so soft she almost missed it—he whispered, "Or maybe not enough."

Sera's stomach twisted. Was that a warning? A confession? Before she could ask, he clapped his hands together, grinning widely again.

"Too much doom and gloom, my darling Guardian!" His grin snapped back into place, and the moment was gone like a breath of wind. His cheer sounded forced as he clapped his hands. "Let's not ruin your grand entrance, shall we?"

Sera's stomach twisted. She had questions—too many—but before she could ask where the portal was, there was a stir in the crowd at her back.

"Here comes the sheriff," someone called. The crowd buzzed with eager anticipation.

The darkness in Fin's eyes shone with wicked pleasure. "Well, dear lady, it's been fun, but I must go. It's showtime."

Before Sera could reply, a deep, rumbling roar reverberated through the air.

# **Chapter Six**

May 21 - Elves, Gnomes & Flying Hats—Oh My!

"Fiiiin!"

Sera whipped around in alarm, her hand flying to her throat, her eyes wide as they fell upon a man who oozed fury in every pore. Barely four feet tall, including a weathered Stetson sitting firmly on his head, he reminded her of Bram with his bulbous nose, thick untamed eyebrows, and a head full of unruly hair.

But where Bram appeared friendly, this man's features rivaled a stormy sky, ready to unleash bolts of lightning on the unwary earth. Or anyone unfortunate enough to cross his path. Clad in faded brown canvas trousers, a worn wool shirt, a leather vest, and worn-out cowboy boots that creaked with age, he stomped his way through the crowd. A red-plaid bandana, snug around his short, stocky neck, clashed spectacularly with his bushy brownish-orange hair.

In one hand, he gripped a dark staff of ironwood topped with a glowing amber crystal, which emitted a low hum. Spotting a five-pointed sheriff badge adorning his chest, Sera lifted one brow. This was Havenwood Cove's sheriff? He might be on the small side, but she had the feeling that what he lacked in size he more than made up for in the authority his mere presence radiated, as he quickly demonstrated.

He pointed a pudgy, stubby finger at Fin, and his voice boomed through the air, resonating with authority. "Fin, get yer arse down from that roof."

Fin's eyes glowed with pure joy. He held his hands up in apology to Sera. "Officer Grumpy Pants, oops, I mean, Sheriff Sam, has arrived to spoil such a delightful visit." He winked at her.

Sera's gaze flipped from Fin to the red-faced sheriff. "Um, perhaps you should listen—"

Fin waved her off, his attention laser-focused on the sheriff. "Trying to catch me again, Sam? You'd have better luck catching fog with a net, but carry on, Sheriff; it's the most exercise you get all week."

The sheriff slammed the end of the staff onto the ground. "Ya know the rules, ya damn Fae." His jaw quivered with anger.

Fin sighed dramatically. In the blink of an eye, he was gone.

Sera's heart skipped a beat as she whirled around in a circle, searching for the mischievous elf. Or Fae. Or whatever he was. "Where did he go?" she stammered. "He just went poof!" Her fingers flicked the air. Everything she once knew and understood about life and the laws of physics felt upside down.

Wild, almost maniacal laughter drew her attention back to the roof of her building. She backed up, shaded her eyes with one hand as she tipped her head back. Fin stood, feet braced on the highest peak of the roof. She just shook her head, beyond asking how.

Fin called down, "I see you're wearing that ridiculous hat again, Sheriff. Does it come with a free bowl of soup or is it just to keep your brains from evaporating?"

Another low, menacing growl erupted from the sheriff. The crowd behind the sheriff scattered, and Sera bit back a squeal of surprise when the man swung his staff out so fast it cut through the air with an angry whine.

"Don't ya worry, Miss Blackthorn," the sheriff said, his voice low and harsh. "I'll deal with this damn prankster." He punched the tip of his staff toward Fin. A flash of golden light exploded from the crystal, followed by the sound of a loud pop.

Fin, with arms windmilling, went soaring through the cloudless sky like a projectile propelled from a cannon. With palms against her cheeks, Sera's first reaction was horror and panic until sensing the excitement in the air warned there was more to come.

The sheriff, with a smug look on his face, nodded at her. "He won't be bothering you." He pivoted on his heel and strode down Main Street, the sound of his boots creaking and the dull thud of the staff hitting the ground as he used it as a walking stick.

Sera's heart continued to pound in her chest. Torn between defending Fin and feeling uncertain whether she should interfere, she debated whether to chase after the sheriff. Would he propel her through the air like a weighty bowling ball? The crowd parted to give the sheriff a wide path. She saw no fear, just humor in the smiles and muffled mirth behind cupped hands. Maybe Fin hadn't been hurt at all. Maybe this was just ... a game? Taking a chance, she followed the sheriff. "Sheriff—"

Out of the blue, a powerful gust of wind rushed down the center of the town, sending her hair flying around her face and forcefully snatching the sheriff's oversized Stetson from his head. The hat shot upward like a kite before gracefully descending onto the lush green grass a few feet ahead.

Gales of laughter broke out from the crowd. Sera breathed a sigh of relief. Fin was—somewhere. Alive and unhurt. Fuming with frustration, the sheriff spun in a circle, staff raised like an extension of his arm as his dark eyes scanned the rooftops. He unleashed a steady stream of curses directed at the unseen Fin.

Sera wrapped her arms around herself, feeling a shiver of anticipation as the furious sheriff stooped down to reclaim his Stetson just as a trail of neon pink shot into the hat. The now bright pink hat sprouted golden wings. Much to the delight of the amused spectators, the hat fluttered across the vibrant expanse of green grass, with the sheriff pursuing it.

Onlookers enthusiastically urged the sheriff to reclaim his elusive headgear. Sera's eyes widened in astonishment; her gaze fixed on the unbelievable scene unfolding before her. Her jaw dropped, and her eyes bugged out.

A hand on her shoulder startled her. "Don't fear, Miss Sera. Just another day in Havenwood."

Sera eyed Tommy, who'd moved to join her. "This is normal?" Her voice ended on a high squeak.

He slapped his knee and nodded vigorously. "Oh my, yes. Our sheriff takes his duties to protect Havenwood seriously, and Fin lives to annoy him. Might say they have a love-hate relationship."

Sera lifted a brow. "Meaning Fin loves to torment the sheriff and the sheriff hates being the brunt of Fin's pranks?"

George and Henry joined them. "Got that right, Miss Sera."

If her answering grin and laugh felt and sounded forced, well, who could blame her? She had a feeling that the town would provide many surprises. She just hoped she could handle what was obviously a magical community.

*And I'm a witch!* Which made her a part of this craziness! The thought was both wild and sobering. Her gaze wandered over the people, noticing for the first time the diversity among them: tall, elegant women with pointed ears, short, stubby figures in all brown, more gnome-like people, and even a child with wings hopping down the cobblestone path. Those who looked human didn't look surprised as they wandered from shop to shop. Were they witches as well?

Sera rubbed her temple where a headache brewed. *And no wonder*, she thought. She feared that if she saw just one more unexplained bit of magic or whatever, her head would explode! She backed up a few steps, feeling overwhelmed. Not just through this brief introduction into Havenwood Cove, but through everything that had happened since the delivery of the flowers and journal. She needed time to process everything.

She glanced at her grandmother's shop. The woman who knew her father hadn't returned. And no wonder. Fin had probably scared away her first customer, which was too bad. Part of her longed to hear about her father, even though at the moment, she didn't think she could absorb any more. *Hopefully, she'll be back.*

"Uh, I should go," Sera announced, taking a step back from the chaos of the town swirling around her. She took one last look at the town and realized for the first time that she wasn't a visitor. She belonged there. That thought spurred her back to her car. Once inside her Mini, she rested her forearms and head on the steering wheel.

"OMG! Did all that truly happen?" Her plan to check out the shop flew out the window, along with her sanity! She, Seraphina Blackthorn, was a coward. "I was once the woman who dictated meeting agendas. Now I'm debating if I just watched a hat *sprout* wings," she moaned.

Impossibilities have become possibilities.

Lifting her head to be sure no one was witnessing her mini meltdown—ha-ha, *in* her Mini—she wondered just what her grandmother had gotten her into. "No, can't blame Nonie," she muttered. "I agreed to this insane plan to take over her yarn shop and become some sort of Guardian. Well, sort of agreed."

Had she really had a choice? Sera felt cheated to learn she had a grandmother and didn't have the chance to meet her. She picked up the thick envelope on the seat beside her. On the journal page, it had been a small square, like a sticker, but once out of the journal, it became a regular-sized envelope stuffed with instructions.

She didn't need to reread it to know that her grandmother had left to go wherever she'd had to go. She leaned her head back. "I hope you come back, Nonie. I need you."

Sera threaded her fingers through her hair. Her mind felt like a whirling tornado, with images, thoughts, and questions swirling wildly. "Focus on the now," she ordered herself. Maybe it would keep her sane. Starting the car, she returned to Vista Cliff Road and headed for her grandmother's house.

She exhaled. She craved normalcy and an escape from the whirlwind of adventures and magic that had suddenly become her norm. No more adventures. No more magic. Not today. Maybe tomorrow she'll figure out what to do next. She headed toward what looked to be another point of land sticking out over the ocean. According to the map on the seat beside her, the house should be on the cliff that jutted out toward the ocean. The map showed only one house labeled *Maude*.

The rhythmic crashing of the ocean waves filled the air, the soothing sound echoing through the surroundings. Glistening sunlight danced upon lines of gently rolling whitecaps headed for the cliffs, and as she curved inland, she spotted a driveway. Leaving Vista Cliff Road, she was eager to see the house in person, not in a mirror.

Her thumb found and rubbed her heart-stone on her wrist. "Thank goodness." Relieved, she blew out a breath of air and eased up on the gas as she crawled up a tree-lined driveway. An air of excitement filled her.

For ten years, this had been her home; a home filled with love and laughter. Though her memories of that part of her life were still hazy, she remembered her grandmother telling her stories at night, and spending time together in the vibrant gardens. She recalled swinging on a swing hung from a branch of a tall tree. Was it still there? And then there were relaxing walks through the forest with both her grandmother and father.

In her mind, Nonie's home came alive: sounds of birds in the gardens, her grandmother's delighted laughter when a limp flower came to life in Sera's hands—

"OMG!" Sera stopped the car to stare at her hands. "I remember being sad that the flower was dying, and I brought it back to life." She also remembered that it had been temporary, as no amount of magic could counter the natural cycle of death.

For a few minutes, she let the memories fill her: leaves scattering before her on a forest path, the solid, reassuring grip of her father's hand in hers. It still felt odd that she couldn't remember what he looked like, but the feeling of being loved felt strong. Eager for her first glimpse of her grandmother's house, she eased the car forward. Smiling, wishing her grandmother was still there to greet her, Sera leaned forward and drew her lower lip between her teeth as her gaze sought the house.

And hit the brakes at the sight of a run-down Victorian. In her mirror vision, her grandmother's house had been a pristine yellow queen, majestic and bright, surrounded by a lush garden where flowers sparkled like gems. What greeted her now was a dull muddy-gray, brown shell—weathered wood, peeling paint, and loose shingles sagging like tired shoulders. The shrubs and trees stood brittle and lifeless, not a single flower in sight.

"No ... no, this can't be Nonie's house," she whispered, her chest tightening as disappointment welled up. Overcome with sadness, she wondered why her grandmother had let such a beauty fade to ruin.

From the time she'd entered Havenwood Cove, the rich, floral landscape had charmed her. But here, everything was brown, as though the very land was barren or had the life sucked out of it. Even the air drifting around her hung heavy with the scent of dampness, age, and years of neglect.

The gems on her bracelet warmed, as though happy to be home. She sank back in her seat, her stomach twisting with unease. This wasn't the house she remembered, or the one that had shimmered to life in the mirror. That house had been vibrant, alive, touched by magic. This one looked tired, as though it had been waiting far too long for someone who never came.

She swallowed hard. *Maybe it's been waiting for me.* The thought lodged deep, refusing to let go. Nonie's letter had spoken of trust, of leaving the shop and this house in her care. Maybe this wasn't just neglect. Maybe the house itself felt her grandmother's absence as much as Sera did.

"Not too late," she whispered, gripping the steering wheel. "I'm here now."

But the words rang hollow against the peeling paint and broken windows. She stared at the house for a long moment before easing the car forward to the garage behind the house. Stepping out of the car, a gentle breeze carried the scent of salt and old wood, and the bright overhead sun enveloped her in a cocoon of warmth. For just a second, she felt a hum in the air—faint and tired but waiting. She drew a deep breath, squaring her shoulders. The house looked tired, but so was she. If it was waiting, then so was she. "Let's wake it up together."

# Chapter Seven



Sera took in her surroundings, forcing herself to trade the brief fantasies she'd clung to for the harsh reality in front of her. Her arrival in Havenwood Cove was far from the idyllic vision of the seaside vacation she'd imagined. And now, her adventure had taken yet another unexpected turn. She shook her head. In her mind, homecoming meant peace and comfort, even if it was just temporary until her grandmother returned.

But instead of peace, her comfort zone had been thoroughly trampled. Was it her fault for expecting too much? She rubbed her arms, glanced back at the car, and almost turned back. Boston had been predictable, safe. But there was nothing left for her there. Except for Pam. She laughed, the sound verging on hysteria. "I'm a forty-year-old woman with no place to call home."

Yet the sense of homecoming still felt as strong as when she'd driven up the drive. "Okay, one day at a time," she counseled herself. The sound of crashing waves mingled with the chirping of birds in the trees eased her misgivings. A flagstone path ran along the side of the house, leading the way toward the front, which faced the sea.

She took a step, then paused. From the corner of her eye, a ripple of color, almost a wrinkle in the air itself, drew her attention. Her head swung around, but in a flash of brightness, the rainbow trail of color zipped through an upper window of the drab house. Her pulse jumped. For one dizzying second, the air seemed to hum, alive. Then, it was gone. "What was that?" she whispered, biting her lip. Had it really been there? Wrinkling her nose, she decided she didn't want to know and returned her attention to the sound of waves and gulls.

Whatever else had gone wrong in her life, she knew she could count on the ocean's beauty; it was one promise that remained unbroken. A strong sea breeze ruffled her hair, tugging at it like an impatient friend urging her to hurry.

She continued on. A row of roses hugged the side of the house. Like everything else in sight, the plants appeared dead, the vines dark and brittle on tall trellises. A single limp leaf fluttered in the breeze. She touched it. Surely, the plants should have recovered from their winter hibernation.

"Nonie, what happened here?" she whispered.

*The destruction of Havenwood Cove and all within ...*

Her grandmother's warning played in her head. Sera turned in a slow circle. A sliver of dread slid up her spine. For the first time since receiving the journal, it hit home that there was danger, that this wasn't just a summer vacation.

"Please," she whispered aloud. "Don't let me be too late!"

Rounding the curve that led to the front of the house, Sera stopped to study the asymmetrical façade and gables of her grandmother's home. "She's still a beauty," she murmured, her voice barely audible as her gaze roamed across the neglected house. In her mind, she envisioned what a fresh coat of paint could do. "I could do this for Nonie. Payback for allowing me to stay the summer." A wave of determination filled her, and she saw the house not as it was, but as it could, and should be.

Tapping her cheek with one finger, she cocked her head to one side and considered her choices. "I think shades of Seafoam or stormy gray blues, colors that would blend with the coastal landscape," she decided, hoping Havenwood Cove had painting services. With her eyes closed, the house came alive in her mind.

"A turret with windows, a bay window with a cozy nook—perfect for getting lost in a book or just watching the waves." Of course, that was a bit more than a new paint job. Opening her eyes, she stuck her hands in her back pockets. A sense of peace chased the tension in her shoulders and neck away. Years of curtailing her penchant for daydreaming receded like the waves rolling back out to sea. She grinned. "I'm free," she said, her voice almost giddy. "If I want to engage in harmless dreaming, why not? There isn't anyone to tell me it's childish."

Her gaze took in the neglected garden. "And I can think of no better place than to indulge in some creative fantasies." Tilting her head back, she closed her eyes, immersing herself in the image of the house of her dreams. Shaking her head, she gave a half-giggle. "If I was Cinderella's godmother, I'd wave my wand and say 'bibbidi-bobbidi-boo.' But I'm not." She sighed. Nor could she wrinkle her nose like Samantha in *Bewitched*. "Oh well."

A breath of sweet air swirled around her, and as it caressed her skin, a curious warmth spread through her, as though the very air recognized her. She felt lighter, as if something deep within the house was responding to her presence, welcoming her home in a way she couldn't quite explain. "Okay, Maude," she addressed the house. "I'll take you as you are, if you accept me as I am."

As though the house heard, Sera felt a subtle shift in the air and an answering vibration beneath her feet. She lifted her arms over her head, welcoming the gentle caress, and felt an overwhelming desire to see the ocean. If memory served—and that was a big *if* at this point—there was a seating area on the cliff overlooking the sea. Taking one last look at the house, her brows rose when she spotted a single rose bloom in the bed alongside the front wall. Her frown deepened.

It hadn't been there before, yet here it was. The rich yellow standing alone among lifeless vines filled her with a curious warmth, as though the house, like the roses, were waiting for her to awaken it. If the plant could bloom despite the odds, perhaps she could too.

Continuing down a path through the leafless trees and shrubs, the tangy, salty air filled her lungs and invigorated her senses, while the ocean wind continued to playfully rustle her hair. The warmth of the sun on her skin felt heavenly, providing a moment of solace and peace.

Above her, seagulls cried, their voices joining the rhythmic heartbeat of the sea. The melody soothed away her lingering doubts and nerves. Nonie was right. She needed to be near the ocean. Needed to be here. The rest? The insane town? A world of magic? Time would tell. Through the trees, she glimpsed the teasing flashes and sparkles of water.

The scent and sounds guided her along the path toward the cliff. Around a gentle curve, the scenery shifted, revealing a semicircle of stone benches with symbols etched into them. Here, everything looked healthy, from the grassy ground and flowering shrubs and plants. One hand went to her mouth as she smiled wistfully.

She took a deep breath, letting the calm of the place settle over her as she traced one of the Celtic runes that looked like two triangles forming a butterfly. The rune seemed familiar, tugging at the edges of her mind like an old dream. She traced it again, her fingers tingling. For a moment, the aestralite on her wrist glowed. "I know this," she whispered. "*Dagaz!*" Her heart raced as the word settled on her tongue. It felt familiar, yet ancient. This was a sacred place. She'd come here often with her grandmother and father.

*The symbol of dawn and awakening.*

The surrounding air seemed to still for a moment, thick with anticipation, and then—like a lightning strike—sharp pain surged through her mind. She staggered back, momentarily blinded, her legs weak beneath her as the world spun and another long-forgotten memory surged through her, overwhelming her senses. She'd been standing too close to the edge of the cliff where the Rootwall still stood.

*"Be careful, my sweet Eldling,"* a voice cautioned.

Sera smiled sadly. *Eldling.* Her father's endearment for her. "I miss you, Da," she said as she sank down onto the bench. For a moment, it felt almost as though her father sat beside her. She lifted a hand to her shoulder as though feeling his hand upon her. "Mom had no right to take this from me," she said, fighting her anger.

It hurt horribly not to remember what her father looked like. What color was his hair? His eyes? Were they filled with mischievous laughter like Fin's? Or were they deep and serious, like hers for most of her life? She jumped to her feet. Hands on her hips, chin tipped defiantly, she narrowed her eyes with fierce determination.

Now that she was back where she'd spent the first ten years of her childhood, surely, she'd remember more. No, she wanted to remember everything. Surely his death at the hands of cancer hadn't been so traumatic that it kept her from remembering him? She rubbed her temples. Touching the rune once again, the sharp pain ebbed. The rune glowed faintly, as if still pulsing with her heartbeat.

Breathing deeply, Sera faced the sea. She kicked a small rock, sending it flying over the flowering hedge. "Anger won't help. Won't get me the answers I need. No, answers I deserve!" Unable to deal with any more disappointment or frustration, she turned her back on the sea and headed back to the house, choosing a path that cut through a stand of trees.

Lost in her own thoughts, she didn't notice that the trees and shrubs were turning green as she strolled along a path of stones with moss growing between them. She skidded to a stop when she found herself in an amazing garden. Colorful blooms in every shade and hue, many so vibrant they nearly hurt her eyes, spread out before her. Her jaw dropped.

"This was not here moments ago! Was it?" She'd taken a different path to the cliff so hadn't seen this garden. She spun around in a circle, scanning the garden in every direction, her pulse quickening. She kneeled, pressing her fingers into the damp earth, feeling its pulse beneath her skin. Alive!

A shiver ran up her spine. Had she wandered into someone else's garden? The beauty of the garden wrapped around her like a blanket, soothing her raw nerves. "More magic," she breathed with awe.

Trees, shrubs, and flowers mixed and mingled and created cozy nooks with benches, chairs, and tables made of rock or wood. There was even a carved-wood swing that looked as though the supporting sides were planted trees.

Sera breathed out her worries and fears and inhaled the sweet, tangy scent of a late spring garden in full bloom. She bent down, brushing her fingers over a bright yellow flower with a crimson center. To her surprise, the bloom seemed to rise higher, leaning toward her hand. A delicate vine brushed against her cheek as if caressing her in greeting. She cupped the rosy-pink bloom of the vine, inhaling its soft, sweet fragrance.

"Oh, my stars! Just incredible," she whispered, a smile tugging at her lips. She promised herself she'd spend more time here, soaking in the peace and beauty. That swing over by the oak tree was calling her name—a good book, a big mug of tea, and maybe a piece or two of chocolate, and she'd be in heaven.

As she strolled through the secluded garden, everything seemed brighter, more alive. Every bloom, every green leaf or stem appeared richer, their colors more vibrant. Flowers seemed to shift as she passed, their heads turning toward her like an audience captivated by her presence. The sensation was strange but soothing, as if the garden itself welcomed her return.

A low rustling on the other side of the garden drew her attention. Stopping, she narrowed her eyes. A chill ran down her arms. Was there someone else in the gardens watching her? Her gaze narrowed, but she didn't see any movement. Still, she scanned the area. Wait! There! A shadow among the shadows? She squinted, and her eyes blurred. The harder she tried to see, the blurrier her sight became, like a painting that refused to stay still.

She blinked against the slight ache from trying to pierce the shadows and rubbed her eyes as she recalled the same odd blurring of her eyesight with the delivery driver. Did she need glasses? "Wow, I must really be tired or stressed," she said. The leaves stilled, as if the garden itself was holding its breath, then the breeze returned as if nothing had happened. The feeling of being watched vanished as she studied the cluster of trees and bushes dotted with orange blooms for a moment longer before continuing down the path. Whatever had been there was no longer there.

"Time to go home," she told herself. With a start, she realized that this place already felt like home. She'd take it one day at a time, especially as she had the feeling that her first day running her grandmother's yarn shop would be filled with surprises.

But not as big a surprise as the sight that greeted her as the garden gave way to the front of the house. She froze, unable to believe her eyes as a coat of fresh paint shimmered beneath the sun. She pinched her arm. Hard. "Ow! Okay, I'm awake. I'm not dreaming" she said as she stared in dumbfounded disbelief at the house.

Gone was the ghastly, run-down brown Victorian. In its place stood a proud queen wearing a royal coat of paint in shades of a mesmerizing, stormy blue-gray that mirrored the hues of an impending storm. As she watched, the brown trim morphed into pristine white while accents of weathered, rusty red added touches of rustic charm. The windows, like beacons of warmth, emitted a soft golden glow, inviting her to step inside.

She blinked. Something more than the paint color had changed. The house was different, but how? The gables seemed to shift when she looked away, settling into new angles when she glanced back. Her gaze flicked over the large bay window that now graced the side of the front door, glowing warmly in the evening light. Her breath hitched.

Bay windows? It was as if her wish had been magically granted. A flash of sunlight on a pane of glass drew her attention. To her delight, the window stretched, reaching for the sky until it became a majestic turret with windows on every side. A third floor materialized, like a hidden secret finally revealing itself.

Fingers pressed to her lips, eyes wide, Sera soaked in the sight and felt the comforting embrace of the house as it whispered promises of coziness and serenity. The scene before her was a symphony of colors, scents, and emotions, inviting her to embark on a new chapter within its walls.

Sera's heart swelled with adoration. She felt lightheaded, almost unable to comprehend the change. Joy filled her until she thought she just might explode. This house captivated and enthralled her more than the cold and rigid mansion she'd called home for fifteen long years.

"How—this isn't possible—is it?" Drawing a shaky breath, she shook her head. Had the house—Maude—read her mind? "The impossible is possible," she said as she clasped one hand over her bracelet. "Magic! Okay, I get it! Might take me time to get used to it though."

A surge of adrenaline left her breathless. "What an extraordinary adventure."

Her statement stopped her from racing to the door to enter and explore. "Adventure?" She rocked back on her heels. She shivered, and her fingers twitched at her side. Was this her choice, or had it already been made for her? One step, and she would be part of it— whatever it was.

She exhaled slowly and hesitated, knowing she was about to cross an unknown threshold. Her heart raced. The house loomed alive, watching. One step would change everything. But hadn't her life already changed? She drew a steady breath. "Okay," she whispered, "let's do this. I accept adventure."

###

A dark figure emerged from the shadows. He turned to his companion. "She almost saw me, Elyn. That should be impossible," Ryker Stormrider mused.

"Her magic is powerful, my friend. Look around you. She did this." He waved his hands, showing the garden now in full bloom.

Ryker shook his head. The air still hummed with her magic, thick and alive. Not only was he amazed by the strength of the magic that transformed the dead into vibrant life, but he was man enough to admit her power made him nervous. He rubbed his tattoo, wincing as the pulse beneath his skin flared again, a molten throb that spread up his arm like liquid fire. Gritting his teeth, he refused to rub at it like some nervous boy—but his fingers twitched toward it anyway. He laughed humorlessly at the thought. It was a brand all right, and one he hadn't asked for.

"Why does she feel familiar?"

A flicker of something—someone—ghosted through his mind. Laughter. Red hair. Green eyes. And a voice—soft, teasing—before it all shattered like mist. Almost close enough to touch. His jaw clenched.

Elyn slapped Ryker on the back. "As she is your landlord for the next few months, you have time to find out."

Ryker shook his head. "I'm not here for her. The elders sent us here for answers."

Elyn smirked. "You, my friend. They sent you." He spread his arms wide. "The rest of us? We're here for the adventure. And to keep you out of trouble." His gaze turned sightless, his voice dropping to something more solemn.

"Your past is tied to hers," Elyn murmured, his gaze distant. "More tightly than you're ready to remember."

Ryker's jaw tightened, but he said nothing. The tattoo burned again, hotter this time—as if agreeing with Elyn.

# Chapter Eight

May 21 - Of Talking Birds & Purring Houses

Sera climbed the weathered granite steps, brushing her fingers along the smooth balustrade. Golden lanterns flanked the doorway, catching the last rays of the setting sun, while a pot of yellow and orange flowers brightened the porch near the threshold.

The double-wide oak doors gleamed as though freshly varnished. Carved details along the oval stained-glass panes caught the light, spilling colorful patterns onto the porch. A majestic dragon-shaped doorknocker greeted her with a blue-green, unblinking gaze.

"Beautiful," she breathed, running a finger over the tiny snout before reaching for the doorknob. "Oh, keys. Dang, left them in the car." She frowned as she realized there was no lock. Reaching out to test the door, she was startled when it opened on its own with a soft creak.

Her pulse quickened. "Okay, this is a bit spooky." She laughed nervously. "But not as spooky as a house transforming itself!" Cautiously, she pushed the door open and peered inside. A long marble table took up one side of the entryway. A tall vase of flowers sat beneath an oval mirror. Relieved that everything looked normal, she hesitantly stepped inside.

Should she call out? Alert Molly, her grandmother's housekeeper, of her arrival? The words died in her throat when she noticed an exquisite compass rose inlay set into the gleaming oak flooring. The intricate design and the rich colors of contrasting wood created a stunning work of art that shimmered in the shaft of afternoon sunlight that poured in through the open door. Each point on the detailed compass pointed in a cardinal direction.

But it was the centerpiece that held her mesmerized gaze. A dragon stared back, cradling a luminous orb. Its opalescent surface shifted from milky white to shimmering silver, light pulsing faintly beneath as though moonlight were trapped inside. "Gorgeous."

Another memory broke free, this one of her grandmother telling her bedtime stories; her favorite had been the love story between a Dragon and a witch. Bending her knees, she reached down and brushed her fingers across the gleaming moon. A tingle of warmth ran up her arm. The gems on her wrist flared, showering the compass rose with a glittering rainbow of sparks. Startled, she fell back, hitting the slightly open door, which shut with a decisive click. The bracelet dimmed.

"More magic," she breathed. She should be used to it, but she had the feeling it would take her a while to accept it as the norm in Havenwood Cove. Jumping to her feet, she avoided walking on the compass rose. "Now what?"

"She's heeerrrreeee!"

The hair on Sera's arms rose. The voice—gravelly, stretched, unnatural—echoed down the empty hallway. A slow chill crept up her spine. She clenched her fists, willing her pulse to slow. Nope. Not creepy at all.

"Seraphina Blackthorn has finally graced us with her presence." Wild, cackling laughter followed.

Oh. My. God. She took a step forward. "Um, hello? Molly?" The hesitant greeting stuck in her throat. The odd voice had to belong to Molly, the housekeeper. Her grandmother's letter only mentioned Molly, and a bird named Syrus. If that voice belonged to Molly, Sera needed to rethink her vision of her as a gentle, kindly, older woman who fussed over her domain.

"Hello?" Her voice came out low and hesitant. She cleared her throat and tried again. "Hello, Molly?"

The voice responded. "Welcome to Maude's delightful loony bin—hope you're ready for what's coming. Come join the fun where the house listens, the walls whisper, and I—well—I squawk!" Another round of maniacal laughter followed.

Squawk? The harsh voice had to belong to Nonie's bird, but Sera had never heard a bird talk like this! "Oh, Nonie, you and I need to talk!" she said, her voice taking on an irritated edge. Her grandmother should have prepared her for what she'd find in Havenwood Cove. Sera had hoped for a quiet, restful evening and time to absorb the craziness of the day, but clearly, that was off the table!

The atmosphere in the entry thickened with anticipation, as if the house itself waited for Sera's response, but she wasn't sure what to say. She crossed the entryway but stopped at the sound of a furious, screeching voice.

"Syrus! A stubborn weed in my garden you are! My job is greeting guests, and yours is stayin' quiet and outta trouble, it is."

"Oh dear, Molly, the tyrant of tidiness has spoken! Brace yourself, Sera—adventure awaits," the bird declared.

Sera slapped her forehead. "What craziness am I stepping into? Though after everything in Havenwood Cove, she shouldn't be shocked that her grandmother's household was just as eccentric. Before she could move, a tiny figure darted into the entryway with the grace of a windstorm through the underbrush.

"*Milady!*" the high-pitched voice squeaked, full of earnest delight. "Welcome you to Maude's, I do. Cross this threshold and let the enchantment of hearth and home fill your spirit." She clasped her hands together and bowed so low her long, thin nose nearly brushed the floor. For the third time that day, Sera came face-to-face with someone not wholly human. Bram and the sheriff, both magical, reminded her of gnomes, yet each had human-like characteristics. And Fin, as an Elf or Fae, looked human, except for his ears. And his unusual abilities!

There was no mistaking this tiny woman for a human. Not with skin the texture of bark and mossy tendrils covering her head, swaying gently as if caught in a private breeze.

Her round, wizened face made her seem ancient, and her bulbous, midnight-dark eyes watched Sera intently.

Recalling her manners, Sera closed her mouth and focused on the woman's unusual attire: a charming tapestry of natural fibers adorned with leaves and petals, as were the tiny shoes shaped like pea pods peeping out from beneath her long skirt.

*I shouldn't be surprised*, she thought to herself. Not after all that she'd encountered in such a short time. Somehow, Sera had envisioned a human housekeeper, a kindly woman like her grandmother. Maybe even someone more like Alice, the wise and loving housekeeper in charge of the Brady household, or if magic was a requirement, how about a Samantha from *Bewitched*?

Sera held out both hands. "Please, call me Sera, and you don't have to bow to me."

The woman shook her head so hard her hair swung from side to side. "Greet you properly, I must."

"Ah, okay." Sera tunneled her fingers through her hair. "You must be Molly?"

The little woman beamed. "Yes. Molly I am."

"And you are the housekeeper?"

Molly placed her hands, one on top of the other, over her heart. "More than a housekeeper or caretaker I am. My bond with Maude is eternal. Share in her joys and sorrows, her secrets, and stories, I do. A haven for those who dwell within, here we create and, in my heart and roots, I am a valued hearth-tender, a Guardian of the warmth and spirit of the home, I am," she finished proudly.

"Oh. I see." In her mind, she called herself a liar as she didn't understand any of this. *I can't believe I thought that coming to Havenwood Cove would be simple: a vacation in a peaceful seaside town where I could plan my future.* The ground beneath her felt as stable as a pool of quicksand, and she was sinking fast.

Needing some air and a few minutes to herself, she jerked her thumb over her shoulder. "Uh, I should go unload my car. Perhaps you can direct me to where I should put my belongings. I'm afraid there are quite a few boxes." *A lot more than should have fit in my Mini!*

Molly waved her hands. "No need. Already taken care of, it is. And your car be safe in the garage, she is."

Sera blinked. "Ah. Magic, right?"

Molly grinned. "Maude, she gave you the room above, the one with the bay window."

"Maude? The house?"

Nodding, eyes wide with pleasure, Molly said, "Takes care of all who live within her walls, she does."

Sera studied the earnest face below her, feeling awkward as she towered over the wizened woman. She resisted the urge to bend down to be on the same level, much as adults did when conversing with young children. She chewed her lower lip.

"I don't mean to be rude, Molly, but may I ask what type of magical being you are?" Never in her wildest imagination did she think she'd ever need to ask that question of anyone.

Molly bowed her head again, her hair falling over her face. "At your service, I am. A *Rootling,* I am called. Draw from magic to strengthen and nurture and protect the heart of this home and ensure it remains a sanctuary of comfort and safety, I do—"

A harsh bark of laughter interrupted Molly's serious and impassioned speech. "Ah, Molly, with her tales longer than a winter's night," the voice screeched. "Should we get comfortable, or will there be an intermission?" Hoots of laughter followed.

Molly spun around, whipped a white cloth from around her waist, and stomped back into the room she'd just come from. "Syrus! The echo of woodpeckers in my grove, you are! Impossible to ignore and twice as annoying, you be!"

"Oh man, don't piss off a Rootling," Sera mumbled as Molly aimed her insults like a pro cocking back a bow. She fired her barbs with deadly accuracy, judging by Syrus's swift retaliatory responses. Sera winced as the shouting and squawking grew louder. For one moment, Sera debated whether to make a run for it.

Hands on her hips, she paced as she considered her options. And go where? Back to Boston? To predictability? No, she'd spent years playing it safe. Now, her life was filled with possibilities. She had to suck it up and see this through. Scrubbing the hair away from her face, she pulled her shoulders back. "Well, I wanted adventure, and here it is. Besides, I'm no coward," she murmured, needing to hear the words.

And someone needed to make sure there was no bloodshed between Syrus and Molly, so she took the decisive steps to the arched doorway. The room before her featured the large bay window she'd seen from outside. Natural light spilled into the room from the expansive window, which gave off a harmonious blend of comfort and enchantment, with the window itself offering a generous view of the lush garden and the distant sea. It framed the outdoors as a living piece of artwork.

Shelves overflowing with books lined the wall facing a grand fireplace. The mantle held oddities and artifacts: a tall, black bottle filled with lights that twinkled like a night sky, an antique compass, and a domed clock with glowing mushrooms inside. In an alcove to one side of the room, Sera's gaze latched onto a massive, wooden birdcage carved out of a tree.

The base was a wide, sturdy trunk, its branches stretching upward to form the bars. Tiny blue-and-white flowers bloomed across the leafy canopy, glowing with soft light. The air around the cage buzzed faintly, thick with unseen magic.

Inside, a bird of incredible majestic beauty held her spellbound. The bird's feathers were a rainbow fusion of fiery oranges and yellows, reminiscent of a mystical phoenix with the blues, greens, and purples of a macaw. Its bright crest stood tall, reminding Sera of a cockatoo.

She took one step into the room. "Syrus?" Her voice sounded breathless. She'd never seen a bird as beautiful as this one, and somehow, she knew he too was a magical creature.

Syrus fluffed his shimmering feathers and let out a dramatic squawk. "Ah, a fresh audience!" His voice carried the smug satisfaction of a performer about to take center stage. "Come to watch Molly flail about in defeat, have you?" His violet, silver-flecked eyes locked onto Sera with a mischievous glint.

Molly scowled and shook a long, twiggy finger at the bird. "One day—"

"You finally admit I'm superior?" Syrus puffed out his colorful chest of feathers.

Molly narrowed her eyes and snapped her towel like a pro with a bullwhip. "Fluff up all you like, you ball of scroungy feathers. You're the one in a cage. Lock the door and toss the key, I will!"

"Doubtful, my dear Rootie-Tootie Rootling. Doubtful." He delivered this in a sing-song voice as he sent a shower of sparks through the wooden bars.

"Careful, Molly! I might just turn up the heat on your towel tricks."

Molly huffed, rolled her enormous eyes, and, using the towel, popped each spark out of existence. She waved one hand and sent a blast of air into the cage. Syrus screeched, his talons gripping the wood and his wings spreading wide as he fought for his balance. When the wind died, his feathers were ruffled. Molly smirked. "Watch it, bird, or blast you into the sky, I will."

Sera slapped both hands on top of her head as the fireworks and insults continued. It was obvious both had forgotten her presence. Syrus had warned her that she was stepping into a madhouse, and she was afraid he was right.

"No, this isn't a madhouse," she corrected herself. "It's a three-ring magical circus!" she exclaimed, her voice filled with a mix of astonishment and disbelief. "Beam me up, Scotty," she muttered. Havenwood Cove was not like any place she'd ever seen or heard of on Earth.

Squaring her shoulders, she marched into the room as though she were back in Boston, facing down stubborn clients. "Molly! Syrus!" Her voice rang with authority. The two froze mid-argument, turning toward her as if seeing her for the first time. Sera's pulse

raced, but she refused to back down. "Now, someone is going to explain to me what in the world is going on."
###
Silence slammed into the room like a door shutting. Two pairs of eyes narrowed on her, sharp and unblinking. Sera's steps faltered. Now that she had their attention, she had no idea what to say—or do. Uncharted waters again. Grabbing the first thought that came to her, she waved a hand toward the cage.

"Sorry to interrupt, but ... won't Syrus burn or chew his way out?" Her mind grappled with the fact that the bird, if he was a bird, could shoot fire like a dragon.

Molly's jaw dropped, and her eyes went so wide, Sera feared those bug orbs might fall out of her head. Then the tiny Rootling doubled over in a fit of laughter. She laughed so hard she fell to the floor, her fists and heels beating on the wood. Her laugh, though wild, sounded like the bubbling of a woodland stream. She finally stumbled to her feet. "Oh, *Milady*. Too much, are you."

Molly gave Syrus one last flick of her towel. "You're like a feather in a whirlwind, Syrus. Beautiful but utterly chaotic. Pop off elsewhere. There is much I must discuss with our mistress." She wiggled her fingers dismissively.

The bird stretched out its huge wings, the tips brushing the wooden sides. "Ah, Queen Molly has decreed! Shall I bow or curtsy this time?" Squawking with obvious humor, the bird lifted its wings over his head and disappeared with a loud pop, leaving a rainbow trail of color to shimmer behind.

"Flying Phoenixes!" Sera stumbled back and clutched her hands to her chest. She turned in a circle, but the bird was gone. Hands planted on her hips, eyes narrowed, she asked, "Where did he go? And how did he do that?" Too many people so far all had the ability to just disappear: Lady Lillian and Fin came to mind.

Molly shrugged. "Away. Like a phoenix rising from the ashes, impossible to ignore he is, and twice as impossible to forget.

With her brows drawn, hips jutting forward, and arms crossed, Sera gave Molly the no-nonsense glare no co-worker ever wanted to receive. "And you? Are you going to disappear as well?"

Molly looked as though she wanted to laugh but thought better of it. She shuffled her foot. "No, Milady." She gulped and twitched her nose. "Well, not when you are looking," she added timidly.

What would Pam say or do if she told her of everything she'd encountered so far? And of course, she'd mention none of this to her mother, although she'd lived here before her father died, so she surely knew what went on in Havenwood Cove.

With Syrus gone, the room seemed quieter, almost too quiet. Sera finally let herself breathe. She ran a finger along the smooth branch of the cage. The leaves and flowers felt real, not fake. Glancing at the floor, she spotted bits of green and white. Her eyes widened. The trunk appeared to be growing right out of the floor as it merged perfectly into the wood flooring with not a single seam showing.

"Uh, Molly, is this cage growing up through the floor of the house?" She bent down to feel the floor and then ran her hand up the trunk.

"The cage is part of Maude. Cares for us, she does, even the pesky bird. Flames and foliage—our banter is as vibrant as it is scorching," she announced with a humorous gleam in her eyes and a low chuckle in her throat.

Standing, Sera waved her hand at the room at large. "So, Maude is the house, and she's alive? Sentient?" Sera pointed to the bay window. "She read my mind and added not just two bay windows, but a turret and changed her colors to what I imagined?" It sounded impossible, but what else could it be?

Molly nodded, her expression earnest. "After my missus left, Maude felt abandoned. But you saw her for what she is—a queen. Live here now, you do. Maude is yours, as you are hers." The overhead light in the room glowed brighter, as though Maude agreed.

"See?" Molly flapped her hands and danced in place like a pleased child. "Glad she is that you are here."

Sera eyed the room. "If I'd wanted neon orange?" The walls creaked ominously, and she laughed, raising her hands. "Kidding— you're perfect as you are." Okay, note to self: Don't insult the house or its housekeeper!

Offering another deep bow, Molly spoke, her voice soft and serious. "May this house wrap around you like a vine, offering comfort and support in every corner."

As if in response to Molly's blessing, a scented breeze, one of cedarwood, oak and the sweetness of wildflowers, swept through the cozy room, ruffling Sera's hair and wrapping her in what felt like a gentle embrace. The lights brightened, and a fire sprang to life in the fireplace.

"Ah, Maude approves of you, she does. Yes, she does." Molly twirled happily in a circle.

Sera chuckled. "Strangely enough, with everything else, that makes sense." She turned in a slow circle. "Uh, thank you, Maude." She addressed the room at large. The floor vibrated, and a hum filled the air.

*A purring house*? Sera giggled. After everything she'd seen today, it felt normal.

Sera felt a sense of disappointment and sighed. "So, it wasn't me. I didn't do this."

Molly tipped her head to one side, her pointed ear poking out as her curtain of moss and vines swung with the movement. "Your connection to Maude it was that allowed it to happen," she explained simply. "A Blackthorn and the new Guardian, you are."

Ignoring the reference to her status as the Guardian, Sera wandered over to the bookcase and ran her fingers along the spines of books, some new, some well-worn. There was a mix of paperback novels and hardbacks, along with rows of non-fiction. One title caught her eye: *Are You a witch? A Beginner's Journey*. Oh yeah, that sounded like a book she needed to read. As she surveyed the offerings, she knew she'd be in heaven if she had time to just sit and read.

"This is a lovely room," she said to Molly, who nodded happily.

Sera eyed the cozy seating area in front of the fireplace. The marble mantel held several photo frames, flanked by fat candles at either end. The flickering flames and crackling fire added warmth to the room.

Walking over, her heart ached as she stared at a photo of a young child with bright, curly, red hair. She picked up the silver frame, gazed into her own laughing eyes, and smiled sadly. It was the first picture she'd seen of herself as a child before moving to California. She hugged the image to her chest. Her mother had told her that all her childhood photos had been lost in the move. Was that a lie? Were there more photos, maybe even some of her father? She'd ask Molly later.

Another double frame caught her eye. Tears rolled down her cheeks as she returned the first photo and picked up the frame containing her high school and college graduation photos. How had her grandmother gotten hold of these? Had her mother sent them to her? Betrayal and confusion churned inside her, but as she gazed at the photos, something deeper settled over her—proof that her grandmother had always loved her.

"The past is past," she murmured, gently setting the photos back on the mantel. Still, a small thread of hope tugged at her. Perhaps there were more pieces of her past waiting to be discovered. She took a deep breath, steadying herself. There would be time to sort through these feelings later. For now, she'd take it as it came. Her gaze drifted across the room, landing on a large, clear crystal ball sitting on a gleaming, dark wood table, surrounded by a trio of candles.

Sera moved closer, her hand hovering over the clear surface. The air felt cooler, and the flickering candles stilled. She felt a strange tugging sensation in her chest as the air shifted around her. Her curiosity swelled, but so did an odd sense of caution. She hesitated for a beat, wondering what she might see or feel.

Taking a deep breath, she lightly touched the ball with the tip of one finger and gasped as the inside swirled into a frosted cloud and a thread of warmth ran up her arm. The stones and crystals on her wrist responded, each glowing in response to the magical object. A faint hum in her ears, along with the warmth, confirmed that this was a magical object, as did the sense of homecoming that slid from her head to her toes, followed by the faint images of pink and blue cats swimming inside the globe in a slow, dreamlike rhythm, as though inside a fishbowl.

"Oh, I used to see colored cats," she remembered. Her grandmother's words floated inside her mind: *Your gift is the ability to see what is not there.* Watching the swirling antics of the cats, Sera wasn't sure how the ability to see make-believe cats was going to help her save the town. "Some gift," she murmured.

Still, Sera felt as though the crystal ball recognized her, accepted her. One by one, the cats faded as other faces winked in and out: her grandmother, several other women, all with the same golden red hair as her own. She grinned. Were these her ancestors, other Witches? Previous Guardians of the Moondragon?

She wanted to reach for them, to beg for answers, but the faces stretched and smeared, bleeding across the glass like spilled ink. A shadow followed, slow and creeping, its smoky fingers searching, seeking. The darkness swallowed the figures and the light until only suffocating blackness remained.

She yanked her finger away and stumbled back, relieved when the crystal ball became a clear orb once more. Molly's happy chatter faded as she caught sight of Sera's face.

"You saw something, you did." Molly's voice was quiet now. Not teasing. Not playful. Just knowing.

Sera forced air into her lungs and pasted on a smile. The warmth in the room had dimmed. Even the fire flickered, as if uncertain. "It was nothing," she lied, but the darkness clung to her thoughts like smoke, curling tighter with every breath—as if it hadn't finished with her yet.

# Chapter Nine

May 21 - So ... About That Portal Problem

Sera shivered and rubbed her arms to shake off the lingering chill from the threat she'd not only seen in the crystal ball but felt in her bones. Though the fire crackled in the hearth, she no longer felt its warmth. For the first time since signing her name in the journal and accepting the role of Guardian, she realized that she truly didn't understand what she'd agreed to. Despite the discovery of the joy and wonder of magic and meeting so many quirky characters, misgivings assailed her. Even the beautiful house couldn't chase the unease that clung to her skin. What had she agreed to?

She'd told Molly she'd seen nothing, she reflected as she wandered the room that took up the entire front of the house. She ignored the housekeeper's worried expression and constant wringing of her tiny hands. Technically, she hadn't lied. Darkness by itself wasn't a threat—was it?

Yet, the darkness and shadows felt threatening. Letting out a huff of air, she jammed her hands on her hips and admitted she wasn't ready for this. She needed time, and lots of it, to come to terms with everything that had happened since the delivery of the journal yesterday.

*Yesterday.* The reminder of how her life had changed in one day was almost frightening. It felt as though days had passed. She glanced around the room, desperately seeking a distraction from the cascade of thoughts and images falling like dominoes in her mind. Her gaze landed on the inlaid coffee table. On its gleaming surface, a dark green crocheted doily drew her attention. Leaning down, she traced the delicate pineapple pattern with her fingers. Hopefully, running a yarn shop would give her lots of time to indulge in her love of both crocheting and knitting. Straightening, she trailed her fingers over the vase of flowers that sat in the center of the low table. A shiny hardcover book graced one edge. Her gaze fell on the book's title:

**Beneath the Dragon Moon**
**by R.S. Rider**
**An Otherworldly Novel**

"Nonie reads fantasy?" Disbelief gave way to the pleasure of discovering something she had in common with her grandmother. Out of work for six months, Sera had caught up on her reading and binge watching her favorite movies and TV shows. Evan and his mother had considered fiction to be a waste of time, so she'd always read her favorite authors in secret on her phone or tablet.

She studied the bookshelves again, noting the worn spines showing this collection of books had been read and reread often. Evan's library held all the right books, with most having never been opened. All show. Just like him and his house, whereas what she'd seen of her grandmother's home was warm and full of character. *And characters*, she added silently with a sidelong glance at Molly hovering in the background.

Grinning, she picked up the novel with a dark, majestic dragon and moon gracing the cover. "I love his novels," she exclaimed to Molly. "They're dark yet filled with hope. This must be his newest." She hadn't realized he had a new book out.

"Whole shelf of his books, there is." Molly joined her. Her hands fluttered with excitement, and her eyes went wide as she leaned forward. "He be here, you know," she nearly squealed. "My missus, she rented the cottage to him and his family for the summer, she did."

Sera's jaw dropped. "You've got to be kidding me. *The* R.S. Ryder, the famous author, is here in Havenwood Cove?"

Molly nodded enthusiastically and pointed toward the far wall. "The cottage, she be hidden among the trees. Came for the Bloom and Moon Festival in two days' time, he did. Signing his books, he is."

"But I heard that he never does book signings or personal appearances." Sera's grip tightened on the book. "Wait, Nonie mentioned a renter in her letter ..." She thought back to the letter of instructions her grandmother had left in the journal. She tapped her fingernails on the hardback cover.

"Ryker something ..." She snapped her fingers. "Stormrider."

Her fingers tightened on the book as she reread the author's name. "R.S. Ryder is Ryker Stormrider?" At Molly's effusive nod, Sera exclaimed, "No. Freaking. Way." The elusive, reclusive author, the writer whose words had once carried her through the worst nights of her life, was currently renting her grandmother's cottage. What a small world! She flipped the book open to the back cover, scanning for the author's photo.

"Holy hootenanny! He is drop-dead gorgeous." Maybe it was shallow, but after the shadows and shivers, a silly distraction felt like taking deep gulps of air after nearly drowning.

The cliché of tall, dark, and handsome fit the man to a T with his flowing, midnight-black hair and mesmerizing eyes, a swirl of blues and greens that made him look both secretive and mysterious. The strong jawline and firm yet sensuous lips put him at the top of her list of fantasy-worthy men.

Her pulse raced, and she felt like a teenager in the presence of an idol. "Wow. And he's here!" Her heart fluttered. *You're forty. And free*, the voice in her head teased, but just as quickly, she shook off all thought of getting involved with the writer. Or any man, for that matter. "I'm free, and I'm staying that way," she announced. The last thing she needed or wanted was another man in her life. This was her time not only to be herself, but to discover who she was and what she wanted in life. Sera snapped the book closed.

The thrill of discovering her renter was the famous author faded as quickly as it came. A bookish crush wouldn't tell her how to save Havenwood Cove. Sera turned to Molly. "Nonie obviously enjoys his work, so why didn't she stay?"

The tiny Rootling's grin faded, and her eyes dimmed. She hesitated, her hands twisting in her apron. Molly sucked in a deep breath and lowered her head. One foot brushed the floor in a back-and-forth motion. "Guardian she is not."

Sera cocked her head to the side. "But she was."

Molly nodded but remained silent.

"Why did she leave, Molly?"

"One Guardian be allowed. If my missus stayed, Guardian she'd remain."

"So, she didn't just abandon me?"

"No. Stay with you if she could."

Molly both bowed and curtseyed, her thin, twig-like arms held out to her sides. "Guardian of the Moondragon, you are."

There it was again. *Guardian of the Moondragon.* Sera felt as though she'd landed in a fantasy movie or role-playing game. Like Frodo must have felt in *The Lord of the Rings*, the responsibility felt too immense for one person to bear. She thought back to the journal.

*I bestow upon you the title of "Guardian of the Moondragon." Accept your birthright, your legacy.* Sera shivered as though an icy finger traced her spine from neck to base. Realization struck. She hadn't inherited a name—she'd inherited a duty.

Recalling her grandmother telling her it was time for the seventh, the most powerful—her—Sera paced. Molly watched with wide eyes as Sera gripped the back of one cozy chair facing the fireplace. "What am I facing, Molly?" She held up a hand to forestall Molly as she recalled her grandmother's message in the mirror.

The destruction of Havenwood Cove and all within.

A power born of shadow and hunger.

Seeing again that vision of shadows and darkness in the crystal ball, Sera's heart raced. Magic coursed through her blood, linking her to an ancient lineage she hadn't known existed. She thumped the back of the chair. *Guardian of the Moondragon.*

The words pressed against her ribs, heavy as iron. She wasn't ready. She'd never be ready. But Nonie had believed in her—and for Havenwood Cove's sake, she'd have to believe too. It was time to learn just what she faced as the seventh Guardian.

Facing Molly, Sera ran her finger through her hair. "What did my grandmother, and the others before her, do as Guardians?"

"Waited they did," Molly said with a firm nod as though that explained everything.

Sera frowned. "Waited? For what?"

"To be called," Molly explained. She twisted her twig-like fingers. "Before you, no need for a Guardian, there was. Held the title, passed the legacy they did, but never faced the threat. First Guardian called upon to act you are, Milady."

The weight of generations pressed down on Sera. She thought of the journal, the bracelet, the legacy she never asked for, and the visions of shadows that haunted her mind. The shadows she'd seen weren't just images in a crystal ball. They were real, and they were waiting for her to fail.

She eyed a plush settee and two antique armchairs, which created a cozy seating area facing the bay window. Outside, the air turned deep purple with thin fingers of golden light spearing the sky from the horizon. "Molly, I need your help."

Her expression solemn, Molly inclined her head. "Yes, Milady. Help you, I will."

Mentally rolling her eyes at Molly's formality, Sera lifted a brow. "Please use my name, Molly. *Milady* makes me feel old. Or from the Victorian era."

Molly frowned. "Honor you, I must. As I did your grandmother and so many others." She tipped her head to one side, thought a moment, and offered a wide grin. "But do as you request, I will, Miss Sera."

"Much better. Let's sit." Sera led the way across the room and took a seat on the edge of the couch. Molly scrambled after her, shoved an ottoman closer to her, and hopped up to sit, legs dangling as her feet didn't reach the colorful rug on the floor.

Deciding to tackle the Guardian role first, she asked, "My task, job, whatever you want to call it, is to save Havenwood Cove, correct?"

A combination of sadness and fear entered Molly's eyes. Clasping her hands tightly, shoulders hunched, she spoke, her voice both formal and quivering. "Yes, Milady," she confirmed, reverting to her more formal form of address.

Tunneling her fingers through her hair, tugging on the strands as though that might organize her scattered thoughts, she nodded. "Okay, I got that part. Not sure how or what I'm supposed to do, but let's come back to that. Since my arrival in Havenwood Cove, I've met some unusual people. Bram, the gatekeeper, the sheriff, and an elf named Fin, and Lady Lillian. And you, Syrus, and let's not forget Maude, of course." She held her hands out, palms up. "None of you are human, or not wholly, and I don't even know what kind of bird Syrus is. Birds don't spit fire." That recollection was mind-boggling. He wasn't just a talking bird. He shimmered, like a creature made of thought and shadow.

Molly giggled, then clapped a hand over her mouth as though realizing Sera was being serious. "No, Mil—Miss Sera. Happy I am to say only one Syrus. Bram and Sheriff Sam be gnomes. Not sure what Fin be. Could be Elf or Fae, and I, of course, am a Rootling. Maude, she be part of the magical forest."

"Magical forest?" Sera quickly held up a hand. "No, don't go there. Not yet. All this magical stuff should be impossible, yet I'm seeing it with my very own eyes. I'm forty, and I've never seen anything like what I've seen so far. Fences, or Rootwalls, that grow, people and birds *poofing,* and even I'm now different." Standing, she paced to the bay window, too restless to sit. Outside, dusk slowly crept over the gardens and obscured the sea.

Molly shrugged. "A Blackthorn you are. A witch you've always been. Sleeping, you were."

Sera nodded. Sleeping? That fit. She felt as though she'd woken from a deep slumber, almost as though the life she'd led was a dream, and now she was awake.

She spun around. "Who was that delivery driver? He spoke some odd words, and right after, I started to remember things. I woke up. I need answers, Molly."

Shifting, Molly looked uncomfortable and refused to meet Sera's eyes. "Cannot say, Miss Sera. Trusted him, my missus did."

"Yet, Nonie didn't come herself. She sent a stranger to deliver the journal. She could have—no—she should have been the one to come. I have so many questions." Returning to the couch, Sera plopped back down and crossed her arms across her chest to hide her shaking hands. Her foot jiggled, a sure sign that she was feeling rattled. She felt as though she'd fallen down a hole in the ground, like poor Alice. All this magic was a wonderland of its own, but her logical mind needed an explanation.

"Tell me the truth, Molly. Is Nonie safe?"

Molly let out a long breath and nodded. "Safe she is."

Sera felt somewhat better. If her grandmother was safe, she had to believe the time would come when they could be reunited.

"Okay, let's get back to all this magic and woo-woo stuff. From what I've seen, Havenwood Cove is a magical town. Is everyone a witch or a magical being?"

Molly chuckled. "No, Miss Sera."

"For the love of my sanity, please tell me how all this is possible." Her voice rose as she fought a combination of panic and wonder, because despite being overwhelmed, she also found it as exciting as it was frightening.

Molly stroked the side of her skinny, long nose, studying Sera, nodding and leaning forward. "Though you wish not to talk about the magical forest, we must. Her roots are the very foundation of Havenwood Cove. The forest, she cares for all who make their home on her land, just as Maude cares for all of us who reside within her walls. And the forest cares for Maude." She held up her hands. "Connected we are. All of us to this land."

"Magical forest," Sera parroted thoughtfully as she recalled how the pines along the highway had given way to a thick wall of forest that framed the road into Havenwood Cove. Trees so tall and majestic, with canopies that looked as though they belonged in some faraway rainforest. And hadn't she felt a surge of power as she drove beneath the canopy, as though power lines ran overhead? Yet she had seen none. Her brows rose. In fact, she hadn't seen a single power line since entering the town.

"Where did the forest come from?"

Molly's eyes grew wide. Almost frightened. She hesitated, leaning so far forward she nearly fell off the ottoman. She cupped her hands around her mouth and whispered, "The Portal, *Milady,*" she squeaked, then quickly covered her mouth with both hands as though to stop herself from saying more.

Sera froze. Her body chilled, and she felt lightheaded, as though she needed air. Realizing she was holding her breath, she exhaled slowly. Her grandmother had mentioned a portal. "Portal, as in leading to another world?" The very thought seemed to twist reality.

Molly suddenly appeared much older. Wizened, as though she'd aged in the blink of an eye. Her thin shoulders hunched, her twig-like fingers plucked at the tunic she wore. Bits of grass drifted to the floor. "It once opened to our home world, the portal did," she whispered. The fear in her voice left her trembling.

"And now?" Sera held her breath, her gaze intent on Molly, noting the look of terror in her eyes.

"Sealed."

Sera waited for more, but Molly remained silent, her fingers twisting strands of her hair. Bits of twigs fell to the carpet.

Sera rubbed the back of her neck as she struggled to believe what she was hearing. Hadn't she had more than enough evidence since her arrival to accept that there was something different about Havenwood Cove and those she'd met so far? Sera leaned forward to calm Molly's nervous fingers. "Never mind, Molly. I'm sure I'll learn what I need to know in due time."

Molly breathed a sigh of relief, and her shoulders relaxed. Until Sera asked, "Where is this portal?"

Hugging her knees to her chest, Molly rested her head on her drawn-up knees. "I know not, Milady," she said, her voice muffled and formal once again. "The forest, she guards her secrets, she does." She glanced up, her eyes wide, black pools. "The portal, sealed it has been for hundreds of your Earth years, but us who belong to the magical forest feel it weakening, we do."

A weakening portal? What did that mean? What was on the other side of that portal, in that other world, that frightened Molly so much? And how was she supposed to keep a portal sealed? Surely there were others with more knowledge and ability, who would be a better choice? Molly's voice drew her back from her panic.

"*Milady—Miss Sera,*" she beseeched, holding out her hands, long fingers stretching toward Sera. "Sealed it must remain. See to that, you must. The Guardian, it is promised, will protect us. Slaves we were. Escaped through the portal to this world. Free we are now. Free we mean to stay." Tears streamed down her face.

"Die we will if they come for us." Shaking, she covered her face with her hands, her body hunched over.

"Oh Molly," Sera spoke softly. Her heart ached for the tiny woman who shivered with fear. She yearned to comfort her or promise that she had nothing to fear, but how could she make that promise? How could she not?

Sera rubbed her aching head. Her task—or quest—had just taken a wild turn. Her stomach felt hollow, almost sick, as though she sat high above the ground in one of those carnival rides that dropped you without warning.

Everyone, from her grandmother to Lady Lillian and Molly, had all hinted that there was something amiss in Havenwood Cove. But Molly had revealed the shocking truth. The sealed portal was failing, and that meant she, Seraphina Blackthorn, was tasked to keep it from opening. Not only that, but she had to protect the magical beings, like Molly.

Sera jumped to her feet and rubbed her temples to ease the pounding there. "Me? Keep a portal from opening? Great galaxies!" She'd asked for a simple explanation as to how the impossible was possible, and she'd received an answer that was literally out of this world.

Spinning around, she shook her head. "Molly, I'm sorry. I know nothing of this world you came from, or any other world aside from this one. Just Earth. I am simply a human—well, witch."

Molly shook her head so hard her nose whipped from side to side. She stood and bowed deeply. "Guardian, you are. Save us, you will. Save Havenwood."

She bowed her head once again, covered her face with her trembling hands, and fell to her knees. "You must, Milady, or all will be lost."

"I understand I'm the Guardian. What is the Moondragon?" Sera held her breath. Information—that's what she needed. Desperately.

Molly brushed the tears from her weathered cheeks as she met Sera's gaze, her dark eyes blazing fiercely. "Know not what a Moondragon is. You come from the first Guardian, Aisling. A great witch was Aisling, and a kind mistress."

Sera went still. Her brows drew together. "You knew her?"

Molly's eyes held a faraway look. "Seventh Guardian you are. Seventh in the twenty generations since Aisling, and her twin sister, Saoirse, walked this land."

Her mind boggled at the thought that Molly had been around that long. "And Nonie passed this title, this role to me," Sera said, her voice cracking with emotion as she recalled the formal words, along with the surge of power she'd felt when she'd read her grandmother's entry in the journal. With hands on her hips, Sera stared out the window. The darkening view offered no comfort. In the garden, golden lights flickered like distant stars. Her stomach continued to churn, her mouth felt dry, and the room seemed to tilt slightly as her mind raced to make sense of everything.

"Oh Nonie, I need you here to explain what is going on." Sera battled with warring emotions: frustration as there was so much she didn't understand, anger that she hadn't been asked if she wanted this role, and edging those two emotions out was pure wonder. For a young girl who'd created fantasy worlds in her head, who devoured books, binged movies that carried her out of reality, Havenwood Cove was a dream come true.

*Magic. Was. Real.* Amazing! And freaking frightening as well. Later, she'd deal with the chaotic emotions swarming for attention. "Molly, what is this world you're from called?" she asked as she turned around. "And who is threatening—"

"*Thyron.*"

The air in the room thickened, pressing against Sera's skin like damp wool. The moment Molly spoke, the fire in the hearth flickered—then froze, the embers trapped in eerie, ice-blue stillness. Beneath her feet, the floor gave a warning tremor.

Molly went deathly still. The color drained from her bark-brown face, her twig-like fingers twitching as if the word itself had burned her. Then, with a squeal of terror, she bolted.

Sera could only stare after her, heart pounding.

The fire crackled back to life, but the warmth was gone. Only the name remained, hanging in the silence like a curse.

*Thyron.*

# Chapter Ten

May 21 - Gifts, Burdens & Zero Survival Guarantees

What just happened?

Sera's fingers dug into her upper arms, needing something solid to grip as her mind scrambled for reason. Of all the scenarios she could've imagined, *another world* wasn't one of them. And yet ... her grandmother had mentioned a portal, so she really shouldn't be so shocked. Still, she was. Not just shocked—rattled to the core.

Outside, darkness pooled against the windows, eerily similar to the vision she'd seen in the crystal ball. She shivered. Her thoughts scattered like leaves in a gale. Across the room, the fire hissed softly, as if echoing Molly's terror.

Slowly, she turned, eyes scanning the room as if expecting the shadows to whisper more forbidden truths.

*Thyron.* The name of the alien world echoed through her bones, stirring something primal. And Molly's last revelation—that they had once been slaves—tightened her chest.

"I'm fighting for freedom," she whispered. Her fingers covered her mouth.

A soft flutter of wings drew her attention, followed by a voice, smooth and dry as smoke: "And more, Guardian. You're fighting for the right to survive."

Syrus perched on the back of the couch, his brilliant plumage dimmed by unease. His violet eyes held none of their usual mischief.

"You're back," she breathed, relieved not to be alone.

"I never left," he murmured. "I've been watching." He tipped his head up and down and extended his wings in what appeared to be a bow. "I am here for you, Guardian," he announced, his normally harsh voice softened. There was something almost ancient in his voice, a weight that didn't quite match the playful, snarky bird she had first met. If she didn't know better, she'd think his demeanor was almost reverent. She grimaced. If he were as old as Molly, and from the magical forest, that might make sense.

"This is meant for you, Seraphina Blackthorn, Guardian of the Moondragon." His words were slow, deliberate. "It is no mere trinket. It is an *oathstone*. Keep it close." He held out one clawed foot and dropped a stone onto her outstretched palm.

Sera closed her hand around the offering, the warmth welcome as her hands were cold as ice. She opened her hand to study the stone. Deep, jagged cracks ran through the smooth amber surface, glowing faintly red, like wounds that had never quite healed. To her surprise, the bracelet on her wrist hummed in response and sent rainbow sparks dancing across the stone. Another piece of her legacy?

Threads of current zapped into her palm and out each finger, not painful, but enough to raise her brows. The stone in her palm flared to life, molten gold swirling beneath its surface. Her breath hitched. It looked old. Ancient. And felt ... *alive,* thrumming with wild magic.

"The Guardian stones are now connected to the oathstone," Syrus whispered, his voice filled with awe. "Past, present, and the future come together."

Drawing her lower lip into her mouth, Sera turned the stone to view each side. At first glance, it seemed like nothing more than stone, its deep amber color flecked with red and gold, but when she tilted it slightly toward the light, she spotted a shadowy fracture running through the center. Though it was faint, it was undeniably the image of a heart. Not quite perfect, not quite intentional, but it resembled a broken heart.

A wave of sadness struck her, as though the stone was communicating its pain. *If the heart inside was once whole, then what broke it?* For just a second, she swore she felt a heart beating.

*A heartbeat that wasn't hers.*

"What is this?" she whispered.

Syrus bowed his head. "A gift. A burden. A choice." He speared her with eyes that flashed molten silver. "Make the right choice."

Startled, Sera glanced at Syrus. "What choice? I thought I made my choice in coming here."

Lifting his wings high above his head, he clicked his hooked beak. "This stone was created by two blood-bound brothers, united by magic. One sacrificed everything for all." His eyes dimmed, snuffing out the silver light. His next words were a whisper that made her blood turn cold. "The other could not."

Her fingers closed around the stone as dread and fear spread through her. What sacrifice had this stone once demanded? Who were the two brothers and what happened to them?

Words from her grandmother's entry in the journal drifted across her mind: *The oldest tales whisper of a love so powerful it sealed the portal, of a sacrifice so great it bound the magic to this place forever. It must remain sealed at all costs* .... She swallowed past the lump in her throat as she brought her fist to her heart. Was that what she felt deep in the oathstone? The love of two brothers? One thing she believed: The oathstone carried more than just magic; it carried expectation, duty, and a connection she couldn't yet fully understand.

"Syrus, who were these brothers? What was sacrificed?"

Syrus's gaze fell. "Love was sacrificed. And life," he whispered. He shook his head as though fighting a deep internal battle. "I cannot say more. Find the portal, Guardian, and destroy it. If you don't, if you don't," he repeated, "everything will be lost."

Startled, Sera's gaze flew to the magical bird. *"Destroy?"* Her voice rose, ending in a shrill shriek. She stumbled back, hit the ottoman, and fell back onto it. Her heart pounded, and her mouth went dry. Taking a deep breath, she lifted her head and glared at the bird. "No one said anything about destroying a portal! A portal to another world! And I bet you don't know where it is either?" Her question was a challenge born of sheer overwhelming fear.

Syrus trembled. "When the portal was sealed, it disappeared. It is here. I feel—many of us feel—it weakening, but it is hidden. You, Seraphina Blackthorn, Guardian of the Moondragon, are the chosen one, and the only one with the ability to find it. Find it and destroy it forever."

Sera knew enough to know that when someone told you that you were "the chosen," things were about to get complicated. And when that *someone* was a talking bird? Even worse.

Gripping the stone hard enough that her fingers ached, Sera shook her head. "You all need to make up your ever-loving minds. First it was 'find the portal and keep it sealed,' and now you and Molly are telling me that I have to destroy it? Got any more impossible tasks?" Her voice dripped with sarcasm. "Or advice?"

Syrus turned his dull gaze onto her, and for a moment, she thought she saw a glimmer of empathy in his eyes. "We thought we'd sealed the portal for all time—my kind, your kind ... all of us. The sacrifices were great, but now the seal is weakening."

"Why? Why is it weakening?" Sera demanded.

Syrus bowed his head. "The sacrifice wasn't complete. It failed, and the magic won't hold much longer." He fixed her with an unnervingly serious stare as he spread his wings. "Find the portal, destroy it—and Sera, try not to die."

The air shimmered where he vanished. The room fell silent, thick with magic and fear. Jumping to her feet, she jammed her hands on her hips. "Perfect. Now I'm in charge of averting the apocalypse."

The stone pulsed against her palm, steady and unrelenting.

*A gift. A burden. A choice.*

*Sacrifices.*

She swallowed hard. What if she made the wrong choice? And what was she going to be asked to sacrifice? Her life? Syrus's ultimate piece of advice played in her mind: *Try not to die.* Was her life on the line?

She held the stone up. As if in response, the gems on her wrist sent soft bands of light flickering across her skin. Another artifact—another piece of a puzzle she didn't understand. She exhaled sharply and rubbed her eyes. No more thinking. Not tonight.

Her steps dragged as she left the room. Exhaustion, both physical and mental, pressed down on her shoulders like a lead blanket. Using the polished wooden handrail, she pulled herself up the stairs. Wall sconces flickered on as she made her way down the dark corridor. The moment she stepped into her bedroom, the fireplace flared to life, golden flames dancing in the dark. Maude's way of offering comfort? Sera sent a silent thank you to the unseen presence. She glanced toward the bay window. The curtain of darkness outside felt suffocating, as if it was pressing against her chest, foreboding and ominous. And menacing.

She didn't bother changing into pajamas. Instead, she slipped under the covers and held the oathstone to her chest, letting its warmth seep into her to chase away a bone-deep chill. Her breath slowed. Her body softened. The world dimmed at the edges.

###

The night stretched endlessly above Havenwood Cove, the silver glow of the moon casting long shadows across the land. Restlessness coiled inside him, a tension that had been building since his arrival. The town was quiet, peaceful, but the silence felt deceptive. His dreams whispered of creeping darkness, fractured magic, and a future hanging by a thread.

A sharp wind cut through the sky, tugging at him, though the chill barely registered. Below, the distant cry of an infant broke the silence, followed by the creak of a weathered sign swinging in the breeze.

He moved with the wind, limbs stretching, tension easing with each smooth, practiced motion. The night wrapped around him—vast, endless, familiar. To anyone below, he'd be nothing more than a ripple of air, a wrinkle in the dark. Behind him, his siblings followed, invisible streaks across the sky.

Each breath came slow and controlled—but the burn beneath his mark betrayed the truth. It pulsed with his unease: a constant reminder that time was slipping away.

A soft hoot split the air. He glanced to the side just as the ghostly form of a white owl glided toward him, its wings utterly silent. Her sharp, knowing gaze locked onto his—assessing, ancient. An equal. A judge. Beneath her, another bird rose, its iridescent plumage catching stray threads of moonlight as it joined them in flight. Together, they moved like sentinels—watching, waiting.

With one last glance at the town below, he turned toward the forest. The two birds followed.

The wind stilled as he descended, a quiet shadow, unnoticed in the stillness of the world below. His limbs stretched, bones realigning, the shift effortless, practiced. The tension bled from his muscles as his power shrank, contained once more. His human form always felt confining—but necessary. Silent and steady, he landed on the forest floor. The moment his feet touched the ground, a presence stirred in the darkness.

A woman in white emerged from the shadows. Pale, luminous against the darkened path, she moved with the eerie grace of someone who had long since stopped being entirely human. He braced himself instinctively, tensing, though he hadn't realized he'd been holding his breath.

"Welcome, Ryker of the Stormriders," she said, her voice as soft as the night, yet carrying the weight of old promises and unspoken truths. "The Mother offers you Her refuge and protection."

The sound of his name, spoken with such familiarity, made Ryker's chest tighten. The Mother was powerful, but even her forest could not stand against the storm that was coming. He inclined his head, silent. Acceptance wasn't surrender—but it was close. The storm was coming. And it carried his name.

###

The night murmured promises of peace as Sera wandered along a moonlit path, each step an echo of her own uncertainties. So many changes and upheavals in her life, starting with the pain of betrayal and the resulting end of her marriage. Yet it was that event that led her to where she now stood, at the brink of new discoveries and adventures. The past faded into insignificance.

Lifting her arms overhead, she reveled in the cool, night air. Dropping her arms, she continued down a pebbled path lit by the glow of the moon and maybe something more, as the ground held a glow of its own. Darkness draped over her shoulders, flowing behind her like black silk. A sigh escaped her lips and merged with the soft rustling of the night breeze. Above her, a multitude of twinkling stars adorned the sky, emanating a sense of solace and familiarity.

Yet the air pulsed with a potent, almost palpable magic. Anticipation—and something else—drew her along the silvery path until she reached the edge of a dense forest of giant and old-as-time trees. The moon, unnaturally large, cast an eerie glow that illuminated the path spearing like an arrow deep into the darkness of the woods. Sera hesitated as an irresistible pull urged her to continue.

"Is this real?" So much had happened, she wasn't sure anymore.

"It's as real as you want it to be, Guardian."

Sera glanced at the woman in white who suddenly materialized beside her. The strange glow beneath their feet reflected in the silver arm cuff the mysterious woman wore. "Lady Lillian. What are you doing here?" This was her dream, wasn't it?

The ethereal woman chuckled. "Yes, it is your dream. I can leave if you wish."

"No." Sera sighed. The farther she went into the forest, the cooler the air became. Too bad her dream self hadn't thought to bring a sweater. Something floated around her shoulders. She lifted her eyebrows as she stroked the shawl.

"Um, thanks."

Lady Lillian chuckled. "I did not gift you that fine garment."

"I did this?"

"You will one day become a powerful witch, like your grandmother and all who came before her."

Sera resisted the urge to shrug. Even though this was her dream, it felt rude to do so. Towering trees on either side of her murmured their secrets in a mysterious language she didn't understand, yet she recognized the whispers that spoke of fear, as though her own fears were projecting on the night air. Leaves danced and rustled, carrying the weight of countless broken and unfulfilled dreams.

The two women strolled in silence. The glowing path gave off enough light for Sera to see. With each stride into the unknown, the atmosphere grew increasingly dense, enveloping her in an electrifying presence. The deeper she ventured into the mystical forest, the scenery shifted, mirroring the turmoil within her. The air around her felt heavy with anticipation; each breath she drew into her lungs felt tinged with both excitement and trepidation.

She hugged herself. "This place frightens me," she whispered.

Lady Lillian rested her hands on Sera's shoulder, halting her. Her palms slid down Sera's arms. She took Sera's hands in hers. "You are wise to be frightened, my daughter. There is much for you to learn, and not much time." She squeezed Sera's fingers gently.

Fear rooted Sera to the spot. She thought of the encroaching shadows and looming darkness she kept seeing. "How—how much time?"

Lady Lillian released her hands and gently brushed the hair from Sera's face. "Three moons."

Heart pounding, the weight of responsibility had her gasping for air. A tremble of fear ran through her. She clenched her fists, her nails digging into her palms. Three moons? Three months? Her voice rose. "A ticking time clock—ninety days—to find and destroy the portal to save Havenwood Cove? Are you kidding me? Three months?"

"Yes, and to save your Earth, for your world is in danger as well," Lady Lillian added.

"Wonderful. No pressure at all." She held out her arms as panic caught in her throat. "I don't know where to begin. Help me, please. I can't do this alone."

Lady Lillian smiled gently and firmly took her trembling hands once again. "My sweet daughter. You're not alone. There is a legend of love, betrayal, and sacrifice. A love that spanned worlds. Seek the truth in your roots, and only then will you find the key. This is your task." She stepped back.

Thinking of the journal and the names of past Guardians she'd seen on a page, like some sort of index, Sera nodded even as she drew in a shaky breath. "How do I destroy a portal to another world? Where is it?"

A sad smile met her question. "I wish I could guide you further, but this is your path now. Trust the magic within you, it's been there all along. You have the strength to complete your quest, and complete it you must." She backed away and faded into the darkness of the forest.

Glancing around, Sera let out a long breath. Had she imagined the conversation with the woman in white? This was, after all, a dream.

She continued her stroll, seeking peace in solitude. Ahead, the narrow path widened, the forest falling behind her to form a shield at her back. A full moon revealed a small lake. The silver of the moon rippled on the surface. In the center, a small island added to the peaceful ambiance. Tall pines reached into the sky, some appearing to touch the low-hanging moon.

An ancient, triangular, stone archway stood like a sentinel in the night, glowing with eerie light. Within the arch, a swirling vortex of vibrant colors shifted and undulated, captivating her gaze. As the colors danced, both awe and dread filled her, sending shivers down her spine.

Sera's heart raced, torn between fear and the yearning for something beyond the confines of the past. The archway before her wasn't just a portal—it was the threshold to the woman she might become, a path from sorrow to something greater.

Mindful of the still water of the lake, she stepped closer, drawn to the world she saw through the portal. Strange shapes flew across the alien sky: large, dark, ominous shapes, too blurred to make out.

A gentle breeze brushed against her skin, carrying with it a faint chill that heightened the sense of foreboding. Her steps faltered, not from hesitation, but from the overwhelming surge of emotions it elicited. Memories of her former life, the one she had left behind to pursue independence and self-discovery, clashed with the emerging realization of her significance in this larger, mystical narrative.

The feel of this otherworldly scene enveloped her and left her both captivated and apprehensive. Whispers, barely audible, came from somewhere deep in the magical forest behind her. The words flowed like a haunting melody and resonated deep within her.

"Two will come to turn the tide. Their fates collide as the portal weakens, and darkness gathers. Waiting. Waiting. Only together can the two succeed where the previous two failed."

Sera's heart quickened. She wasn't alone on this quest. But who was this other person? How were their fates tied? In response to the spoken words, the ground trembled beneath her feet. The lake quivered, its placid face disrupted by sudden, concentric ripples racing outward as though strong winds shoved at the water.

A second tremor struck, deeper, stronger. The lake bucked as though waking from a dream, its smooth skin splitting into chaotic waves. The shoreline trembled, pebbles skittering into the frothing water. Trees groaned, their roots pulling at the heaving earth. Then came the rupture, an explosion that shattered the stillness of the night. Loud roaring, as though from a thousand furious predators, filled her ears.

In a heartbeat, a shimmering seal snapped over the portal's opening, cutting off the noise and plunging the world into an eerie stillness. The portal's glow convulsed, twisting inward as though it were struggling against itself. The air thickened, pressing against Sera's chest, heavy and unmoving. A deep, unnatural silence fell. Something was coming.

Then, the seal exploded outward in a violent explosion, sending shards of magical light in all directions. Shrill shrieks and ear-splitting screeches rent the air as shadow-wraiths burst free, their jagged, twisting forms as dark as the shadows she'd seen in the crystal ball.

Sera's stomach twisted. The malevolent energy of the creatures coiled around her like invisible tendrils, sinking into her skin, draining the warmth from the air. Each shriek sliced through her, sharp as a thousand tiny knives. The world dimmed, shadows stretching unnaturally, as if reality itself recoiled from their presence.

Everything within her screamed for her to run. But she forced herself to stand and face the danger. Defiant, she tipped her chin up and fisted her hands at her sides. A voice echoed in her mind. Face them. Face the portal. Face yourself.

Sera forced herself to truly look at the writhing mass of horrors flitting above her. They circled, a seething, living storm, their formless bodies merging into one massive, undulating cloud of darkness. But something inside her shifted.

An awakening.

She had spent so much of her life running—from her past, from herself—but no more. The fear was there, but it no longer ruled her.

Syrus said she had choices.

This was her moment. Her choice. And she chose to fight.

With a surge of defiance, she lifted her hands over her head and screamed, "NO!"

It wasn't just a rejection of the creatures—it was a rejection of everything that had ever tried to break her. Her breath came in ragged bursts, her heartbeat pounding in her ears. The darkness surrounding her wavered, shifting like a living thing.

An answering scream followed her shout. For one moment, she thought the wraiths would descend. Then something shot out of the forest and streaked over her head, its massive presence blocking out the stars. A rush of wind whipped her hair around her face as she lifted her arms to shield herself.

A fiery roar ripped through the night, raw and unbridled, shaking the earth beneath her feet.

# Chapter Eleven

May 22 - Darkness, Drama & the Dawn That Follows

Ryker hunched over his laptop, fingers flying over the keyboard, seeing not the words, but the images in his mind. His brows furrowed as he fought for every word.

His latest dark fantasy novel, *Beneath the Dragon Moon*, consumed him. The tension in his words deepened, his breath quickening as ancient wyrms stirred beneath a blood-red moon, their eyes alight with madness and fury as they took to the sky. Their wings blotted out the stars, and their screeches filled the night. In their path, the earth cracked open, and fire devoured all that dared stand in their way.

His vision blurred, the glow of the screen growing distant as exhaustion pulled him deeper into the story, no longer just writing it, but living it. As weariness slowly enveloped him, he leaned back in his chair, closed his eyes, and propped his feet up on the desk, seeking just a few precious moments to rest and gather the scattered threads of his story. The weight of unwritten words pressed on him, urging him to push on before dawn.

Unwilling to release his grip on the story, he allowed his mind to immerse itself in the vivid scene. His subconscious sifted through the details, separating the essence from the superfluous. Suddenly, the atmosphere shifted instantly, altering everything. The battle vanished, replaced by an ancient stone portal. The intricate runes encircling the opening radiated a mesmerizing glow, while the triangular stone structure pulsed with an otherworldly vitality.

He shook his head, denying the truth. He'd lived this nightmare night after night, drawn deeper into the darkness. A chink of light appeared around the edges of the sealed center of the portal. Sinister eyes, ablaze in hues of red, yellow, and green, glowed through the emerging cracks. Talons slipped through the cracks, and the center shivered, but the magical shield, put in place hundreds of years before, held. Beyond the cracks, something writhed, twisting through the dark like living smoke—hungry, waiting.

"You shall not cross," he vehemently shouted. "Earth is not yours."

"Surrender," a chorus of voices whispered, each syllable slicing into him like a blade, twisting deep. "Come home," other voices enticed.

He shot his fist high in the air in defiance. "NO," he shouted. "To surrender is certain death."

Shadowy Dragons, no more substantial than smoke, flew toward him. They weren't real, just illusions, yet they stung and burned. "Free us."

His world tilted, and he found himself high upon a cliff, watching the world burn under the Dragon Moon. He spotted a still figure standing in the distance—a woman with hair as red as the fire consuming the earth beneath him. He couldn't make out her features, but her presence tugged at him, and he knew she was important—no, vital—to preventing what was coming.

Suddenly, the dark Dragon illusions shifted their attention away from him and focused on the woman. Ryker tried to shout and warn her, but his voice caught in his throat. His entire body froze, yet his mind raced. One of the largest Dragons launched forward, aiming straight for the woman.

The woman, her golden-red hair glowing beneath the moon, lifted both hands—one holding a book, the other a stone. "I am the Guardian of the Moondragon. I protect what is mine." Twin beams of light shot into the sky, illuminating the darkness of the nightmare.

A burning ball of flame answered. It descended toward the woman.

"NO!"

His scream echoed off the walls, and he shot out of the dream. His Dragon scale tattoo burned like a hot poker, a searing reminder of the destiny he had tried so hard to escape. Breathing raggedly, the dream's intensity gripped him like a shadow he couldn't shake. The woman. The portal. The creatures. It wasn't just a dream—it never was.

The burning tattoo seared into his skin, forcing him to confront the truth he'd been avoiding. He could not fight the call of fate. He staggered to his feet, knees buckling. "No," he muttered as the evil images of wyrms continued to swarm his mind—taunting, suffocating, attacking.

He clapped a hand over the burning tattoo, the pain lancing through him—an undeniable confirmation of what he had been running from. "I never asked for this," he said through gritted teeth. "It was never supposed to be me."

The door to his room burst open. "Ryker!" Elyn rushed inside.

Still shaken from a nightmare that felt less like a dream and more like a warning, Ryker turned toward the familiar voice of his best friend. His breath came in uneven gasps as he pressed a hand over his burning tattoo, grounding himself in the present. Then, voice raw, he rasped, "The time draws near. The elders were right. Gather the others."

### 

Sera jolted awake, gasping, her body shaking with a bone-deep chill. She swiped at her eyes, but the nightmare clung to her, a ghost of something real—the glowing portal, the shrieking wraiths, the weight of something dark pressing down on her chest.

Pushing herself up into a sitting position, she wrapped her arms around her knees. "Nightmare or vision?" she asked the silent room, her voice barely audible. Her grandmother said she possessed veil sight, the ability to see beyond the visible world. Did that apply to dreams as well? The dream started out pleasantly enough but ended in terror. Everything she knew about her quest, her role as Guardian, crashed into her mind. Portals with weakening seals, tyranny, slavery ...

She rested her head on her knees. Her conversation with Lady Lillian felt real. Veil sight? Three months was all the time she had to find and destroy a portal that led to another world where something waited just beyond the edges of reality, something dark, fearsome, and dangerous.

Her plans for a peaceful summer in Havenwood Cove slipped away, replaced by a new reality pulsing with magic—and danger. This wasn't some sweet Cinderella tale with a happy ending, or even the twisted wonder of Alice's rabbit hole. No, this felt like Pan's Labyrinth—a world both breathtaking and terrifying, where shadows whispered from the trees and myths wore masks of truth.

Escaped slavery.

Oppression.

Death.

Her head dropped to her knees. "What freaking universe have I landed in?" The magical beings she'd met so far weren't monsters, but what of the ones Molly feared? The ones who wanted Earth for their own?

Slaves.

And Syrus had confirmed that the portal was weakening. But why now? And why her? The thought of an unseen enemy destroying Havenwood Cove and the rest of the world chilled her to her very soul. Syrus's words echoed in the frozen state of her mind:

"You must find the portal. And destroy it."

From the moment she'd opened the door to an odd delivery driver, her life had spiraled out of control, and each new revelation threatened to unravel her. Yet somehow, she held on.

Shivers continued to wrack her body, chills that emanated from fear, not the lack of warmth in the bedroom. A glance at the fireplace confirmed the embers glowed softly. She clenched her teeth together to stop them from chattering. The lines between reality and dream blurred as she relived her dream in her mind: The shrieking wraiths felt real, as did the danger and the fire-breathing beast at the end. Had the portal truly opened? Was Havenwood Cove even now under attack?

Driven by the need to see for herself if Havenwood Cove was under attack, she scrambled out of bed and ran down the hall to the turret room. As she passed, the wall sconces flared to life, providing a soft glow to light her way. Inside the circular room, soft golden light dispelled the shadows. Windows formed a 180-degree view of sea and harbor, but it was the forest she desperately needed to check. Frustrated that the back of the house blocked her view, she ran a hand through her hair.

A flash of light across the room illuminated a narrow, circular staircase almost hidden by the shelves that lined the other half of the room. Climbing quickly, Sera found herself on the third floor of the turret. She hurried to the curved window seat. The windows offered a full 360-degree view.

Kneeling on the cushions, she opened the window, and though still cold outside, she welcomed the brush of brisk night air on her face and drew in a deep breath. The remnants of fear from the nightmare faded. Everything looked normal. No shadows or wraiths, and no fire burning the forest. Palms resting on the narrow windowsill, Sera breathed a sigh of relief as she stared into the clear night.

Above, stars shone brightly, and the moon, nearly full, bathed everything in its silvery light. Winking lights in the harbor from anchored ships added their golden glow. Turning from the sea, she focused on the distant forest, watching as golden orbs darted among the trees like dancing fireflies—but they were much too large to be fireflies.

Her heart quickened. The lights weren't the only unusual thing she saw. The air above the forest rippled with energy, faint streaks of light tracing patterns that faded as quickly as they appeared. It was as if the veil between worlds was thin tonight, the magic pulsing just beneath the surface. Was it the nearly full moon? Or her veil sight awakening?

Glancing downward, she spotted the same flickering lights in the garden below. Suddenly, her vision shifted, pulling her into another layer of reality. She blinked, the ordinary night fading around the edges. The glowing orbs became sharper, more distinct, and within them, she swore she saw tiny, shimmering creatures flitting through the air, their wings glinting like gold dust in the moonlight. She blinked hard, the tiny orbs shifting in and out of focus. Her pulse pounded—was she hallucinating?

"No," she cried out. "Glimmerlings." She recognized the tiny sprites who tended gardens. And with recognition came another memory—of visiting the gardens at night with her father or grandmother to leave little gifts for the magical creatures.

As her gaze swept over the night below, Sera felt the pull of something familiar—something alive. She reached out, her hand pressed against the cold windowpane. Her fingers tingled with warmth, and for a moment, she thought she could feel the pulse of the earth humming with quiet magic.

Her gaze returned to the forest in the distance, and she swore she heard whispered voices on the night breeze. Sera's breath caught in her throat. Closing her eyes, she reached out with her senses. The magic of Havenwood Cove pulsed around her, a faint vibration in the air, and with it came a sense of something ... watching ... waiting. Her body stiffened as she remembered her dream and the shadows escaping the portal. Her fear that something had crossed through it returned.

What if she failed? "I don't know what I'm doing," she whispered, her voice trembling.

The lights in the room dimmed.

Sighing, Sera nodded. "I'll do my best, Maude."

Her gaze returned to the magical forest. What secrets did it hold? Though tired, she knew she wouldn't sleep. How could she after what she'd seen and experienced? Crazy as it seemed, another world threatened all she knew.

Her dream made that clear. She didn't understand how or why it involved her bloodline, and that was her starting point. Researching her roots. Her ancestors, starting with the first Guardian.

Absently, she turned the bracelet on her wrist and found and rubbed her heart stone. She missed wearing it as a pendant. She raised her wrist and allowed the beam of moonlight streaming into the room to spark off the stones. Each magical stone was a gift from a past Guardian, an ancestor. She had a journal that contained a diary from each woman.

Drawing a deep breath, Sera knew that was where she needed to start. Previous Guardians hopefully knew more about the legend. And someone who lived there must know the history of the town. She snapped her fingers. "A library." She assumed the town had a library.

Feeling relieved to have a plan of action in place, she was about to return to her bedroom when she spotted a ghostly white shape flying in a circular pattern, growing closer to the house. It flew past her window on silent wings, close enough to allow Sera to see the feathered face of an owl. Another bird joined the first, its larger body flying protectively above the owl.

Syrus.

The two birds continued to fly over and around the house, a pair of silent Guardians. Oddly soothed by the sight of the birds after her nightmare, Sera felt the lingering chill in her bones ease. The silent flight of the owl and Syrus, along with Lady Lillian's words of wisdom, reminded her she wasn't alone in this strange new world. Her breathing slowed, and for the first time since waking from the nightmare, the panic subsided.

Mesmerized, she tracked the flight of the birds over the garage. Each dipped and flew over a shimmering silhouette of a cat that appeared to be nothing more substantial than mist. For just a moment, the cat came into focus. Tiny motes of light flickered in the air like embers, and a pair of silvery eyes met hers.

Watch the signs, Little Human. The past stirs.

Before Sera could question whether she'd heard a voice or imagined it, the cat's tail flicked, creating a ripple of energy that creased the air. With a leap off the roof, the cat vanished mid-air, leaving a trail of silver and blue streaks fading into the night.

"Wow, what was that?" She rubbed her eyes and exhaled slowly. Sighing, she admitted that there would be many strange sights to process in her new life. She stood, filled with purpose, and headed back to her room. Her mind wandered to some people she had met so far—Bram, Fin, Molly, Syrus, and Lady Lillian, all of whom had welcomed her in their own quirky ways. Each also knew her role. So, what did they know of the past, of the dangers, of the portal? They were also resources, and she planned to explore every avenue that opened to her.

She still didn't understand why two Guardians couldn't coexist in Havenwood Cove together, but after the nightmare, Sera was suddenly glad Nonie wasn't here. At least she was safe. Time would tell if the same could be said of herself.

Back in her room, she picked up the oathstone. She clutched it in her hand, felt its warmth, its weight. Part of her longed for her very simple and boring life, but that part was shrinking. The woman she was becoming couldn't run away, not now. She'd opened Pandora's box, and it was too late to return to a normal world and pretend magic didn't exist or ignore an entire town under threat.

"I won't let you down, Nonie," she whispered. "Or Molly. Or Maude." It sounded weird to make a promise to a house, but it felt right to include her. She changed into a soft sleep shirt and crawled under the thick comforter and stared up at the ceiling, her mind racing with questions. She might not know the full truth yet, but one thing was clear: she wouldn't fail. No matter the cost. Whatever the danger, whatever the sacrifice, she would deal with it. As it started with a legend and the magical power of this strange town, she'd learn all she could. And be ready for the final showdown with whomever or whatever lay on the other side of that portal. A battle for freedom and survival was coming.

# Chapter Twelve

May 22 - Of Whiskers, Widgets & Waffles

The light of day streamed into Sera's bedroom. The events of the night before lay like a crushing weight on her chest, making breathing difficult. Wrinkling her nose, Sera lifted her hands to shove the heavy comforter off and encountered fur. Her eyes flew open, and panicking, she bolted upright with a startled scream. The beast launched into the air, vanishing in a shimmering ripple.

"What in Merlin's name?" Sera exclaimed as she frantically glanced around the room. A blur of movement in front of the fireplace drew her attention. Her jaw dropped when she spotted a huge, fluffy, white cat calmly washing its face. Scrambling to her knees, she blinked, unsure if she was seeing what she was pretty sure she was seeing. She stared, her thoughts tangled. The fog of fear cracked apart, leaving only memory—the tearful day her mother took her away from Havenwood Cove. With her heart breaking, she'd said goodbye to the cat that no one had ever seen.

"No way," she whispered. "This isn't real."

At the sound of her voice, the cat froze, one paw held up as if in greeting. Twin blue orbs, brilliant as cut crystal, locked onto her. The eyes narrowed to mere slits as the cat turned its back on her. Though fluffy by nature, the animal's fur stuck out as though from an electric shock.

"Wil-Willow?" Sera squeaked. She leaned forward on her hands.

The cat swiveled her head, reproach in her diamond-bright eyes. "Scared the life out of me, *Little Human*." Nose in the air, the cat stretched out her front paws and went into a full body stretch with rump high and fat tail curved over her back.

"Uh, Willow, I hate to break this to you, but I'm not so little anymore."

"Compared to me? Still a child," Willow sniffed, then swiped a paw over one ear.

Sera scrambled off the bed and crouched beside her childhood companion. "I can't believe—I thought you were my imaginary pet. Maybe I'm still imagining you?"

The cat stood, tail flicking, eyes narrowed. "Imagined me?" Scorn laced her tone. "Hardly. You've always seen what others couldn't, Little Human."

Sera ran her hands through the soft fur, warmed from the fire, and sighed with pleasure and wonder. "You feel real. Solid." She remembered wishing others could see her big, beautiful cat, especially her mother, if only to prove it wasn't all in her head. Thinking back, she realized both her grandmother and father had believed her. That memory made her sigh. Now that her memories were returning, she realized her mother, from the time they'd left Havenwood Cove, had denounced anything magical, anything not rooted in logic and realism. She sighed and wondered why.

Willow flopped down and rolled from side to side. "Hungry," the cat mewed pathetically.

Sera giggled, feeling like a kid again as she stroked her fingers over the cat's exposed belly. "Look at this. You don't need food."

The cat's eyes narrowed to slits. "You calling me fat, Human?" The cat growled low in its throat.

Tipping her head to the side, Sera frowned as her fingers continued to dig into the cat's luscious coat. Sighing, she rubbed the cat's velvety-soft ears. "I wish you were real." She longed for a companion, a friend, especially in this strange town.

If a cat could roll its eyes, Willow's would have rolled up into her brain. She butted her head against Sera's palm. "I'm as real as you, Human."

Tipping her head to the side, Sera considered. "I remember you walking through walls and disappearing. Like a ghost." Suddenly, she recalled seeing an image of a cat on the roof while in the turret room. Both the owl and Syrus had flown over and around the animal. She also recalled how the cat, almost translucent in the night, had leaped off the roof. And disappeared! And Willow had done it again that morning when she kicked off her chest and vanished, the air rippling in her wake—like heat rising off sunbaked asphalt.

Her voice held wonder. "That was you I saw last night, wasn't it? You spoke to me."

"Very good. Your gift grows." Willow rolled gracefully to her feet. "I've always been real. But I'm more than just a cat."

Sera studied Willow. "That I believe. So, what magical being are you?"

The cat placed its front paws on Sera's thighs. "If you must have a name, you can call me an eidolon."

"Why did you never tell me?" Sera sat, crossing her legs. The fire felt good as the morning was chilly.

Willow climbed onto Sera's lap and curled up. "You weren't ready for the truth before. Easier for you to believe I was a ghost or an imaginary pet." She flicked her tail. "But you're back now, and it's time for the truth."

"What truth?"

"Timing is everything, Little Human. You'll learn when it's time. For now, know that I chose you a long time ago. You were and are the answer."

Needing to do something with her hands while she absorbed yet more information, Sera picked up her very real cat and glanced around the room. Filtered light from the clouds outside highlighted the worn but polished floor. A large throw rug in warm blues added a calming color. One wall held floor-to-ceiling shelves. Her brows rose when she spotted one shelf devoted to R.S. Ryder. "Thanks, Maude," she muttered with a smirk. Apparently, the house had picked up on her fangirl moment last night.

The air smelled faintly of lavender and vanilla, which tugged at something deep inside her. The room felt both strange and familiar, as if it had been waiting for her to return. Sera gently deposited Willow onto the bed and went to her closet, where she found her clothes hung neatly. Molly? She'd have to thank her for unpacking her things.

Laying her choice for the day on the bed, she studied the cat. "Chose me? Why? Because I'm the Guardian?" She almost didn't want to know the answer, afraid if it tied into her being the Guardian, that would mean all of this was ordained long ago.

"You were always meant for something bigger, but you were too young. You are now ready."

Sera frowned. Hadn't her grandmother said the same thing? "Ready for what? I'm not like Nonie ... I'm not a trained witch, so why choose me over her?"

Willow settled into a loaf. Her tail lashed back and forth, and her pupils narrowed. "You're more than just a witch, Little Human. You'll figure it out soon enough. All you need to know for now is that I'm here for you."

Though filled with questions and doubts, Sera embraced her joy at being reunited with her companion. Maybe, just maybe, she didn't want to know more yet. She scooped the cat back into her arms and buried her face in Willow's soft fur. The cat's purr vibrated into her chest. "I'm so glad you're here," she said, her voice muffled by the fur.

Sera stood and walked toward the bay window. She exhaled. "I forgot all of this: Nonie, this town, you. My father—still can't remember much of him—so much I've forgotten. She butted her forehead against the cat's. "And speaking of real, what was with that kick! That hurt."

A paw tapped her cheek. "What was with that scream?"

She chuckled. "What you get for scaring me." She rubbed one of Willow's silky ears. For the first time since her arrival, she felt calm and not lost. With Willow, she wasn't alone. "I'm sorry, Willow. I guess I've had a few too many surprises and shocks and a horrible nightmare to top it all off." With her life in turmoil, Sera breathed deeply as she appreciated the view, though fog obscured most of the ocean and a fine mist coated the land. Down below, the gardens, with their greens and vibrant colors, promised sanctuary. "So beautiful. I could get used to seeing this every morning."

Another memory brought a smile to her lips. "Did you used to turn blue or pink for me?"

Willow purred with amusement. "Figured you needed a bit of color in your life, and you had such an imagination, so I indulged it." The cat's eyes sparked with mischief as she turned blue. Then a pink that merged into violet.

Sera laughed with sheer delight. A pool of happiness settled deep inside as the cat turned white again. How long had it been since she'd laughed out of sheer enjoyment? The emotion that washed over and through her was joy. Despite the enormous task being laid at her feet, she was happy.

She glanced at her watch. "I'd better get a move on. Need to open the shop for a crochet group that meets early."

Willow's ears flicked forward, then back, as though she heard something Sera couldn't. For a moment, the cat's eyes narrowed as she gazed out the window, but then she relaxed and jumped down.

"I'm going with you," the cat declared, winding between, around, and then fading to almost nothing to go through Sera's legs. Sera shivered.

"Ugh! Willow! You know I hate that! Stay solid!" Sera swore the cat smirked as she went into the bathroom to get ready for the day. After a quick shower, one where she didn't run out of hot water, she dressed. A glance in the mirror surprised her. The golden-red strands, wavy with curl, framed her face and made her green eyes appear brighter. Her lips curved into a pleased grin that felt foreign.

She scooped up the strands of hair and held them up. Should she put her hair up, tame the wildness so she appeared more businesslike and not like a wild woman? "No," she told her reflection as she dropped the strands and watched them fall below her shoulders. She'd hidden her hair with plaits and buns to become the image others demanded. "No," she repeated. "This is who I am." She kissed her fingers and touched the mirror.

"Thank you, Nonie, wherever you are." She waited, hoping her grandmother would appear in the mirror here, as she had in the condo. The mirror held only her reflection—until she turned away. A faint ripple shimmered, a whisper of fingers trailing after hers, fading into shadow.

"Hurry up, Human. I'm hungry," Willow demanded.

Sera shook her head. In the bedroom, she gathered her briefcase and made sure she had everything she needed for her first day as a shopkeeper. "I'm ready."

"About time." Willow smirked, tail swishing as she stepped forward—then faded through the door. Sera shuddered, opened the door, and followed.

The hallway stretched before her, its walls paneled in rich wood carved with spiraling patterns—vines, stars, and something that might have been runes. A long runner in mossy green muffled her steps.

"Something smells good," Sera murmured, sniffing the air. "Someone's been baking."

The wall sconces flashed with a rainbow of color. "Wow. Does this mean Maude is happy?"

"Means breakfast is nearly ready," the cat announced, her tail a fluffy plume of fur. "So move it, Little Human. Some of us need to eat before we fade away."

Willow glanced over her shoulder—and did exactly that. She faded into nothing.

"Ha-ha. Very funny, Willow."

The cat reappeared slowly—body first, head last—wearing a huge grin.

Sera clapped a hand over her eyes. "For crying out loud, Willow! That is truly terrifying. Don't do that. You look like the evil version of the Cheshire Cat."

Willow snickered, though it sounded more like she was about to cough up a hairball. Shaking her head, Sera started down the stairs. Once again, she felt anxious about what lay ahead of her. She grimaced and rubbed her stomach, which felt hollow with nerves. "Think I'll just head to the shop."

Willow flew down the rest of the stairs. Glaring up at Sera, she narrowed her eyes and thumped her tail repeatedly on the wooden floor. "You want to tell Molly and Maude they cooked for nothing?"

Recalling Molly's temper with Syrus the night before, and even the feeling of sadness that came from Maude, Sera held up her hand in surrender. "Okay, good point." Despite the joy of being reunited with Willow, a weight settled on her shoulders as she trudged down the stairs.

The shop, the town, even the air she breathed—everything felt bigger now, as though the entire town was watching to see what she would do next. She fingered the oathstone resting beneath her sweater. The need to keep it close was too strong to ignore, so she'd envisioned a simple silver wire wrap to make it into a pendant. Surprised that her attempt at witchcraft had worked, she'd put it on the chain she'd used for her heart-stone.

She tried to stay lighthearted and positive, but the idea of being the Guardian felt overwhelming, like it was pressing in from all sides. Everyone thought she was ready, but what if she wasn't? What if she failed? She gave herself a mental shake. Nope. Not going there. Failure was not an option.

Pulling her shoulders back, she followed Willow to the kitchen, though she had to detour a few times when the cat went through the walls. "I'm here, Molly," she sang out as she entered the warm, spacious kitchen.

Molly pointed to the small table nestled in a sunny nook. "Sit."

The nook was tucked into a curved corner of the kitchen beneath a trio of paned windows dressed in gauzy, cream curtains. Cushioned bench seats lined the walls, each covered in a mismatched patchwork of hand-sewn fabric—florals, moons, and stars. A small round table sat in the center, its wooden surface worn smooth by years of use and love. A vase of fresh-cut wildflowers swayed gently, though there was no breeze. It felt like time slowed down here, just enough to let a person breathe.

As she sat, Molly rushed over to set a large mug of coffee in front of her.

"Your food, almost done it is. Yes, almost." She hurried to the stove, and with hands on her hips, tapped her tiny foot.

"Slow you are this morning, Maude. Our girl is here and waiting, she is."

Wrapping her hands around the warm mug, Sera took in the large kitchen. The bright, open floor plan made her sigh with longing. After nearly a year in her cramped and dreary condo, the space, the light, and the color of her grandmother's kitchen calmed the anxiety building inside her. She resisted the urge to get up and explore. As Molly muttered in the background, Sera took in the view from the back corner of the house.

The windows sparkled as if freshly cleaned, and through a break in the clouds, a single shaft of sunlight speared the table. Sera cradled the steaming mug in her hands and drank in not just the brew, but the flowering landscape that stretched to the cliffs curving around the house. Instead of the open ocean, her gaze followed the rugged coastline as it wound out of sight.

A crack in the land from the edge of her property and the other side created a narrow river that ended at the edge of the cliff. Water spilled down into the ocean below. And in the far distance lay the towering magical forest. In the light of day, even in dawn's overcast sky, it shimmered with greens, browns, and a sprinkling of golden lights, like a net over the canopies.

"If only Nonie was here, we could share this view together." Sera removed her phone from her back pocket and snapped a few pictures—she never wanted to forget this place in case her stay was temporary. Setting her phone on the table, she turned back to Molly. The top of the Rootling housekeeper's head barely reached the stovetop. For a moment, Sera wondered if she should offer to help.

Her eyes widened when the pan on the stove rose unaided into the air and flipped two eggs over, deftly caught them, and returned to the burner. Before she could comment, the oven door opened, forcing Molly back. A tray of mouth-watering scones floated onto a wooden board on the counter. Molly quickly plated the eggs and scones.

"Wow. Okay, no help needed." She chuckled. As she wondered if she'd ever get used to magic like this, a small bowl of fruit appeared on the table to her right. Molly set the eggs and scones in front of her.

"Double wow. I don't normally eat this much for breakfast!" Her stomach rumbled, reminding her that she hadn't eaten much the day before. "But today, I think I can eat," she said with a grin.

"Too thin, you are," Molly said with a firm head jerk.

Hungry, Sera bit into a steamy, perfectly flaky scone. The eggs were next. When she was nearly done, her phone let out a soft beep. Curious, she wiped her fingers on a napkin that appeared out of nowhere. The screen lit up with a notification. She read:

A new app is ready to install. Maude's Magic. Install now? Sera blinked. "What on Earth?" She scrunched her nose. "Well, considering all things, maybe not Earth! "An app? The house has an app?" she muttered. How was Maude able to communicate with her phone? Just what else could Maude do?

She tapped the notification, and a small app icon appeared: a tiny, intricate illustration of the turret from Maude's roof, complete with swirling stars and a glowing moon. The title beneath it read *Maude's Magic*. Install?

Curious, Sera tapped it. "Well, why not?" she said. The app loaded, its whimsical graphics swirling across the screen like tiny fireflies before opening fully to reveal a dashboard with a small orb of light glowing at the center—a magical pulse that shifted from gold to pink, as if reflecting the house's contentment.

An elegant script flowed across the screen. *Good morning, Sera. Welcome to your new home. I am Maude, your home's guide and companion. Shall we begin?*

Sera's jaw dropped as she stared at the message. The house clearly had a personality, one that seemed to extend beyond its walls. It was strange, but ... oddly comforting. She couldn't help chuckling. Did she type her answer? There was no text box. Then she rolled her eyes. Maude was the house, so she said, "Yes."

At the top of the screen, a playful message appeared: *Add a hint of lavender honey to the scones. Trust me. Pure magic.*

Engrossed in exploring the app, Sera finished her eggs and scones with a dash of lavender honey—Maude was right. They were purely magical. The app included a Mood Ring indicator with a helpful legend. Right now, Maude's mood appeared golden, meaning happy. "Okay, that's cool."

Nibbling on the fruit, she explored quickly—Mood Ring, Magical Advice, Spell Suggester, even a chat room. The map revealed glowing icons, sparkling paths, and strange shifting markers. Sera clicked on the interactive map, watching as tiny icons appeared—shops, paths, even strange, shifting markers she hadn't noticed before. What were those? She made a mental note to explore later. Enlarging the image, she spotted Yarns of Wonder. "So much to explore in your app, Maude. But later. Need to get moving." She stood and gathered her plate, but Molly rushed over, her mossy hair swinging side to side.

"You go." She took the dishes from Sera and hurried back to the sink, where water was running, bubbles floating in the air.

"Okay, thank you, Molly." Living with magic was going to take some getting used to, and heaven help her, if she returned to a normal, mortal world, she was afraid she'd miss it.

Sera gathered her stuffed tote bag holding her computer, Nonie's notes, and the journal. Despite the warmth of the house, she shivered. Running the shop wasn't just a temporary job—it was the first step to something bigger. With Willow padding after her, Sera opened the map. "Let's go, Willow," she called out as she headed for the front door.

"Off to save the world? Or just escaping my charming company?"

Sera backtracked a couple of steps to peer into the living room. Syrus perched on top of his cage, preening his feathers.

"You're back. Again." She fingered the hidden stone Syrus had given her the night before. He'd been so serious, almost sad when he offered it to her, but today, he appeared to be his snarky, sarcastic self. She rolled her eyes at the bird. "You, I'm afraid, will take some getting used to, Syrus."

Molly rushed into the room and flicked her fingers dismissively. "Work to do, no time for snark, we have."

"Molly, your voice is like a spell—it makes me want to disappear!" Syrus rasped.

Shaking her head, Sera waved her hand. "I'm out of here. Carry on." She laughed, but then a thought occurred to her. "By the way, what am I supposed to feed you? What do you eat? I don't think I'll find any information on the internet about your care."

"Eat whatever I want," the bird replied in a singsong, albeit harsh, voice. He did a little dance, bobbing his head up and down as he laughed uproariously.

"Er, okay. Going to the shop, but I'll be back—"

Before she could finish her sentence, Syrus disappeared with a shimmer and squawk. Sera pinched the bridge of her nose, drawing in a deep breath. "A lot of getting used to," she muttered, her mind racing to keep up with all the changes.

Around her, the house seemed to settle into an odd stillness. As the soft scent of wildflowers filled the air, a wave of calm washed over her. Maude was always there, always knowing when to step in. Sera smiled in appreciation. "Thanks, Maude," she whispered, letting the magic of the house ease her anxiety, if only for a moment. But with each step toward the door, the weight of her additional responsibilities grew heavier, and somehow, she knew today would be anything but ordinary.

"I'll get through it," she murmured softly as she drew in a deep breath of fresh sea-scented air to steady her nerves, "Where there's a will, there's a way," she reminded herself as she squared her shoulders and stepped into the day.

# Chapter Thirteen

May 22 - Petals, Pixies & Pesky Priorities

Sera hurried down the driveway, eager to see her grandmother's shop. She made a face when she remembered how a certain prankster elf had thwarted her plans yesterday. Looking back, she chuckled. Yesterday had been unforgettable—her first actual glimpse of the town's magic. But today, she planned to be all business.

Having never run an actual shop—just handled the books for other businesses—she felt the weight of responsibility and didn't want to let her grandmother down by making a mess of things. "It's just yarn and customers," she muttered. But even she didn't believe that. Not here. Not in a town where houses created apps and flowers hummed. Crossing the road, she recalled her encounter with the Rootwall. She shook her head. "Yesterday was a total eye-opener!" Willow darted ahead, leaving the road to scoot down a path chasing and batting at butterflies.

Though she trusted the cat knew the way, Sera checked her phone. "How cool!" Faint, glowing footprints followed the path the cat took, even showing the cat with a "W" in the lead. "Wow, Maude."

A mixture of open fields and clusters of trees and shrubs broke up the gentle downhill path. She tapped the weather icon, which promised a chilly but clear day once the cloud cover burned off. A glance upward revealed bits of blue splitting the gray, overcast sky.

What didn't thrill her was the app's insistence on revealing the phases of the moon, especially the reminder that tomorrow marked the first day of the full moon. Her stomach tightened. If she believed Lady Lillian had truly appeared in her dream—and she had no reason to doubt it—she had three months, or three full moons, to find and destroy the portal. That gave her until August, as May's full moon was almost upon her, and surely it didn't count but served as the countdown marker.

Pushing aside the worry and fear, she vowed to concentrate on her grandmother's yarn shop today. She focused on the map of the town, using her fingers to enlarge the businesses on Main Street. Sera couldn't help but feel a sense of intrigue and anticipation. Havenwood Cove was a place where cars and a fast-paced life took a backseat to the charm and simplicity of a bygone era.

Once again, she thought briefly of her life in Boston: the streets clogged with traffic, hordes of people rushing from shop to shop, and the brutal pace of work, with the need to be the best and on top driving out the simple joy of living.

A shadow fell across her path. Heart hammering, she froze, the dark wraiths of her nightmare returning. She glanced up, then laughed nervously when she spotted a jagged cloud moving inland. Several feet in front of her, Willow stopped and regarded her.

"You are safe, Little Human." The cat studied the sky. "For now."

Sera gripped the strap of her tote. "Not sure that helps, Willow." She kicked a rock in her path. In her dream, she'd stood at the edge of a lake with an island, and on the island sat a glowing portal, its surface swirling like liquid glass. Was it real, or just fear playing tricks on her? If it were real, where was it? How could she find out where it was, if it existed?

Her hope that the portal wasn't real, that maybe it was symbolic, had died with the dream. It haunted her and reminded her that she was out of her element. How did Veil Sight help? Did it mean she'd find it using her gift? *Even if it does, that doesn't tell me how to destroy it.* Her thoughts spiraled, the sickness and dread creeping up her throat like smoke.

"The answers will come, Little Human," Willow offered.

Sera nearly tripped over the cat, who'd stopped in front of her. "Ack! Don't stop like that!" She glared at the cat. "Instead of platitudes, answers would be more helpful, Cat." She stepped around Willow. "One thing at a time," Sera muttered. "Just survive your first day without burning the place down."

Ahead, a stand of oaks broke up the wide expanse of green field. Muted light filtered through the ancient canopies, their limbs entwined high above to form a vaulted ceiling. The path wound through them like a ribbon.

Willow paused, tail and whiskers twitching. "Mind your step."

"Because of roots?"

"Because the forest watches."

Sera laughed uneasily. "You mean that poetically, right?"

Willow's eyes gleamed. "Do I?" She turned and trotted ahead.

Following the cat, Sera studied the trees that appeared ancient and gnarled, their branches and trunks twisted from the strong breeze that blew off the ocean. The air smelled of moss, brine, and memory.

One great bough stretched overhead like a crooked arm, heavy with leaves that whispered secrets in the breeze. It hung low enough that Sera reached up and brushed her fingertips across the rough bark. A leaf spiraled down, landing on her shoulder, where it glowed faintly. She glanced to her right, where the magical forest rose like a living wall. She plucked the leaf off her shawl and twirled it between her fingers.

"Okay, it's watching," she murmured. That begged the question: What was it waiting for? She slowed, the hush of the moment pressing in, as though the tree paused with her.

The path continued across a velvet-green meadow, jeweled with tiny blooms that shimmered in the filtered light. A stiff breeze off the sea teased the hem of her calf-length skirt, the woodland brown print blending with the earth. In deference to the chilly spring morning, she'd chosen a warm beige sweater with a darker cable pattern, her calf-high brown leather boots finishing the look. A heavy shawl hugged her shoulders. Sera let out a deep breath. "You've got this," she whispered. "Just don't screw it up."

As the meadow leveled out, a soft, musical lowing broke through her whirling thoughts. Sera blinked and, glancing around, spotted a herd of cow-like animals. Her breath caught in her throat. "Are those baby cows?" The small, dog-size creatures reminded her of shaggy Highland cows with long, flowing hair and horns that curved outward then spiraled inward like tree branches. But unlike normal cows, their fur was multi-colored and their eyes glowed with a soft blue bioluminescence.

"Oh goodness," she exclaimed, stepping back as several of the creatures trotted toward her. Her pulse quickened, a sharp pang of uncertainty tightening her chest. "Tell me they are friendly," she squeaked as she stumbled back and nearly fell. "Are they ... are they charging us?"

Willow snickered. "Won't attack unless you steal their flowers." Willow's tail slapped the ground, and her eyes danced with humor. "These are Velwynths," she said matter-of-factly. "Friendly as a dog. They bring good luck and make you feel good. Your grandmother gathered their wool," she added as she trotted forward to greet the lead animal with a nose butt.

The Velwynths surrounded Sera, their glowing eyes blinking curiously. Instantly, a wave of calm washed over her. Her breathing leveled out, and her heartbeat returned to normal. Bravely, she reached down to stroke the smallest one, her fingers sinking into its soft, colorful fur. One by one, the animals moved toward her to butt her gently, as though each animal wanted to touch her. The last of the tension in her shoulders faded.

Sera fingered an ear tag decorated with runes and symbols. The horns of each animal were adorned with moss, vines, and flowers. Some wore braided leather with beads, bells, and shiny crystals dangling, adding a charming tinkle to the air. She grinned appreciatively. "How charming," she murmured, stroking and petting each animal. "Who decorates them?"

"Owners," Willow replied, rubbing her head against a Velwynth with fur streaked in blue, green, and pink. "And the kids from the Clover and Charm Club. The school teaches the children how to care for them."

Curiosity satisfied, the herd wandered to a patch of blue flowers. As they munched, their coats shimmered and took on a bluish tint.

"Okay, they're cool—uh Velwynths. But if I don't hurry, I'll never make it to the shop."

Willow swished her tail, her eyes narrowed. "Priorities, Human."

Sera rolled her eyes. "Yeah, if I'm late opening the shop, Nonie will not be pleased!"

Feeling an unexpected surge of happiness, Sera continued toward the town, following the route that glowed on her phone. Rounding a slight bend, she strolled past a neighborhood of homes that reminded her of English cottages, complete with thatched roofs and gardens in full bloom. To her delight, she spotted a few hobbit abodes—with grass roofs dotted with wildflowers and small, round doors. She chuckled at the sight of a couple Velwynths enjoying a tasty snack.

One woman gathering blooms waved. Sera smiled and waved in return.

"You Elowen's girl?" the woman called out.

Tipping her head to one side, Sera replied, "Yes, I'm Sera, her granddaughter." She waited for the woman to comment on her being the Guardian, but to her surprise, the short, squat woman hurried over. "Welcome. Have a magical day," she offered. "I'm Martha Hawkins. Sam's wife."

Sera's eyes went wide. "Sheriff Sam?"

"Yep. Understand you met him." She paused. "And Fin yesterday."

"Um, yes, I met them," she answered hesitantly.

Martha let out a bark of laughter. "Don't mind them. Fin keeps Sam on his toes," she said, grinning mischievously. She plucked a long-stemmed flower from her basket and held it out to Sera.

To cover her awkwardness, she brought the flower to her nose and inhaled the sweet scent of roses with notes of lilacs. The petals shimmered faintly in the sunlight, and for the briefest second, Sera thought she heard a soft hum—like a lullaby half-remembered. She blinked, uncertain. "Did it ... just hum?"

Martha chuckled. "Maybe. Those blooms are moody. Keep it with you today, it might bring luck. Or at least keep the pixies away."

"Pixies?"

Martha waved a hand dismissively. "Don't worry, dear. You'll meet the pixies soon enough." She snapped her fingers. "Oh! Have you seen today's paper?"

Sera frowned. "No."

Rolling her eyes, Martha grinned. "You made the front page, sweetheart."

She reached into a deep pocket and pulled out a folded sheet of enchanted parchment. "Here—have mine. Penelope Winters wrote it."

Sera hesitated, taking the paper. The golden headline glittered:
**Elowen Blackthorn Takes Sudden Vacation.**

Her stomach gave a small twist.

"Don't let it rattle you," Martha said with a wink. "Penelope's more fluff than fact. She means well, but she does love her gossip. You'll be fine."

She tucked the sheet into her tote bag. She'd read it later. Whatever it said, she'd deal with it when she had more energy. She had enough swirling inside her without borrowing trouble from gold-ink headlines. Right now, she had a job to get to. She quickened her pace. Ahead, a figure in a cart flung letters and parcels at each shop door. The mail went through slots in the door that magically grew to fit whatever was being delivered.

As she neared Main Street, Sera noticed a hive of activity behind the row of shops. Tents and booths crowded the open field along A Street, their colorful awnings fluttering in the breeze. "What's going on?" she asked.

"Festival," Willow commented. "Bloom and Moon. Starts Friday."

The name tugged at something deep in her mind. She was eight or nine the last time she'd been here for it, and the memory was hazy—a blur of bright colors, music, crowds, and the faint scent of something sweet in the air. And magic. So much magic.

Her lips curved before she realized it. "It does sound fun," she murmured, though her thoughts were still tangled in the flickers of memory. She'd explore it later—right now, she needed to focus on work.

Reaching the front of her shop, she paused and gave herself a moment to admire the elegant old Victorian that housed Yarns of Wonder. In Boston, yarn shops were wedged between dry cleaners and donut chains. This one ... this one belonged in a make-believe setting. She laughed as she glanced around at all the fantasy-inspired buildings. "Okay, it fits right here in Havenwood Cove. She took a deep breath and eyed her roof. No prankster elf.

"Perfect," she murmured. Petals, pixies, and priorities, she thought. Let's see if I can handle all three.

It was still early, with only a few people wandering down Main Street, likely fellow shop owners preparing for the day. Spotting a few folks with go-cups, she grinned. Boston or Havenwood Cove, people, human or otherwise, needed that morning jolt of caffeine. She quickened her steps, following Willow, who, as expected, slipped through the door without a care. Sera pulled out the ornate silver key that had come from the journal. She frowned at the doorknob. No keyhole. "Okay. How do I get in?"

Willow's head appeared through the door. "It already knows you belong."

Recalling how Maude's door had opened automatically for her, Sera put her hand on the latch. The door opened. With a shrug and a glance at the silver key, which was not the key to either house or shop, she stepped inside.

# Chapter Fourteen

May 22 - Of Reunions, Runes & Rootcurrents

"Cool ... but spooky," Sera muttered, nudging the door open. A chime rang softly, its echo gentle and welcoming. As she stepped inside, the overhead lights flashed on.

Cleverly hidden spotlights revealed floor-to-ceiling shelves filled with neatly arranged skeins of every imaginable color. The shop smelled of cedarwood, with hints of lavender and lanolin—warm, familiar, and inviting. Sunlight streamed through sparkling windows. Floating dust motes shimmered like glitter caught mid-spell.

"Wow." Standing in the doorway, Sera took a moment to absorb the layout of the shop. Arranged around the open area in the center, armchairs draped with colorful afghans invited customers to sit and relax.

Straight ahead, a 'Y' shaped staircase led to the second floor. Her gaze tracked the railings that ran down each side of the second-story galley. The wood spindles formed different colorways. Two doors, one on either side, led into other rooms. Storage? She assumed the shop had at one time been a house because of the presence of bay windows, even upstairs.

"Sera!"

The sound of her name pulled her away from her perusal of the shop. She turned and stepped back outside to see who was shouting her name. Across the street, a woman dressed in hues of purple waved madly. Balancing two go-cups, she rushed toward Sera, her feet barely touching the ground. Sera's eyes went wide when she caught the sheen of iridescent wings.

Time zipped her back thirty years. Her eyes widened, and a wide grin bloomed across her face when she recognized her childhood friend. "Lila!" she shrieked, joy surging through her as she set her tote down just inside the shop and ran to meet her friend. In that moment, her world steadied.

Lilura Primrose stopped at the fountain and set two go-cups down onto the stone. She held out her arms, and the two women hugged, jumped up and down, and danced in a circle as they clung together, crying each other's names.

Finally, their wild laughter and shrieks faded, and quiet settled between them. "Lila. I can't believe it's you. You're still here."

"And where else would I go, Sera?" She lifted a hand to dry the tears on Sera's cheek. "Havenwood is home. And now you're back where you belong."

Nodding, Sera drew a shaky breath. "Yes, I'm back. I've come home," she said, and for the first time, she felt the truth of the words. Even with all the strangeness and uncertainty, that was the one truth Sera felt deep in her bones. This was home.

Lila's violet gaze held a trace of sadness. "You never came back," she said softly, her hands rubbing up and down Sera's arm.

Sera's heart ached at the thought of all the wasted years. "Oh Lila, until a couple of days ago, I didn't remember this place. My past was gone, but I'm slowly remembering my childhood. Well, a bit here and there."

They stepped back but gripped hands as though neither could bear to release the other. Lila's smile was gentle. "It'll come back. Give it time. You look well, Sera."

"Thanks." Sera pointed at her friend's dress. "I see purple is still your favorite color," she said fondly. Lila's white-blonde hair faded into soft purples and pinks, like the sky at dawn. The hem of her flowing dress glistened with countless sparkles. As she moved, the fabric swayed gently around her thighs, creating a melodic rustle that whispered of magic and enchantment.

"I saw your wings." Sera sighed with remembered longing. An image of the two of them at the beach came to her. She remembered Lila had taken her first short flight there, and Sera had run after her, flapping her arms, pretending she too had wings.

"I wanted wings of my own." She arched an amused brow. "Shouldn't you be flitting around spreading flower petals or granting wishes?"

Lila rolled her eyes and snorted. "Please. Fairies do that. I'm Fae—very different species. Less glitter, more grit."

Surprised, Sera cocked her head to one side. "Wait, I thought fairies were Fae?"

Lila waved her hands in denial. "Fairies *are* Fae, but not all Fae are fairies. I may have been blessed with wings, but I don't do dewdrop tiaras or sugarplum dreams. I'm something in between. More woodland than flower garden." A mischievous grin appeared.

"Think ancient forests and questionable bargains. That's me. And yes, I do bite."

Sera chuckled. "So noted." She remembered the intense longing she'd had as a child, the longing to be special, to be somebody. Becoming a Guardian tasked with destroying a portal wasn't quite what she'd had in mind, though. Unwilling to spoil their reunion, she pointed toward her shop.

"Got time to come in with me? There is a group of crafters that meet here in the mornings. I want to get settled before I open for business."

"Sure." Lila waved a hand toward the cups she'd set down. They floated toward her, the air shimmering beneath them.

Sera laughed. "Seriously cool move, Lila. Admit it. There's glitter in your magic, isn't there?" Her own finger itched to levitate something again.

"I admit nothing!" Lila teased with a wink. "Fancy a Mystic Meadow Mocha? It's my creation. Rich, chocolaty mocha infused with lavender and a hint of mint. Topped with whipped cream and a sprinkle of edible silver dust."

Taking a cautious sip, Sera moaned with pleasure as the warm, creamy liquid slid down her throat. "You created this sinful drink?"

"Yep. I own Fae Brews & Tales." Lila turned and pointed to the building across from the yarn shop with her cup.

"Wow! That's cool. I'm going to gain five pounds just walking past your shop." But secretly, she was thrilled. Having Lila—and her coffee shop—just across the street felt like a minor miracle. She had a feeling she was going to need her friend more than ever. For a moment, she also wished Pam were there. The joyful reunion felt a little lopsided without her. But Pam would totally freak out. She made a promise to call her soon.

Arm in arm, she and Lila headed toward the yarn shop. "You have no idea how happy I am to see you again, Lila." Sera's heart swelled with gratitude. She'd been lonely as a child in California. Until college, when she'd met Pam, who'd become the sister she'd never had. Now she had another sister. Sisters of the heart. The thought made her smile. It was a day of reunions.

Back inside the shop, she wandered, checking out the inventory. She couldn't resist squeezing the balls of yarn—petting, as her grandmother used to say. "So many wonderful skeins of yarn."

Lila studied the cardigan on display. She fingered the soft wool. "I was sorry to hear about your divorce."

Sera shrugged as she explored. "Don't be. It was for the best, and good riddance to the conniving creep. I'm free to be me again." Facing Lila, she asked, "What about you?" It hurt to realize that she knew nothing about her friend's life.

Lila's amused gaze met hers. She shrugged. "Same. Divorced. Five years now. And having the time of my life." She fingered the knitted sweater with intricate cables in different hues of a lilac in bloom. "I love this cardigan," she murmured.

"It's purple so no surprise there." Sera laughed. As a child, her friend had been obsessed with purple: pens, paper, notebooks, clothes, and hats. It pleased her that some things hadn't changed.

Sera spotted a table that held the point-of-sale cash register. She planted her hands on her hips and nodded. "Shouldn't take me long to figure it out." Setting her mocha down, she pulled her laptop and power cord out of her bag and set them on the gleaming, wooden surface. Crouching down, she searched for a free plug. "No outlet? Seriously?" She frowned. "Don't tell me this place runs on moonlight and miracles."

Standing, she checked behind the table. There had to be a power strip or outlet behind the equipment, but there was nothing but smooth, rune-etched wood that ran from one side to the other. She swore one knot in the golden wood blinked at her. Sentient dust?

"Looking for something, sweetheart?" Lila asked as she came and stood close to Sera, her amusement barely hidden in her smile, but her lively eyes sparkled with suppressed laughter.

Hands on her hips, Sera glanced around. "An outlet. A plug. Anything. I'd settle for an extension cord at this point. I'm down to six percent battery and fading fast."

Lila burst out laughing, the sort of laugh only a best friend could get away with. "Oh, *Boston girl*. You're adorable when you try to think like a human here."

Sera narrowed her eyes and fisted her hands on her hips, then jabbed a finger at the register. "Logically, there should be an outlet close to that machine unless everything runs on batteries. If so, I'm toast."

Lila sauntered over and leaned over the table. She tapped a polished nail on the faint silver spiral inlaid at one corner. "Pay attention. This rune is your power source." She pressed her palm on the wooden surface. Faint lines shimmered beneath the wood grain — a tangle of branches and roots forming a circle. Along one edge, other runes lit up. Lila pointed. "Those are your plugs."

Sera's jaw dropped. "Are you kidding me? Where are the wires?" She frowned. "Come to think of it, I haven't seen a single power line at all since I arrived." *Or any cords at Maude's*, she thought to herself.

"And you won't, my dear friend. Havenwood has its own source of power. Each building sits atop a Rootcurrent node. Just set your stuff down, and the forest will take care of your electronics."

"The forest?" Sera hesitated.

"This is your first lesson, Little Human." Willow appeared on the desktop.

Sera glared at the cat. "Can't you just jump up like a normal cat?"

Lila giggled. With an exasperated sigh, Sera lowered her open laptop onto the table and waited. Nothing. No glow. No buzz. No magical humming chorus of power. Just silence.

"This town runs on invisible nonsense," she muttered, poking at the runes. From somewhere above, a dry, unimpressed voice cut in. "Invisible nonsense? How dare you insult our life source."

A gust of air startled Sera, and her heart jumped when Syrus swooped down from the rafters and landed on the counter with theatrical flair.

"Ah, the talking bird returns," Willow intoned. "Welcome, Old One."

Syrus bowed. "Ancient One."

"Merlin's mother," Sera groaned. "Why are you here, Syrus?"

Syrus preened one vibrant wing. "Fun to observe. And eavesdrop. And judge you with great enthusiasm."

Lila smirked. "Be nice, Syrus. She's adapting."

"She's poking at ancient power conduits like they're broken toasters. Forgive me if I'm less than optimistic." He clicked his beak and fluffed his feathers.

Sera crossed her arms and eyed her amused audience. Even Willow's bright gaze gleamed with humor. "If someone would explain how this works—without mocking me into an early grave—I might be more cooperative."

Syrus bobbed his head up and down. "Fine. Lesson time. Listen closely: Havenwood is wired not with cables, but with roots. The forest beneath our feet is alive, magical, and highly opinionated. That magic—Rootcurrent—flows through ley lines like blood through veins. The buildings here are built on the intersections of those lines, and rune-bound wood like this," he tapped gently at the table with one clawed foot, "acts as a conduit."

Sera stared at the glowing rune next to her laptop. Lila waved her hand, and the laptop shifted slightly to the right until it sat on the rune. The surface of the table vibrated with a soft *whirr*, almost like a heartbeat beneath the wood. The laptop screen flickered to life.

"Ding," Syrus said, his voice high and amused. "You are now connected to the local network."

Peering at the icons, Sera saw that the battery was now charging. She blinked. "That actually worked."

"Told ya." Lila laughed.

"You're welcome," Syrus added. "Though I suspect you'll break something before the week is out."

"You're very smug for someone with feathers," Sera muttered.

Syrus tilted his head. "And you're very skeptical for someone living on top of a sentient power grid."

Lila nodded, turning serious. "This isn't Boston, Sera. This is Havenwood. You're not just living among magic. You're part of it now."

Sera's gaze swept across the table. Her reflection shimmered faintly on the polished surface. Maybe she was part of it. Maybe she had always been, but one thing was clear: She had a lot to learn.

Lila, Syrus, and Willow continued their playful banter as Sera wrestled with the point-of-sale register. Just as she relaxed into the strange wonder of it all, a sharp *clack-clack-clack* shattered the calm. The sound echoed from the back of the shop, metallic and rhythmic—like wooden bones snapping in time.

Syrus straightened, feathers puffing. "Ah," he said with a knowing gleam in his eye, "she's awake."

# Chapter Fifteen

May 22 - A Touch of Fae ... and Trouble

She? She who?" Sera followed the sounds to a cozy alcove at the back of the shop where an antique-looking spinning wheel sat beside an equally old loom. Both were of dark wood with intricate carved runes. The loom was weaving on its own. "What the heck?"

The two women glanced at one another and approached cautiously. Willow ran ahead. The surrounding air hummed with anticipation as the shuttle danced from one side to the other as though invisible hands guided it. Back and forth it went, the warp and weft intertwining in an ancient rhythm.

A magical loom? Sera watched the shuttle pass through the linen threads, a creamy hue of pure natural beauty that quickly transformed. With each pass of the shuttle, vibrant colors bloomed across the fabric, revealing words in pink and gold.

**WELCOME SERAPHINA**

She felt it—not a ghost, but a presence. Ancient and alive, like the heartbeat of the forest, it had reached through the loom to speak. *Welcome, Seraphina.* The message flickered and vanished, but the air hummed with magic that felt very much alive. She grabbed Lila by the arm. "Did you see that?"

"I did. Wow, Sera, I've never seen the loom do this," Lila said, her voice softening with awe. "Some say the loom was carved from the oldest root of the forest itself," Lila whispered. "It listens. And sometimes... it speaks."

The shuttle continued. Sera, transfixed, watched as new colors flowed like a river of light, deep blues melting into emeralds, shifting seamlessly into the golden warmth of a sunset, only to cool once more into the tranquil purples of twilight. It was as if the loom captured the sky's ever-changing palette, weaving a fabric that was a piece of the heavens themselves.

As Sera studied the emerging landscape, chills skittered up her spine when not one moon appeared, but three. The moons, the violent pink sky—she'd seen this in her dream last night. Sera hugged herself. This wasn't a landscape found anywhere on Earth.

"*Thyron,*" she rasped out, her heart racing. Her gaze sought Syrus. He gave a tiny nod.

The loom stopped abruptly. The threads glowed and then slowly faded, erasing the image. A cold draft made Sera shiver. Her heart pounded in her chest, her breath coming in quick gasps. The shop felt suddenly too small, too full of ancient magic she didn't understand. She backed away, her throat tight, fighting the rising tide of panic. She bit her lower lip and swallowed a bubble of nervous laughter.

"Sera, are you alright?" Lila glanced from the loom to Sera.

Hugging herself, Sera hurried over to the large table by the front window—as far from the loom as she could get without going out the door. She plopped down onto one of the wooden chairs and put her head in her hands. "Not just a dream," she moaned.

Lila scooted a chair close. Her hand hovered above the table, uncertain. "Sera ...?"

Sera reached out and grasped Lila's hand. "My dream. I saw that place in my dream. It's real."

Confused, Lila asked, "What place?"

"Thyron," she repeated. "Those moons ... they belong to another world."

"Thy—" Lila let go and sat back, a dumbfounded expression on her face. "Sera—" Her voice faltered.

Gripping her fingers in her lap, Sera took several deep, calming breaths before meeting Lila's eyes. "Do you know why I'm here?"

Lila tipped her head to one side. "You are the new Guardian of the Moondragon. Your grandmother passed the legacy to you." She paused, plucked at her skirt. "Most of us in Havenwood know, Sera. We also know we are in danger, but we don't truly understand who or what is threatening our town."

Sera ran her hands through her hair, pulling, using the bite of pain to keep her from panicking. "I'm not exactly sure either, except it's something dark. And evil." She hugged herself. "You know about Thyron, right?"

Lila nodded. "According to legends, it's where many of us, or our ancestors, came from originally. Like the Fae and the magical forest. Havenwood exists because of those who came from another world. But it's just a legend. A myth."

"No, it's real. Somewhere in Havenwood Cove, there is a portal from Earth to Thyron. Do the legends say where it might be?" Sera leaned forward. Maybe she'd get some much-needed answers.

Lila shook her head. "According to the legend, it was sealed a long time ago. Most don't even care about the old legends."

"Well, this old legend is about to make itself known. From what I've learned, the seal is weakening. The threat you all face comes from this other world, and I'm here to save the town. Maybe the world." She stared down at her hands to take a deep, steady breath before glancing back at her stunned friend.

"Wild, right?" The silence grew heavy until Lila broke it, her voice hesitant.

"Sera, I don't know what to say?"

Sera leaned back in the chair and stared at the dust motes floating in a beam of light streaming in from the window. Through her sweater, she fingered the oathstone. As much as she wanted to blurt out everything that had happened since her arrival—Molly and Syrus's revelations, the dream, Lady Lillian—she didn't. Nor did she confess that her quest required her not only to find the portal but to destroy it.

"There's more, but I can't go there. Not yet." But she couldn't hold all her fears inside. With Lila, she wasn't afraid to admit it. "Lila, I don't know how to save the town. I may be a witch, but the only talent I seem to have is seeing things others cannot."

Just then, Willow jumped onto the table. Sera pointed. "Like my formerly-imaginary cat."

Lila cocked her head to one side. "Oh, I see a white cat. Saw and heard her at your desk with Syrus."

Sera frowned at the cat. "Really? I thought I was the only one who could see you."

Willow wrapped her fluffy tail around her feet and stuck her nose in the air. "I choose who sees me, Little Human. The time has come for truth and revelations." The cat plopped down on its side in the middle of the table.

Lila's eyes went wide, the pale color deepening with surprise. She waved her hand toward Willow. "This is the ghost cat you used to talk about—the one that turned colors and walked through walls." She grinned sheepishly. "I thought you made her up." She reached out and gently stroked the cat. "Wow, she's real. Sera," she breathed, her voice low with awe and eyes wide with wonder. "You've got veil sight."

Sera nodded. "That's what Nonie said." Her stomach tightened at the thought, and she wondered just what else she would see.

Lila sat back. "Sera, do you know how incredibly rare it is to see through the very fabric that separates our world from the other realms—the in-betweens, the hidden, the things that move in the shadows but leave no trace? Most Witches, and Fae, would give anything to have that kind of gift. Fae like me live in the spaces between, so I know how powerful veil sight can be."

"And scary," Sera said, thinking about the shadows in the mirror and the wraiths in her dream. It seemed less of a gift and more of a curse. Seeing things others couldn't suddenly made the world feel too big, too filled with shadows and whispers she didn't understand.

A soft tap on her cheek from Willow drew her from her fears. She smiled hesitantly. "But good too, as it brought Willow back into my life." She touched her forehead to the cat's.

Elbows on the table, Lila rested her chin on her fist. "I remember how much you loved magic, Sera. It was a part of you."

"Truthfully, I don't remember much still and I'm not even sure what all I can do yet." Or how being a witch would help her with her quest. Her greatest fear was failing. Not just everyone in Havenwood, but herself.

What if she couldn't live up to the expectations laid at her doorstep? She'd seen others with powerful magic—Nonie, Fin, and the sheriff with his staff that could zap people and send them flying. But what did she have in her arsenal to fight evil? She turned her wrist and studied the gleaming gems from her ancestors—or, if she believed, gifts from the magical forest. She also had a magical journal and an oathstone. The magic others wielded seemed so natural, and she still felt like an outsider wanting into the club. Could she destroy the portal without magic? Assuming she could find it, of course. She stared at her hands wrapped around the now-cool cup to hide their trembling.

"Compared to what I've seen, I'm barely a blip on the magical radar. No spells, no wand, nothing flashy. Just eyes that see too much." She tried to laugh, to inject some lightness into the conversation, but fear gnawed at her.

"Stop it, Sera." Lila's voice sharpened. "It's never too late. Like most things in life, you need to learn how to use it. Veil sight can show you things that others can't see—the hidden threats, things that move between worlds. It's like ... your vision walks behind the curtain, where the rest of us can only guess."

Lila reached out and gripped Sera's hand. "Besides, you're more than a witch, you know."

"Yeah, I'm divorced and an out-of-work accountant. What more can I be?" She glanced at Willow, who'd said almost the same thing earlier. Willow blinked back.

Lila shook her head, her eyes dancing with both humor and wisdom. "Sera, have you forgotten? You're Fae. Your father was Faekin and a bit of a legend around here."

Sera blinked. Everything froze: her thoughts, her heartbeat, even her hearing. *Fae?* Her heart thudded against her chest. She blinked once, twice, as if the word itself couldn't land. "He's what?" She swallowed hard, the shop blurring around her as she tried to grasp what Lila was telling her.

Witch and *Fae*. The word buzzed in her ears like static. Her pulse skittered. Was she part of this other world, like Lila or other creatures that existed in the spaces between? What did it mean for who she was?

She took a deep breath, but it didn't help. She'd spent her whole life believing she was just ... ordinary. Boring. Human. And then to learn she was not just a witch but also part mystical being?

Why hadn't her grandmother said anything? Or her mother, for that matter. She had to have known that if she'd married a Fae, Sera would also carry Fae blood. The news hit her like a ton of bricks. She wasn't ready for this—she barely understood her own powers as a witch, let alone a heritage based on magic. Witches were human, but Fae were magical creatures.

"I'm Fae, like you?" The revelation stunned Sera.

Lila chuckled. "No exactly. I'm Fae, but you are Faekin, an ancient line of Fae. Faekins are royalty among the Fae."

"Lila, I'm speechless. Coming to terms with being a witch was a shock but Fae—Faekin?

"I thought you knew, Sera." Lila covered Sera's hands, stilling her restless fingers. "Before you went away, your magical powers were already stronger than those of many older children, me included. Adolescence is when a child's powers start to reveal themselves, but you bloomed early."

She shook her head ruefully. "You wanted my wings, but I envied your magic," Lila said. "Remember this? You taught me this trick. Lila lifted her hands and flicked her fingers. Purple sparks danced in the air. Yours were bigger and so colorful and sparkly."

Sera studied her hands. "I don't remember—" Something awakened inside her, like muscle memory. She couldn't say how she knew; she just did. She flicked her fingers, and silvery sparks floated and mingled with Lila's. "How could I forget this?"

The voice of the delivery driver echoed in her mind. She whispered the words aloud, as if recalling a dream: "Old truths wrapped in silence ... gifts once lost, now returned. Let memory bloom, and the new take root."

Lila drew her brows together. "That sounds like a spell, Sera."

Sera's fists clenched on the table. "It was. A stranger spoke them to me and told me to remember. He gave me—" She hesitated, not wanting to mention the journal. Not yet. "He gave me a message from my grandmother, whom I knew nothing about. But after he left, I started to remember." She stared at her hands. "Magic returned, along with memories of this place. Why was this taken from me?"

Lila considered. "Your mom took you away. Maybe it was to protect you."

Anger simmered, along with feelings of betrayal. "Yeah, I can see that. She hates anything magical and didn't want me to return to Havenwood Cove. That doesn't change the fact that she, or whoever else, stole from me. They had no right."

Willow tapped her shoulder. "Little Human," she began, her voice almost harsh, "we don't always know why, and you can argue all day and night how unfair it was, but you've got your memories back, or at least they are returning when you need them most."

Sera lowered her head. "You're right, my friend." She sighed. "Past is past. I have enough on my plate with today and the future." She stroked the cat. "Thank you."

Lila's gentle gaze warmed Sera. "She's right. And being Fae will give you strength in ways you can't imagine yet. And trust me, I think you're going to need it."

Wanting to lighten things up, and to hide her shock as she struggled with her emotions, she caught one spark on her palm. "You know, I still want wings," she said with a forced smile.

Lila rolled her eyes. "I'll buy you a pair to wear," she joked.

The two laughed, the tension easing in the shop. Sera sobered. "I have so many questions, Lila. I'm still just the woman who balanced books and drank too much coffee. Not some witch-Fae Guardian expected to save the town."

Standing, Lila drew Sera into a warm embrace. "It's a lot to process. I'm here for you, Sera. And so are others. You won't be alone." She paused and sighed. "I've got to get back, and I bet you have lots to do. We'll talk later."

Sera stood as well. "Definitely." Having a friend she could talk to reassured her as nothing else had done. She walked Lila to the door. As Lila stepped out, she turned and snapped her fingers.

"The Bloom and Moon Festival is this weekend. Starts the night of the full moon with a bonfire at midnight, which is tomorrow and goes on all day Friday and Saturday. You'll come, right?"

Sera shrugged. "I suppose I should. You know, support the community and all."

"We'll go together. It'll be fun. Like old times." Lila grew serious once more. "You'll find your way, Sera." With one last glance, she hurried down the path toward her own shop.

Sera closed the door, leaning against it as her thoughts swirled. The yarns on the shelves shimmered softly in the light, as if the magic in the shop mirrored the buzzing in her mind. Being a witch or Fae seemed overwhelming enough, but learning she was both witch and Fae? Add Guardian—and each identity felt like the world rested on her shoulders. How could she balance them all without breaking under the pressure? Everything she thought she knew about herself had just gone *poof*. Like Syrus.

The silence pressed around her. Only the soft ticking of the shop clock reminded her that time wouldn't stay still and wait for her to figure things out. She ran her fingers over the stones of her bracelet. At her touch, her aestralite stone glowed brightly. An answering warmth came from the oathstone beneath her sweater. Across the room, stretched out on the table, Willow's eyes blazed. Sera pressed her hands into her stomach to still the flutters.

Beneath her feet, the faintest vibration thrummed through the floorboards—a pulse, slow and steady. Rootcurrent. As if the living magic that ran beneath Havenwood Cove had felt her awakening. Guardian. witch. Fae. And the fate of a magical town rested on her shoulders. Ready or not, the ticking clock was about to start. She didn't yet believe she could do this.

But the forest did. And maybe ... that was enough.

# Chapter Sixteen

May 22 - Stitched Truths & Tangled Lies

"It's a good thing brains don't explode," Sera told Willow. "Or mine would have done that days ago!" Hands on hips, she stared at her cat. "Any other surprises for me? You could have warned me."

Willow swiped a paw over her ear. "You are who you've always been, Little Human."

Sera jabbed a finger at Willow. "I'm not totally Human! When were you going to tell me?" Her mind felt like a fried motherboard. Willow drew herself up, looking as regal as a queen. Her eyes glowed with an otherworldly—

"Nope." Sera slashed her hand through the air. "Go away." She whipped around. "I have a shop to run."

*"No one speak. Boss Lady wants quiet."*

Sera ran her hands through her hair, gripping the roots as if she could tug away the madness or release her chaotic thoughts. "And you are not here! Go away."

Syrus stretched out his wings, flapped them, and faded to nothing. *"Hellooo? Invisible bird here speaking!"* His harsh cackle of laughter heralded his reappearance—on the second-floor rail.

She threw her hands up into the air. "I give up." There was no escaping the magical madness her life had become. With a resigned sigh, she rolled her shoulders and breathed in the scents of lavender, wool, and the lemon tang of furniture polish. There was even peppermint from the wooden candy dish on the counter that reminded her of her father.

She returned to her desk and ran her fingers across the smooth wooden surface, tracing the faint carvings—tiny swirls that pulsed with warmth, a reminder that magic lived in every corner of the shop. It wasn't just the shop's charm or her grandmother's care that kept it running; the same unseen force flowed through the Rootcurrent connections and the loom in the back.

A clock chimed eight musical tones followed by a knock on the front door. Glancing over, she spotted a group of women on the porch.

"Oh yeah, first on the opening check list: Unlock the door!" Sera hesitated for a moment, her hand on the latch. This was her first test of stepping into Nonie's shoes. Taking a deep breath, she pulled the door open with a smile. "You must be the Yarn Whisperers," she greeted the group of stitchers that met every morning before the shop opened for business. A thrill of excitement ran through her.

A few of the women exchanged glances—not unkind, but ... wary. One murmured, "So it's true then. She's the new Guardian."

Another added under her breath, "The seventh."

Sera smiled, pretending not to hear—but the knot in her stomach tightened. This marked her first official encounter with the townsfolk, though it felt like she'd already met half of Havenwood Cove in just one day. It was a far cry from Boston, where you could walk a mile without knowing or speaking to a soul. Everyone here seemed friendly—well, almost everyone. The sheriff had a bit of a sour streak, but after meeting Fin, she could understand why. She chewed her lower lip as a small knot of tension twisted in her gut.

She wanted to belong here and become part of the community. After all, it wasn't just magic she was looking for in Havenwood, but a place where she truly belonged. Before the ladies waiting could enter, a loud, firm voice from the rear of the group rang out. "Move aside. Make way. In a hurry here."

Sera craned her neck to see who the impatient woman was. A tall, formidable woman in her fifties split the group of women like Moses and the Red Sea. "Need to get the library opened." Huffing, the woman with silver-streaked auburn hair worn in a braided crown hurried up the path. She carried an intricately carved walking stick adorned with crystals.

She tapped the end of her stick on the stone path. Hazel eyes with flecks of gold regarded Sera in a no-nonsense manner. "Rowena Thistlewood. Head librarian. Council meeting at the bookstore tonight, Seraphina. Seven sharp. Be there, and don't be late." Two taps emphasized her command.

Caught like a deer in headlights, the woman's absolute authority froze Sera to the spot. It took a moment for the woman's command to register. Rowena was halfway down the path before Sera found her voice.

"Wait, what meeting? City council?" Nonie hadn't mentioned any council meetings.

Rowena turned, her lips compressed into a thin line. "Did Elowen not explain this to you?"

Feeling like an errant schoolgirl, Sera snapped her jaw closed at the woman's cold, disapproving voice. "Explain what?" Her voice ended in a squeak. She felt like a child facing an irate principal.

"Your position, of course. With Elowen gone, you are now the head of the magical council."

*Head of the magical council* echoed in her head and felt as foreign as though she'd been asked to lead a royal court. "The—what? Magical—*head*?" She ran her fingers through her hair, the tips catching in the tangled curls. "I'm sorry, but I don't know anything about the magical council. I just arrived yesterday."

A loud, disapproving sigh followed by a firmer tap. "No excuse. We need to finalize the opening of the Bloom & Moon Festival. The moon ritual is tomorrow night. Opening ceremony is Friday morning, and we need to make sure everything and everyone is organized. Don't be late."

Feeling blindsided, Sera blinked when, with one last tap, Rowena hurried away from the shop, the crystals on her staff catching the morning light. Sera's stomach churned. Head of the magical council? Absurd. That was comparable to being thrust into the pilot seat of a plane and being told to fly. The thought of the upcoming meeting made her hands tremble slightly. She wasn't ready for this, not even close. She was so new to this world, how could she possibly lead others?

No one spoke. In the corporate world, Sera had once commanded boardrooms with a single glance. But this? This was different. Rowena's authority and control didn't stem from fear or one's position in the company. It was absolute, part of the woman herself. Her gaze alone could still the air in the room.

*I was good,* Sera thought, *but she's better*. With hands on her hips, she voiced her thoughts. "She could probably command an army of magical creatures as easily as she organizes her book collections."

The group stared at her for a beat. Surprise flickered across their faces before laughter broke out. Sera's face flushed, and she clapped a hand over her mouth. "Oh no, I didn't mean to say that out loud." *Good going, Sera. Way to make a good first impression!*

The laughter subsided. A tall, thin woman with silver-white hair tied back with a magenta ribbon that matched her sweater stepped forward and held out a hand. "Daisy O'Connell." Her eyes, deep sage green, were warm and friendly, somewhat calming like a soothing breeze.

"No need to apologize, Seraphina. You'll get used to her," Daisy offered, chuckling softly while squeezing Sera's arm in a friendly manner. "Rowena has a way of making even the most confident witch feel like a schoolgirl. She's a bit bossy, but she's also the go-to person for magical research."

That answered Sera's question about a library. And she now knew who she might go to for answers—maybe. She grinned. "Please, no formalities. Call me Sera, and welcome. Come on in."

Daisy entered the shop, and another woman came forward, her brown eyes sparkling with humor. "Marti Clarkson, just a plain-Jane human who found her way to the cove after her husband died. I prefer crocheting. Since it's faster than knitting."

Sera immediately liked the no-nonsense woman with a practical bob with silver strands weaving through her dark brown hair.

"Move it along, Marti. Fern Verdanthis. Head of RC Management."

Sera smiled. Fern's silver hair bore a subtle brownish-green-golden sheen, but what drew her attention was the simple woven tunic that shimmered with hidden threads woven throughout. "I love the outfit!"

Fern smiled. "My sister owns Earthen Elegance. She makes everything we sell."

"Nice. I definitely need to visit your shop." And soon, Sera promised herself.

"Thank you, Sera. Please do. She'd be pleased to design something just for you!"

One by one, the rest of the group introduced themselves and filed inside. Just as she turned to follow, a large man burst through the door before she closed it. He ushered three children in before him. Her brows rose. In one hand, he carried a tote bag with the name of the yarn shop across one side, and in his other, he gripped the handle of a wicker basket with a tiny brown Chihuahua inside. The dog's ears perked forward.

"Morning, ladies. Sorry I'm late. My daughter was a bit of a sleepyhead this morning." He grinned at Sera's welcoming smile. "Jake Weatherby. I do hope it's okay to bring Tiny?" He held the basket up and lifted a bushy brow.

Sera leaned forward and stroked the dog's golden-brown head. "Of course, she said as she struggled to swallow her laughter. Jake was an enormous man who could give any lumberjack a run for his money, and to see him with a dog that could fit in his palm seemed comical.

Jake set the basket down. "You mind your manners, Tiny." The dog leaped out and ran to the girl.

"That child with the crown—"

"Tiara, Dad!"

"Ah, right you are, Ella. She insists on being called Princess Ella. The two boys are not my sons, but as they practically live at our house, I reserve the right to claim them." He pointed. "Nate and Liam."

Sera hid her grin when all three children glanced at her. Their eyes went huge, as though remembering their impromptu meeting yesterday on the road and Nate's literal run-in with the Rootwall. Nate's face turned beet red.

"It's nice to meet each of you. I think I saw you riding your bikes yesterday."

"Um, yep. Uh, we got homework," Liam said, scuffing his foot on the wooden floor. The trio ran over to a small corner of the shop where a child's size table and chairs sat. A basket of books and toys was tucked beneath it.

She followed the group of crafters to the table. The ease with which they all found a chair told Sera they each had their spot. She felt awkward standing there, her fingers intertwined. About to excuse herself, Daisy addressed Sera. "What are you working on?"

"Working on? Oh, nothing right now. She took a step back, not wanting to intrude. "I'll leave you all to your projects." She felt a stab of envy upon seeing Daisy's partially completed lacy shawl, which was every bit as exquisite as her grandmother's.

Marti shook her head and grinned. "Nope. Not allowed." She pulled out a crocheted scarf done in colorful stripes. "We didn't allow your grandmother to do her books or whatever, either. This is our time before the workday swallows us up."

Sera scrunched her nose. "Not even sure where I'd start. All my hooks and needles are still packed, and I don't have any yarn."

Hoots of good-natured laughter rang out. Fern rolled her eyes. "Child, you have an entire shop at your disposal. Is knitting or crocheting your poison?"

Sera grinned sheepishly, feeling an immediate liking to these crafters. "I used to do both, but I've done more crocheting recently." She shrugged, her gaze meeting Marti's. "It's faster." The two laughed.

Fern tapped her chin. "How about the timeless granny square? You can make a scarf, or an afghan, or a lap blanket, or even a tote."

Marti piped up. "Table cover, baby blanket, or even just squares for coasters, or potholders. Very versatile pattern. Come on, I'll help you get started." She set her work down and hurried around the table.

Accompanied by Marti, with opinions tossed out from the others, Sera, in short order, had yarn, a pattern book of variations of the granny square, and a set of wooden crochet hooks. Taking the chair between Fern and Marti, she spread out her supplies. Excited, as much for the project as the warm acceptance, she held up the photo of the pattern she'd decided on.

"A triangular shawl pattern called *Dawn's Embrace*." She had a weakness for shawls and scarves. For this project, she'd chosen a gradient yarn; the colors flowed from a pale gold to rosy pink and ended with rich blues and deep greens. It reminded her of the coloring of both dawn and dusk over the ocean.

"Very fitting as this is the dawn of a new era for you," Fern agreed.

"Oh, that will be gorgeous," Emily, the tech-savvy young woman who managed her grandmother's website, said, her needles moving smoothly through the loops of yarn. She had half a sock completed in a marbled green and brown yarn.

"Well, I'm only here for the summer," Sera said. "When Nonie returns, I'll have to figure out what to do with my life."

Daisy took a sip from her go-cup. "Plenty here for you, Sera. You might just discover this is where you're supposed to be."

Sera frowned, thinking of what lay ahead. Feeling her anxiety rising, she inhaled deeply. A flash of blue caught her eye. Glancing up, she spotted two brilliant orbs glowing softly. A white paw, held level with the cat's eyes, flashed as though Willow was giving her a thumbs up and telling her, "You got this, Human."

"Thanks," she whispered so softly no one else heard. With another deep breath, she punched her worry aside. Willow was right. There was no sense in panicking: One, she didn't have enough information, and two, she had three months, and this was only day one for her.

Even so, the questions swirled in her mind: What if she failed? The weight of her responsibilities pressed deep into her chest, her breath growing shallow as her thoughts spun faster than she could keep up with.

She glanced at the wooden crochet hook in her hand. Her fingers itched to move, to create. She scanned the pattern. "Okay, here goes." Sera smiled. This wasn't just a shawl—it was a journey. A promise, a small, tangible reminder that she was stitching her life back together, one row at a time.

She began with a magic ring, the yarn looping easily around her fingers. *Fitting,* she thought as the circle tightened with a pull. It was like the center of her own life, a knot of pain, but also of strength. Her hook moved with purpose and with the familiar rhythm, the tension slowly unwound from her chest. The repetitive motion steadied her mind, as if each stitch helped anchor her to the present.

The granny stitch was simple, familiar, yet with each stitch, it felt like more than just a pattern. It was a reminder that she could reshape what was broken, bit by bit. Each cluster of stitches became a small victory, a steady beat pulling her away from the past and toward something new.

"Daisy, how is Bessie? Heard she went to see Amelia." Emily posed the question without glancing up from her work.

"No! She didn't," Fern gasped as she sat back in her seat.

Daisy pulled yarn free from her skein and sighed. "Yep, she did. Wanted an elixir to give her courage to address the school board at the meeting last night, so she asked Amelia for a potion to help with public speaking. But Amelia, the poor deaf dear, thought she wanted a potion to help with public squeaking. Bessie could only speak in random high-pitched squeaks and squeals. Got her to the Healing Center right away. She's fine now."

Daisy grinned and glanced up from her work. "We're calling this latest fail of Amelia's, The Squeak-Speak Potion."

Everyone laughed and groaned at the same time. Sera gathered that Amelia's potion mix-ups were legendary as more stories of mix-ups circulated around the table. She vowed not to drink anything from the unknown woman.

"Uh, Sera?"

The speaker was another young woman with colorful hair and gentle, almond-brown eyes. "Yes, Grace? Right?"

The young girl nodded shyly. "Is it true what people are saying? That you're the new Guardian and your grandmother—"

"Grace," Daisy interrupted firmly. "Let Sera get used to us before we ply her with questions."

"Oh. Sorry. I tend to blurt out what I'm thinking," Grace said, her cheeks turning pink.

"No, it's all right," Sera said as she glanced around the table. "For better or worse, I am the Guardian. There's a lot I don't understand." She drew her lower lip into her mouth and then sighed. "I've been told there's a legend of love, betrayal and sacrifice. I thought to check out the library, but would any of you know of it?" She smiled weakly.

Daisy nodded. "Most folk here know some of it." She smiled. "Living in Havenwood, you'd have to have at least some understanding of its history or how life operates here. Rowena is a good person to check with as there might be actual historical accounts." She lifted her brows toward Fern.

Sighing, Fern set down her needles. "I can help some. You've already figured out there are magical beings in Havenwood. Some are part human, but not all of us. Some, like me, come from magical lines—creations of the magical forest. Like your housekeeper, Molly, Fin—none of us are sure what he is. Most of the gnomes have interbred with humans."

She waved a hand. "I digress. I am a Verdan. In your world of mythology, you could say I'm a mix of druid and dryad. And more. My family line goes back to the beginnings of Havenwood. We are tied to the land, to the forest, and to the Rootcurrent."

"Havenwood is truly a unique place," Sera murmured. It felt like pieces of the puzzle falling into place, connecting, and the forest was that missing piece. Everything made sense if you considered that the forest, or The Mother, was the center of all life here. "So, the Rootcurrent is like the blood, and the forest is the air, both feeding or sustaining life in Havenwood?"

Nodding agreed. "That is a good way to look at it. Now, the legend you seek is older than most here remember or know. After all, most legends or myths aren't real." Fern paused and took a sip of water from her bottle. "But the legend about Saoirse and Drakon is true. Saoirse, her family, and many others settled here long ago.

They were shipbuilders, sailed here and stayed. Saoirse fell in love with a man named Drakon. Trouble followed the lovers for he was not of this world."

Sera, her project forgotten, nodded. "He was from Thyron."

Fern dipped her head. "You know that much. That is good. Yes. Saoirse was a witch. Her twin sister, Aisling, was the first Blackthorn, and first Guardian. Drakon wished to remain with the woman he loved, but he was promised to another."

Everyone paused in their work. The clicking of needles and the slide of yarn fell silent. The air was still, as though everyone held their breath. "He didn't go back, did he?"

Fern shook her head and drew a deep breath. "No. And because of his refusal, Thyron declared war on his followers, and that included all the magical beings on Earth, and the Humans. To protect the innocent, he and Saoirse sacrificed their lives. Their love sealed the portal. That is all I know. No one knows how they sealed the portal. But most of us feel it weakening."

Sera's breath caught in her throat at the thought of two lovers sacrificing everything they had to save others. She tried to absorb the information—that her ancestor had given her life to protect Havenwood Cove—but how?

Staring at her work, the stitches blurred as her mind tried to process what she'd just learned. She blinked hard, steadying her hands. Her next step was to discover how they'd sealed the portal. Maybe then she could prevent it from opening—without destroying it. But no matter what, she owed it to Drakon and Saoirse to do whatever it took so their sacrifices were not in vain.

"Mrs. Blackthorn?"

Startled from her thoughts by the formal address, yet relieved at the interruption, Sera glanced at Ella, who stood at her elbow. "Sera or Miss Sera will do, Ella. What'cha need?"

"I'd like a tiny ball of the color changing yarn. Not too much. I just want to decorate my Velwynth for the parade on Friday."

"Okay, do you know where it is?"

The child nodded. "Yes, you have to ask the spinning wheel for it."

Sera's eyes went wide. "Ask—"

Jake rested his plate-sized hands on the table as if to stand. "I'll help her, Sera."

Pulling herself together, Sera shook her head. "Thanks. How about if Ella shows me?" she suggested as she got to her feet. "Lead the way, Princess Ella."

Ella giggled. The two boys were whispering. Nate shook his head. "No, that's not right. We need—"

"You look hard at work," Sera commented with a smile.

Both boys jumped. "Uh, yeah, sure," Liam stammered.

"Science." Nate nodded as if that explained everything.

Sera lifted a brow. Both boys looked to Ella for help, which told her they were up to something.

"Velwynth's wool is special," Ella chimed in. "Their fur changes color with what they eat, and it holds the magic from all the places they've been." Ella smiled sweetly. "We're experimenting with something for a contest. Plus, Sweet Pea needs to look festive for the parade," she said with a glint of determination in her eye.

Sera sensed mischief in the making. "I see." A sound from the alcove drew her attention.

"Look," Ella cried out with glee. "Nellie is spinning." She rushed into the alcove.

Sera watched in amazement as the gleaming antique wheel turned on its own, the gray roving twisting into colorful yarn like magic—duh—because it was magic. Her breath caught. "Wow," she whispered.

The spinning wheel stopped and cut the yarn.

Ella took the small ball of yarn, her grin wide. "Perfect," she said.

"Can it make any color?" Sera asked, still amazed.

Ella nodded eagerly. "You just tell it what you want."

"That's such a tiny ball of yarn. Is it enough?"

"Oh yes. Thank you." Ella ran off to rejoin the boys.

Sera returned to the table, shaking her head in disbelief. A magical loom and spinning wheel. Amazing. She picked up her project and resumed where she'd left off. "I don't think Ella can get even one tiny braid out of that tiny ball."

Emily smiled, holding up her own small ball of yarn. "It doesn't look like much, but it's always enough. Just picture your project and the wheel gives you exactly what you need. Doesn't look like I'll get a second sock out of this, but I will."

Sera smiled. "Guess I have a lot to learn."

As she returned to her shawl, she felt the rhythm of working with the yarn settle her nerves. The noise of her past quieted as her hands worked, and her breathing slowed to match the steady pulse of the yarn.

"You're fast, Sera," Fern commented, glancing over from her own project.

Sera smiled. "I've missed this," she breathed. The pattern was simple enough, but in its simplicity, she found solace. As she worked, she found her thoughts drifting, not to the pain of her past, but to the promise of the future. The finished shawl would become a symbol of her resilience and strength. Her magic might be unknown and unpredictable, her future uncertain, but this ... this she could control. She could shape it, mold it, and make it hers. For the first time in a long while, Sera believed in the beauty of what could be.

Sera paused, her nose wrinkling. For a fleeting moment, the air in the shop carried a scent she couldn't place—sharp, metallic, and slightly sweet, like the air after a thunderstorm. A faint hum vibrated from the floor, and across the room, her laptop went dark.

Fern froze mid-stitch, nose twitching, head turning to study the shop.

"What's wrong, Fern?" Daisy paused her work.

Fern drew her shoulders up in a shiver. "The current trembled." She tipped her nose into the air. "Smell that? Burnt sugar and sage ..." The lights in the room flickered.

Grace's needles stopped. "The Rootcurrent never fails. What does this mean?" She glanced anxiously around the table.

Pale, Fern rested a trembling hand on the table and drew in a deep breath. "It's starting. The forest trembles, the shield weakens." Her tone was tight as she glanced at Sera.

Sera set her hook on the table as she absorbed the various degrees of fear and confusion among her companions. "The magical forest is a shield?"

"Yes. It protects Havenwood," Daisy explained. "It's old magic, and it has never faltered. Until recently." She held Fern's gaze. "It's happening more often."

Sera sought Willow and, from the cat's perch on the hutch, gasped when she winked in and out of existence. "Willow?"

After a moment, the cat solidified. She blinked slowly. "I taste it in the ley lines." She tucked her paws neatly beneath her, as if that ended the matter.

The familiar, comforting scent of wool and lemon returned. Fern visibly relaxed, and her color returned.

"There, it steadied." She reached out and laid a hand on Sera's. "I fear you don't have a lot of time, Guardian."

The impact of being addressed as Guardian shook Sera. No one looked at her, said anything further. "Three months," she whispered.

Fern sighed. "I'm connected to the forest. She'll fight to protect Havenwood, as will I and others. The Mother may tremble—but she is still strong.

Sera chewed her lower lip. What would happen if the forest failed? Would the seal on the portal also fail? And if it opened, what would come through? Sera resumed her crochet, but her hands moved slower now, the rhythm thrown off by the quiet tension that lingered in the room.

She glanced back up at the cat, now feigning sleep in a perfect curl atop the hutch. But Sera knew better. Willow wasn't resting. She was *listening.* As though no one wanted to discuss the actual possibility of the forest failing, including her, everyone set about packing up. Talk was hushed as the air of unease became the elephant in the room.

The walls felt too still after everyone left, as though the building itself was holding its breath. Sera tidied up. The relaxation she'd felt faded back to fear and worry. Willow flew down from her high perch and landed on the table. "You have time, Human."

Sera stared at her hands until their trembling stopped. "The trees groaned when I came through the gate," Sera said aloud, mostly to herself. "Bram said the shield was ... twitching?"

Willow flicked her tail once. "They did more than groan. The shield pulled tight, like a thread snagged on a nail."

Glancing at Willow, Sera drew a deep breath. "You felt it?"

"Of course I did. So did the forest. So did Bram. And if you'd listened closely, so did you."

Willow jumped down, her blue eyes gleaming. "You're not just here to inherit a shop, Guardian. You've woken up old magic. And it's watching to see what you'll do."

Feeling unsettled, and if she admitted it, scared, Sera rang up her purchases, including a delightful tote bag with the name of the shop, to stow her supplies and project. She paid with her debit card and stowed the bag beneath the counter. She eyed the table. Would the crafters return after the festival ended?

She hoped so. She'd found acceptance and a shared love of her craft. Evan, her snobby ex, had scoffed at her handmade sweaters, scarves, and hats. They weren't polished or sophisticated. Or designer labels. She vowed to allow no one to dictate her personality, her likes or dislikes. It was time to be Seraphina Blackthorn, whoever that person might be, and one thing she knew—working with her hands to create was a big part of who she was.

"Incoming. Incoming," Syrus called out with gleeful enthusiasm moments before the door crashed open. Frowning, Sera turned toward the door, her welcoming smile dying as the sheriff stomped inside, his stormy expression warning her that something was up.

"Seraphina Blackthorn, I need your help!" With one hand on his hip, the other gripping his staff, he glared at her, his boots thudding against the floor. "Well, wha' are ya waiting for! Let's go!" He punctuated the command with a sharp crack of his staff against the wood. He stomped out.

# Chapter Seventeen

May 22 - The Trouble with Quilts (Curses & Complications Included)

Sera hurried after the sheriff. "Sheriff," she called out. "Wait! I can't leave the shop unattended."

Sam whirled, hands on hips, glowering. "Wha'? Ya think you'll get robbed?" His tone made it clear no one would dare.

"Well ..." She glanced around. "What if a customer comes and I'm not here?"

He rolled his eyes. "Let 'em wait."

Sera jammed her hands on her hips. "Not a way to run a business, Sheriff. What's this about?"

The sheriff's face reddened, his jaw clenched, and Sera thought steam just might shoot out his ears. Lifting his staff, he sent a ball of sizzling blue light into the air. "Fiiinn!" he shouted, his voice louder than thunder. Across the street, a group of women paused.

Before Sera could blink, the air split with a soft rip, like a seam giving way, and Fin stepped through. "Honestly, Sheriff, with lungs like that, you could moonlight as the town foghorn."

Sam's eyes narrowed to furious slits. "Careful, Elf, or I'll find you a job that actually *requires* yelling."

Smirking, Fin shrugged. "Tempting offer, but I'd hate to put you out of work."

"Watch. The. Shop." Sam jabbed his staff toward the door, each word like a hammer.

Fin tipped an imaginary hat. "Aye aye, Captain Foghorn. Yarn's in excellent hands."

Hands gripping his staff hard enough to whiten his knuckles, the glare the sheriff sent Fin could have melted glass. He eyed Sera, his brows furrowed in a line. "Satisfied? Let's go before 'em women kill each other." Spinning on his well-worn heels, he took off without waiting for Sera's answer.

"Women killing each other?" Sera muttered, but the sheriff was already storming away. With a last warning to Fin—"No pranks"— she jogged after him.

Fin bowed. "As you wish, Guardian. Your shop will be safe."

"And my customers," she muttered as she ran after the steaming sheriff, who was already rounding the side of her building and setting off across the grassy field toward a large tent. As she drew close, she could hear shouting coming from within. A sizeable crowd had gathered at the far end.

"Sheriff," she said when she caught up with Sam. "Give me a clue here. What is going on?"

Sam glanced over his shoulder as he quickened his pace. "Top two quilters—Siobhan Fitzgerald and Deirdre Quinn—are at each other's throats." He didn't elaborate.

Confused, Sera asked, "Why?" And wondered what it had to do with her.

"Better you see for yourself."

Inside the ginormous tent, the space housed various sections that reminded Sera of a fair where a large building showcased local talent vying for ribbons and top honors. She passed a stall with garments hanging on the walls and displayed neatly on tables. Some held colored ribbons that glittered and sparkled. Shooting stars announced the first-place winner. "Oh, that's cool." Sam ignored her commentary, so she hurried past exhibits showcasing baking, flowers, and monstrous-sized vegetables and vowed to return to check each display more thoroughly. She also spotted several Rootlings bustling around, each wearing tags that proclaimed they were judges.

Ahead, the sounds of arguing grew louder, the voices shrill. "Move out of the way afore I blast my way through," the Sherrif growled as he shoved his way through the crowd, even jabbing a few slow bystanders with his staff. With yelps of pain, a path quickly cleared. He stopped in front of a display of quilts where two angry women yelled at a Rootling who was rounder than he was tall.

Like Molly, his skin was bark-brown with a fine mossy undertone. He wore a brightly patterned vest over a cream shirt with rolled sleeves, and a polished acorn gavel on a cord hung around his neck. He stood on a table, and even then, the two women towered over him.

The irritated sheriff jerked his thumb at a woman with long, glossy, chestnut waves wearing a bold jewel-tone dress. "That be Siobhan Fitzgerald. She and her sister own Woven Threads Cottage. The other is Deirdre Quinn. Them two compete fiercely every year for first prize."

Deirdre, dressed in a deep green dress with a brown leather apron stained with dye, jammed her stained hands on her hips and whipped around at the sound of the gruff voice. "About time you got here, Sheriff. I want her arrested!"

The sheriff ignored her and pointed his staff at the Rootling on the table. "Head judge, Perrin Thistledown. You runnin' a quilting contest or hostin' a brawl?"

Perrin narrowed his bulging eyes and adjusted his vest. "You try judging quilts while two she-devils aim to unravel each other—see how long your nerves last."

After eyeing the angry women and the frazzled judge, Sera glared at the sheriff. "You took me away from my shop to watch a cat fight?" she asked incredulously.

"Cat—" He looked confused but shrugged it off. "Do something," he ordered her.

"Me?" Sera squeaked, then choked and went into a coughing fit. When she could breathe, she shook her head. "You're the law," she reminded him.

He jabbed her with his staff. "And you be the head witch. This is a case of magical malice, and that means it's your problem." He banged his staff on the ground. The crystal tip let out a high-pitched whine. People cried out and covered their ears. Silence fell. Sam pushed Sera forward.

"The Guardian, and head of the magical council, will settle this," he announced.

"No way, Sheriff. I'm not ready to solve town disputes," she protested, planting her feet to remain where she stood. Head of the magical council was one thing, but head witch expected to solve problems where magic was involved? Too much!

Sam waved off her protest. "Too bad. You're head of the magical council. Comes with responsibilities." His next shove sent her stumbling forward, and while she regained her footing, he pivoted on his heels and stomped his way back through the crowd, muttering about difficult females.

Sera wasn't sure what to do or say. She smiled weakly at the judge, but before she could say anything, he bowed so low she feared he'd take a header off the table.

"Guardian Blackthorn. Head witch of Havenwood, your judgment will be our thread of truth. Now, if you'd be so kind, my ears could use your wisdom before these two fray each other to bits."

Seeing that she had no choice but to get involved, Sera sighed and clasped her hands loosely in front of her as she stepped forward. "What is the issue here?"

Siobhan pointed at Deirdre. "She destroyed my quilt! Look at it. Ruined." She waved a hand toward one quilt hanging on the makeshift wall.

Sera studied the quilt in question, titled *Moon Over the Bay*. At first, it glowed with luminous blues and silvers, the metallic threads catching the light so perfectly the moon seemed to rise out of the fabric itself. Then, without warning, the image rippled—like a stone dropped into still water. A dark shimmer spread across the surface, muting the colors, draining the moon's glow, and fraying the scalloped edges into ragged tatters. A faint tug brushed at the edge of her vision, making her blink, but the beauty she'd first seen was gone.

Deirdre's shrill cry pulled her attention back to the women. "I did not. You ruined mine!" She glanced at her quilt, also on display, with tears in her eyes.

She turned to Deirdre's quilt, *Evergreen Shore*, its deep emerald forests flowing seamlessly into a sea of rich blues. The applique work was intricate, alive with texture, and for a moment, she could almost hear the waves. Then the surface wavered—subtle at first, then undeniable—as a shadowed shimmer rolled across it. The greens dulled to lifeless gray, the blues curdled into muddy brown, and the fine details blurred as though someone had smudged the stitches with ash. Again came that faint tug at the edge of her vision, leaving a prickling at the back of her neck, and once more the beauty was gone.

Siobhan, unaware of Sera's confusion in what she was seeing, crossed her arms and went nose to nose with her competition. "Why would I touch your quilt when mine was clearly superior. Admit it! You've always been jealous—now you've ruined my work!"

"Your arrogance is showing again. My skill's worth more than your glamor spells. I would have won this year, but you couldn't stand to lose your winning streak, so you destroyed my quilt!"

The two women hurled insults and accusations at each other faster than a tennis star lobs a ball.

Perrin clapped his hands sharply. "If you two don't hush, I'll dock points for noise pollution." He grabbed tufts of silvery-green lichen that covered his nearly bald head and addressed Sera.

"What did you see, Guardian?" he asked, his mossy brows drawing together.

Sera rubbed a spot between her eyes as though trying to order her thoughts. "At first ... they were both beautiful," she admitted slowly. "But then something came over them. Like a shadow, or a shimmer, something just ... wrong. As though what I first saw was still there but hidden."

Perrin's gaze sharpened. "Veil sight," he murmured, as if naming it settled something in his mind. "A rare gift, Guardian."

"Veil sight?" Sera echoed under her breath. Lila and her grandmother had both said she could see what others could not—like Willow. *So ... am I seeing the quilts as they were before the damage?* A chill prickled along her arms. *Why does seeing what isn't there make me nervous?*

"They feel the same," she told the judge. "As though the same hand destroyed them—a signature maybe?"

"Is someone destroying our quilts?" a small voice asked. "How about mine? Is it also tainted?"

"Marla, dear, why would anyone destroy your work?" Deirdre shook her head and smiled kindly. "As lovely as your quilt is, it doesn't hold a candle to either of ours."

The woman pouted. "It could win." Her voice conveyed her own doubt.

Sera turned to the fearful woman with short, dark blonde hair streaked with silver. Small, gold, thimble earrings dangled from her ears. "You are?"

"Marla Densmore." She stood uncertain, shoulders hunched, hands behind her back.

"Which one is yours?"

The woman jerked her chin toward a warm, cozy patchwork quilt in golds, reds, and creams. The title read, *Hearth Light*.

Staring up at it, Sera felt a bit of nostalgia radiating from the work. Neat stitching but not dazzling like what she'd observed in the other two before seeing the actual damage. And no shadowy shimmer. "No. I don't see any damage here."

Marla sighed with relief.

"Well, what is it, Head witch?" Perrin nervously fingered his acorn gavel.

Sera shook her head. "I honestly don't know, but I don't think either of these women sabotaged the other's quilt." She glanced from one to the other. "And why would anyone destroy their own quilt? This was done by another's hand."

"What are you going to do about it?" Siobhan demanded. "The quilts are being judged tonight."

"I will look into it. I need to do some research." She glanced between the two ruined quilts, the shimmer still lingering in her mind like an afterimage. "This wasn't an accident."

Perrin's mossy brows drew tight. "Then best be quick, Guardian. Judging's tonight, and I'd rather not hand out ribbons for sabotage."

Siobhan's eyes flashed. "Just make sure you find the right culprit, Head witch. I won't have my name dragged through the mud."

"Nor mine," Deirdre snapped, folding her arms. "But don't take too long—first prize won't wait forever."

The crowd murmured, the air thick with rivalry as Sera stepped back. She addressed Perrin. "Perhaps it would be best to delay the quilt judging awards."

Marla shifted on her feet, her hands tightening behind her back. "Does ... does that mean none of us will win tonight?" she asked, her voice small.

"It means," Sera said evenly, "that I intend to find out what really happened before any ribbons are handed out."

Siobhan huffed. Deirdre muttered under her breath. And somewhere in the tense hush that followed, Sera realized she'd just taken hold of the first loose thread in a tangle of truth and pride.

###

Sera descended the stairs from the second story of the shop. The rooms she'd explored held supplies: roving, yarn, accessories, even boxes of tote bags imprinted with the shop's name. The third floor comprised one large open room with windows on all sides, offering breathtaking views of the sea and of downtown. It enabled her to see each shop's unique personality. She could also see the forest, the harbor, and even the point where Maude's house sat. Sera was eager to explore Havenwood.

A flutter of wings drew her attention. She ignored Syrus as he soared down the stairs ahead of her. "Cursed quilts," he sang. "Mysteries abound for our beloved Guardian."

"Not helping, Syrus. Go away."

A chime on her phone drew her attention. She hurried to the counter where she'd left her phone to charge on one of the glowing nodes. "Notification from Maude." She chuckled and swiped to open the message. "Imagine, communication with a house via technology." It blew her mind.

*Council meeting in thirty minutes.*

"Oh geez, what do I know about being on this council?"

From his perch near the register, Syrus piped up: "Cue the violins and the sob story. Do you want some cheese with that whine?"

"Really not helping, Syrus!" Sera sent the bird a disgusted look and flicked her fingers. "Go bother someone else."

To her surprise, he disappeared. She glanced at her fingers. "Did I do that, or did he just go poof?"

Willow tossed her head back and let loose with a wild cackle. "No one makes Syrus disappear, Silly Human. He has more magic in that sarcastic beak of his than half of Havenwood together." Willow stretched long and languid, her tail high, her razor-sharp nails clicking on the counter.

"Okay, you do not need to do that again, Willow. Truly frightening." A purple feather floated down and landed on her shoulder, followed by a loud squawk that echoed throughout the shop. "Okay, got it, Syrus." With a sigh, she gave Maude's message a thumbs up. As much as she didn't want to attend, she couldn't disappoint her grandmother, not to mention incurring the ire of Rowena, so she'd just have to put off her plan to delve into the journal in front of the cozy fireplace. Aside from needing help with the sabotaged quilts, there was the whole Guardian-portal-save-the-world task.

Sera blew out a breath. She wasn't just an out-of-work accountant or temporary shop owner. Fate had decreed her to be part of something larger, and though she wasn't sure she was ready for what lay ahead, she'd do whatever she needed to do.

Another message scrolled across the screen. *It will be dark when the meeting is over. Sending Cricket to pick you up. She'll be waiting behind your shop.*

"How?" She eyed Willow. "Magic, right?"

Willow yawned. Rolling her eyes, Sera typed, "Thanks, Maude." While her relationship with a sentient house was as weird as weird could get, Sera found comfort in Maude's gentle watchfulness. Gathering her things, Sera headed for the door. She turned back and lifted a brow as she addressed Willow. "You coming?"

"Couldn't keep me away," Willow replied as she jumped down, landing gracefully on the floor. With a mischievous grin, the cat ran through the door.

Sera winced. "Wish she wouldn't do that. Says she's not a ghost, yet she sure acts like one. If not a ghost, what the heck is she?"

Syrus popped into view. "Ghost, cat, poltergeist with fur? Does it really matter? She's a walking mystery wrapped in sass, just like half the people around here. You'll drive yourself mad trying to figure her out."

Sera slapped her hand on top of her head. "Good point, Syrus. Sorry I asked."

The bird cocked its head, one beady eye watching her with mock seriousness. "Maybe she's the afterlife's idea of a practical joke." He fluffed his feathers and added with a snicker, "Face it, Sera, she's probably here to haunt you for your terrible taste in shoes. Those are so last year!"

Biting back a groan, Sera picked up her tote bag with her laptop. From the corner of her eye, a shadow drew her attention. She paused. Something moved—just a flicker, low and quick near the corner of one of the front display windows. Was someone outside? She blinked, but the space was empty. Still, something about that flicker clung to her thoughts as she pulled her shawl tighter ...

Probably someone checking to see if she was still open, she decided, or someone curious to see the new Guardian. Half the people who'd come into the shop that day had been there to check out the Guardian.

She focused on the window but saw only dust motes and fading light. Pulling her shawl tighter around her shoulders, she had enough to worry about without conjuring imaginary shadows.

"Night, Syrus. I trust you'll find your way home." She pulled the door shut and took a moment to breathe and steady her nerves. Across the way, Lila's coffee shop blazed with light. A group of teens spilled out through the door, their laughter ringing into the evening.

Sera smiled, wishing there was time to get herself another of Lila's sinful concoctions. "Tomorrow," she promised herself as she adjusted her grip on her tote. As nightfall approached, the brightness of day gave way to the purplish hues of dusk. Something bright, like a star or firework, soared into the air, leaving behind a glittering trail of energy the shade of a healing bruise. It headed toward her shop.

The trail shimmered like heat above pavement, carrying a faint metallic tang that made the hairs on her arms lift. It was subtle, almost hidden. Watching it fly overhead, the air warped, the way it might above a candle's flame. But instead of going over her roof, it slammed into the gable above the porch.

CRACK.

Sera froze, heart thudding, as the angled section of roof tore free. Panic and fear ripped through her. She dropped her tote, raised her arms to shield her head—but the crash never came.

*"Sera! Move!"*

*No time,* she thought. Heart pounding, mouth dry, she glanced up. The roof hovered, trembling, above her. She stumbled forward, out from beneath the porch, and nearly tripped when she saw Fin on the path ahead, feet planted wide, arms straining to hold the massive piece aloft.

"What are you doing, Fin?" Her voice broke on her scream. If this was his idea of a joke or a prank .... Before she could order him to stop, another voice boomed out.

"Fin! Ya damn elf!" The sheriff huffed over, his staff pointed at Fin.

Fin, his face red with strain, shouted, "Not me, Sam. Not me. Help me. Can't hold it much longer."

Sera, hands on her pounding chest, stared at Fin. He held his hands high, his arms shaking as though he held a great weight. Beads of sweat dripped down the sides of his face. An intense look of concentration, almost a contortion of pain, twisted his handsome features as he stared at the roof.

"Finley, I'm warning you. Put. It. Back." Sam ordered, his voice a low, threatening growl.

"Sheriff, I think he's telling the truth," Sera interrupted. She gasped in alarm when Fin staggered and went down on one knee.

"Sam!" Fin pleaded, sounding out of breath. "Yell later. Help now!"

Sam studied his Fae nemesis. The sheriff swung his staff up so fast, it hummed. A blast of light flared, cupping the bottom of the roof. Slowly, the fallen piece rose and shifted back into place. Fin fell to his hands and knees, panting and gasping.

"Okay, what in tarnation happened here?" Sam demanded, thumping his staff on the ground. Red sparks flew from the embedded crystal.

"Magic," Fin gasped, his eyes shifting from the sheriff to Sera and back. "Somebody used magic to tear the roof off." Fin glanced at Sam. "You know my magic. If I'd caused that, I'd have been able to restore it, but I could barely hold it."

Sera frowned, her gaze studying Fin. She glanced up at the repaired roof. "What are you saying, Fin?"

Sam thumped his staff again. Harder, sending sparks soaring. "He's saying that wasn't an accident, Sera. Someone meant to hurt you."

"Hurt? That would have killed me."

###

Concealed by shrubs between two buildings, a lone figure watched from the shadows. The wind tugged at her dark cloak and whispered through the leaves like an old secret. Her eyes narrowed at Finley. How had he just appeared? She'd cast the spell carefully—no witnesses. But the elf always had a flair for dramatic timing. Always playing the hero. Always getting in the way. She clenched her fists, long nails biting into her palms.

The spell had worked. Seraphina Blackthorn didn't belong here. "Should've stayed away," she murmured.

Her gaze lingered on the trio across the green. Had Sera truly seen her ... or only sensed her? Either way, there was too much power in that look.

Unease crept in as she slipped behind a group of giggling girls drinking from cups that sparkled. She blended effortlessly. When they crossed the street, she slipped into the space between the buildings, disappearing into the deeper shadows like breath on glass.

# **Chapter Eighteen**

May 22 - Guardians, Guards & a Grumpy Gnome

Sera trembled with shock as she glanced from one man to the other. Fin alone could not have held the roof. It had taken both men to put it back where it belonged, and that meant she'd likely not have survived.

Glancing around the street, she saw nothing out of the ordinary. "I don't understand," she murmured. The thought that someone— anyone—meant her harm left her shaken and confused. "Who would want to kill me?" How could she, in her short time in Havenwood, have gained an enemy?

Fin, back on his feet, hands on his hips, glanced from her to Sam. "I'd say someone doesn't want you here, Guardian."

"Why, Fin?"

His eyes dimmed, or was that just a trick of the light? He shrugged. "Maybe some want the portal open."

Before she could ask why, Sam jabbed Fin. "No one wants to be enslaved again, you damn elf. No one wants war. Everyone here is a refugee."

"Yes, you are right as always, Sheriff," he mocked as he bowed.

Sam narrowed his eyes, his bushy brows forming a straight line across his forehead as he studied his longtime nemesis. "Why are you here, Fin? We got back from that cursed quilt business hours ago." He straightened his Stetson and crossed his arms; his staff held across his body.

Fin shrugged. "Why not?"

Sera frowned. Had he been the shadow at her window? Was he spying on her? She also recalled he'd been at her shop yesterday when she arrived. Coincidence? What was going on?

Sam's tone turned sharp. "Still playing Guardian to the Guardians, are you?"

Fin's smirk faltered, and his gaze turned inward. "Old habits, Sheriff. And good thing I was hanging around!"

"Who did this? Did you see?"

For a moment, the happy-go-lucky elf looked furious. "No, I was on the roof across the way and saw the blast hit. Winked over, barely in time. Had I not seen it hit, I wouldn't have been here in time."

Fin glanced from Sera to Sam. "It is in my best interest to protect the Guardians, Sam. Whatever my faults, whatever you think of me, protecting the Guardians is vital."

Sera felt the tension mounting between the two and wasn't sure she could handle any more drama. Oddly, she felt safe around Fin—frustrated, yes, but safe. "Sheriff, I'm grateful Fin was here, no matter his reason. It may have been accidental—a wayward blast of magic."

She breathed deeply and decided she'd try later to figure out if this was a deliberate attempt on her life. A glance at her watch showed she was going to be late for the meeting. With one last glance at the roof, she suppressed a shudder, adjusted her tote, and turned away. "I've got to go, or I'll be late for the council meeting." She took a step away.

"Hold on," Sam barked.

Sera turned back. Fin stood uncharacteristically quiet while Sam glowered. "Not safe for you to go alone."

Truthfully, Sera really didn't want to walk alone, even though she felt confident her would-be killer was long gone, especially with the sheriff and his magical staff there. But she wasn't a coward. Yesterday, she'd have said she had no choice, but after another glance at the yarn shop, it was her choice. Come hell or high water, she was here to stay.

"I'll be fine, Sheriff. Just going to the bookstore." She waved one hand toward the shop a short distance from hers.

Sam smacked Fin on his thigh with his staff. "Well, go with her. Do what you do. Guard the Guardian."

Sera tipped her head to one side. "What do you mean? Does Fin work for you? Is he some sort of guard?"

At her question, Fin looked horrified, and Sam barked out a laugh. "Fancies himself a guard to each new Guardian." He marched away, thumping the end of his staff on the ground, sending glowing amber sparks from the crystal into the air.

Fin's eyes held something—a flicker of guilt? Or worry? She couldn't tell. Sighing, Sera shook her head. "You really don't have to walk me to the meeting, Fin."

Fin waved a hand, dismissing her concern. "You heard the bossman. Don't want him mad at us, do we?" He wagged his brows.

Sera rolled her eyes. "Somehow, Fin, I don't think you care if he gets mad at you."

Laughing, Fin doffed his elf-hat and bowed with a flourish. "Right you are, Miss Sera. But it would be an honor to walk with you. Besides, I'm on the council as well. Now, if you'd rather not be seen with me, I can make myself invisible." He offered her an arm.

Sera grinned. "No, not necessary." She hooked her arm through his.

Though the bookstore was her nearest neighbor, a wide, open space flowed to the open grassy area behind the shops where festival booths were popping up. Her footsteps echoed softly against the cobbled path as she and Fin made their way to the bookstore. Despite nearly meeting death head on, a stillness that felt almost magical clung to the air.

The shadows stretched and merged with the lingering light, creating a blend of darkness and faint illumination, a perfect backdrop for strange and mystical events. Sera glanced around. A few people still strolled up and down the street. Sera spotted a group of children playing tag on the grass in the center of the main street. They darted around fountains or stopped to splash each other with water.

Was her would-be killer still out here, hiding? Watching? What should have been a pleasant stroll left her tight with both fear and tension. Who had tried to kill or harm her? And why? She bit her lower lip. It couldn't be anything she'd said or done. Even she couldn't get into trouble that fast. That left her role as Guardian. But if she was the only person to save the town, why kill her?

"You're safe, Miss Sera." Fin broke the cycle of worry and fear.

She nodded. "Thank you, Fin." There was no point in thinking about the incident now. Instead, her thoughts turned to the upcoming meeting. "I don't know anything about the festival." She kicked a small, white pebble. What did she have? A yarn shop, a snarky parrot, and a ghosting cat with attitude.

"Tonight's meeting is mostly a last-minute check, but as you are now the head, you need to be here so you know what is going on. Rowena has it well in hand," Fin said with a grin. "And hey, don't let her railroad you into anything."

Drawing her shawl tighter around her shoulders, Sera nodded. Glancing up at a sky shrouded in thick layers of gray clouds, the air felt heavy with the scent of damp earth and the tang of salt from the ocean. Faint hints of twilight shone through the cloud cover, casting a dull, silvery light over the cobbled path. The wind ruffled her hair, sending the red strands dancing around her face.

Sera breathed deeply and found her calm. She'd truly come home. And that gave her even more determination not to fail. Across the way, music poured out of what looked like a tavern. Laughter spilled out into the fading day. Ahead, next to the bookstore, a sandwich shop offered outdoor seating. The aroma of freshly baked bread made her stomach rumble.

They strode past an old copper tub of pink, purple, and blue flowers with tiny white heads mixed throughout. As she passed, every delicate head turned to follow her progress. Frowning, she glanced over her shoulder. "Okay, that's strange."

Fin lifted a brow as he glanced from her to the tub of blooms. He grinned. "I'd say that was magical."

Reaching the bookstore, Sera forgot about all her worries and fears. The bookstore stood like a hidden gem, its ivy-clad stone walls and weathered bricks whispering of ancient secrets. The wooden sign above the door swayed gently in the sea breeze while its golden letters glinted in the light: *Mystic Pages*. Through the large arched windows, a soft golden glow spilled out into the deepening dusk, offering a glimpse of the shop's heart—a labyrinth of towering bookshelves stuffed with books to tempt any reader.

A cart of books on sale sat to one side, along with a couple of wooden chairs. In front of a double archway sat a black cat with fluffy fur and a smokey black ruff. He blinked, his deep, coppery eyes gleamed with a hint of mystical knowledge. Willow sat regally beside him.

Fin released her arm. "I'll see you inside, Miss Sera." He strode through the doors.

Willow strolled toward her. "Ah, my Human has arrived," she announced.

Sera rolled her eyes. "Your Human has a name, Willow."

"You'll always be my Little Human." She stretched and yawned. "At least I dropped the little," the white cat scoffed.

Reaching down, Sera picked up the cat, needing to feel her warmth and the comforting softness of her fur. "Your Human nearly became a ghost tonight."

Willow's eyes darkened. *"The Mother* won't let anything happen to her Guardian."

It was the second time someone had referred to The Mother almost as though she were a person or a magical being. "Who is The Mother?"

"She is the magical forest. She is life," the cat said, her voice mysterious as a breeze curled around Sera's ankles, feeling like a gentle hug.

"Okay, Havenwood Cove's version of a god then," she decided as she set Willow down next to the black cat. Squatting, she held out her hand and grinned when the cat arched his back under her touch. "Aren't you a beauty. What's your name?"

"Ink," the cat answered, his voice a low, harsh rumble as he head-butted her hand for more pets. "'Cause I'm all black."

"You talk?"

The cat flopped on its side and rolled. "Of course I speak. How else would we familiars communicate?"

The cat talked so fast Sera had a hard time following him.

"Don't mind her," Willow told Ink. "She's new. Has some catching up to do."

Sera arched her brow at Willow. "So, you're my familiar?"

Willow licked a paw and swiped it over her ears. "That's as good a title as any. For now. But I'm more, so much more."

Sera shook her head. "Nothing like a cat to make you feel silly," she muttered. Standing, she brushed her palms down her skirt. "Well, I've got to go." Her confidence dipped. There was sure to be a room full of seasoned Witches and other magical beings—people who would judge her and find her lacking. Not only did she not know much about Witches or witchcraft, she definitely did not know how to destroy a portal and save a town.

"Watch out for Sylvie," Ink called out. "Not too happy. Came in and gave my Human a hard time. Doesn't—"

Willow smacked the black cat on the head. "Enough, Ink. You're such a gossip. Let's go." She all but shoved the black cat into the store.

Frowning, Sera asked, "Who is Sylvie?"

Ink glanced sideways at Willow. "Her family is one of the original human settlers: witch families. Thinks her family is just as important as yours. Or more so. Full of resentment and entitlement."

"Ah, okay, thanks for the warning. I've dealt with people like that." Especially her ex-husband, who believed money and family status gave him privileges he didn't deserve. She turned to the arch, and as soon as she stepped through the open doors, she forgot about Ink's warning and her own self-doubts.

Inside, the scent of old parchment mingled with the crisp scent of newly printed books. Subtle perfume from the herbs hung above the door, and the candles placed all over the store added to the charm. Comfortable armchairs, well-worn and inviting, were tucked into a cozy reading nook near the hearth, with a small wooden table beside them, perfect for holding that cup of tea.

The store exuded a gentle magic, subtle but ever-present. As she strolled past tall bookshelves, the books seemed to shift on the shelves. Low, almost inaudible whispers came from the shelves as though the books were speaking, enticing visitors to pick them up and explore their contents.

"Wow," Sera breathed, her voice hushed. To her amazement, lanterns floated just above eye level, casting a soft, flickering light across the room. She gave in to the desire to browse, running her finger across spines, reading titles and breathing in the atmosphere.

She nodded at a young woman wearing dark jeans and a thigh-length sweater—handmade if she wasn't mistaken. The woman glanced up from flipping through the pages of the book in her hand. Sera grinned. "This is a wonderful bookstore," she said as a thrill of pleasure warmed her from the inside out. It was pure heaven to behold, and each book offered the reader possibilities.

The woman froze. Her eyes narrowed, and her lips compressed into a hard line. "If you say so." She shoved the book back onto the shelf and strode off, her shoulders stiff.

"Okay," Sera said. "That's rude. Someone's not having a good day," she said to Willow, who rubbed against her shin. Ink stood beside her. Both cats stared in the direction the woman went. An excited voice drew Sera's attention as she wandered back to the main aisle.

"Mom! This is the book. It spoke to me. I need this one for my report." A teen held up a book to her mother. "*Magical Properties of Mushrooms.*"

"Ah, Good choice, Lana." An older woman with silver-streaked hair tied back loosely and wearing an apron with the store's name on it hustled over. "Take it to the register now. We're about to close for the day."

"The book spoke to her?" Sera cocked her head. She still heard indistinct murmurs but couldn't make out the words. Were the books reading their contents aloud?

"Of course. If you need a book, just think about it and then listen." She pointed to the floor. "And follow the footsteps. By the way, I'm Ellie, owner of Mystic Pages. You must be Seraphina? Elowen's granddaughter? Rowena said you'd be here for the council meeting."

Sera grinned and held out her hand, relieved to meet another friendly person. "Please, call me Sera. What a wonderful bookstore. Absolutely enchanting." She pointed to the floating lantern in front of her. When her finger got close, the magical lamp shifted out of reach. "I've never seen anything like this. Well, except for in movies." She laughed.

Ellie joined her. "It does add to the ambiance, doesn't it?"

Sera spotted a table covered with books by R.S. Rider along with a winking sign that announced a book signing on Friday. Her brows rose. "His signing is Friday?"

"Yes, but not in here. We'll have a booth outside for the festival."

A pile of books floated past, re-shelving themselves as they went. Sera's eyes followed them, widening as the tiny figure with wine and mossy hair darted between two bookcases. Another Rootling. Havenwood truly was magical ... in ways that felt both new and familiar all at once. Had she really forgotten all this?

Ellie's smile was full of understanding. "It can take a while to get used to it if you weren't raised here."

Sera frowned. "I lived here for the first ten years of my life, but I don't remember anything magical. What about humans—or maybe I should say, non-magical people? Do they come to Havenwood Cove? And how do you explain the floating lanterns and books, or the Rootlings?" She thought of her own magical shop with the loom and spinning wheel and wondered what other magical surprises were in store for her.

Ellie nodded, smiling gently. "People come from all over, especially for the festivals. But most won't even notice the lanterns or Rootlings. People tend to see only what they want to see, and even if they do glimpse something magical, it's gone from their minds once they leave."

That gave Sera pause. Had she lost all her memories because she left? And if so, would she get them back? She frowned, her thoughts racing. What if she left after the summer was over? Would she forget everything again? The thought lingered, unsettling her in ways she hadn't expected. It was a sobering thought, one she wasn't ready to explore just yet.

"Ellie, is Talia in here?" A tall, barrel-chested man with wide shoulders strode into the shop. He wore a green polo shirt featuring a logo with a stein and an overflowing head with the words *Mystic Brew* framing it.

"Yes, Frankie—"

"Talia!" he bellowed. "Come fetch your mother and take her home before the deputies cart her off to jail to sleep it off." Frankie ran a hand through his ginger hair in frustration.

Ellie jammed her hands on her hips and hissed, "Frank O'Mallery. You lower your voice. I'll thank you not to bellow like a bull in my shop!"

"Sorry, Ellie, I hate doing this, but her mother is causing a scene. As mayor, I have to think about the whole town."

The rude woman Sera had spoken to earlier darted out from behind a bookshelf. Her features were taut as she glared at each of them. Sera shivered as she studied the woman. There was something there—a faint recognition—oh, she was the customer that Fin scared away the day she arrived. Without a word, Talia bolted out the door.

"Okay, that's one unhappy woman," Sera commented.

"Can't blame her, not with her drunk mother. So sad, and such a waste." Ellie jabbed a finger into Frankie's arm. "Frankie, you're the mayor—show some compassion. Talia's had it rough. No father and a mother who drinks too much. It's not her fault."

Frankie sighed deeply. "I know, Ellie. It's not fair to Talia, but I have a town to look after. I'm just doing what I can."

"As we all try to do," Ellie agreed. Frankie nodded to Sera and strode off toward the back of the shop.

"Ellie!" A loud, insistent voice called out. "Meeting's about to start. Chat later."

Ellie leaned closer. "Rowena is a stickler for starting on time. Come on, I'll show you the way." She led Sera toward a set of double doors carved with ancient runes. "Your seat is at the head," she whispered.

She squared her shoulders. Ready or not, she'd face whatever waited beyond those doors.

# Chapter Nineteen

May 22 - Magic, Meetings & Mild Panic

Shoulders squared, Sera entered a meeting room with a long golden table, polished to a mirror shine, that dominated the center of the space. The wood seemed almost alive, its grain shifting in subtle waves as though it had been carved from a single, ancient tree. Chairs, each slightly different in design but matching in warmth of tone, were spaced evenly all around as if awaiting a council of equals.

Taking her place at the head, her gaze fell to the center of the table where a Tree of Life surrounded by a Celtic spiral shimmered with a soft, silver glow, pulsing faintly in rhythm with the Rootcurrent. The air above it hummed with quiet energy.

Against two walls, books, with their spines gleaming under lantern light, filled bookcases out of the same wood as the table, and woven tapestries of forests and moons hung on one wall and softened the space. Extra chairs were stacked against the wall behind Sera's chair. The room carried an odd duality: the practical air of a meeting place paired with an undercurrent of the arcane, as if business and magic were meant to coexist here.

She studied the assembled council, noting the air of mystery that surrounded each member, as if Havenwood Cove's magic ran through every person in ways she still barely understood. The town's magical depth was greater than she had realized, and the weight of that knowledge pressed on her shoulders.

She felt a small sense of relief that she knew—or at least had briefly met—a few of those gathered. Rowena occupied the chair on her right, and Frank, the mayor sat to her left. Bram, the gatekeeper, gave her a friendly nod, while Fin grinned. Across from him, Sam glowered as though this was not where he wanted to be. There were two members she didn't know, along with one empty chair.

Rowena clapped her hands to signal silence. "I'd like to introduce Seraphina Blackthorn, Elowen's granddaughter and the new head of our council."

Although Sera didn't feel she was the person to lead this group, she kept her doubts to herself. "Thank you. Please bear with me as I get caught up to speed on council business."

A stylish young woman wearing a dark maroon cloak swept into the room. She removed the hood, releasing a mass of blonde curls that fell to her waist. "Sorry I'm late," she announced. "Sylvie Star, owner of Enchanted Elegance. And I must protest Ms. Blackthorn's position." She stared at Sera as though memorizing the enemy. "Nothing personal, you understand," she added.

"Now Sylvie," Fin began.

Sylvie waved him off with a perfectly manicured hand. The smile she sent Sera was false and full of condescension. "She was not raised here. We need a leader with more knowledge to head this council."

Although uncomfortable and a little put out by the woman's air of superiority, Sera would have agreed with her. But after dealing with the quilters and accepting that this was another responsibility her grandmother had entrusted to her, she clasped her hands on the table and nodded. "You have a valid point," she began.

Sylvie interrupted. "Yes, I do, and she even agrees with me. I offer my experience and expertise."

"No," Sera corrected. "I said you had a valid point, but that doesn't change the fact that I am here and willing to fulfill my responsibilities."

"Sylvie," Sam growled.

The woman narrowed her eyes at the sheriff. "Sam, you think we should just hand over control to someone we don't know? Does she even have any magical talent?"

Fin chuckled. "More than you know, Sylvie dear. More than you know."

Bram placed both hands on the table and half rose, but Rowena interrupted the arguing by tapping her pen on the table, much as she'd tapped her cane that morning. "A Blackthorn has always been head of the magical council. You know this, Sylvie."

Sylvie rested her arms on the table in a classic I-am-in-charge posture. She glanced around, taking her time to meet everyone's gaze. When she got to Sera, she lifted her chin. "Why should we cling to the old precedent in these uncertain times?" she asked, her voice deceptively sweet. "My family came over with the Blackthorns. What right do they have to claim more power?"

"Your family are not Guardians, Sylvie." Rowena's voice cracked like a whip.

Sylvie waved a dismissive hand. "Guardians have done nothing for Havenwood. We need someone we know and trust."

"Can't fool me, Sylvie," Sam growled. "You've been after this position for years. How many times have you tried to take it from Elowen? None of your ploys worked then, and this latest weak attempt to gain power won't either."

Bram spoke up. "Elowen trusts Sera, and so do I."

Sylvie rolled her eyes. "Of course you do," she muttered sarcastically. She clenched her hands into tight fists. Her brown eyes blazed. "This is different, and you all know it." Her smile didn't reach her eyes as she once again addressed Sera. "Again, no offense, Ms. Blackthorn, but how are you going to save our town?"

Sera straightened in her chair and leaned forward, arms on the table, hands clasped loosely. Sylvie's smugness grated on her nerves, but instead of making her feel small and uncertain, a quiet strength rose within Sera. She had faced hostile boardrooms before, and this—magic or not—was no different. Dropping her shoulders, she tilted her head slightly and lifted one brow. "Are you suggesting that you take my place?" she asked softly, her voice steady.

Before Sylvie, who was preening and about to speak, could do so, Sera asked, "Tell me, Sylvie, *where* is this threat coming from?" Sylvie snapped her mouth shut. Sera waited several beats and then asked, "*What* is the threat?"

Sylvie shifted in her seat. She stared straight ahead, not meeting Sera's gaze. "No one knows."

Sera pursed her lips and nodded. "Then how is it that you are more qualified than I? What knowledge do you have—do any of you have—that I do not?" Her gaze swept around the table, meeting every council member's gaze. She might not feel equipped to be head of this council, but she wasn't about to be intimidated and driven out. She was a Blackthorn, and this was her town and her home. Just admitting the words to herself gave her peace and strength.

Rowena stood and leaned on her cane. "Sera isn't just a Blackthorn. She is the seventh Guardian. Like it or not." Her gaze swept the table and included Sera. "Like it or not," she repeated, "Sera is both Guardian and head of this council.

Sylvie drummed her nails on the table and narrowed her eyes at Rowena. "Just where did Elowen go, and why did she leave so quickly? Rather a sudden decision to just up and abandon her duties."

"Who are any of us to question the Guardian and head of the council? She didn't abandon anyone. She passed her duties to her rightful heir." Fin shrugged his narrow shoulders. "It doesn't matter why. The legacy now belongs to Sera."

Sera had a feeling they could hash this out all night and not come to any satisfying answers. For better or worse, she was the Guardian of the Moondragon—a title that held weight beyond what she could fully grasp. A role that tied her to Havenwood Cove's fate, and to a legacy of power and danger.

The room buzzed with bickering until Sera lifted her hand. She allowed it to hold for a heartbeat before she spoke. "I am here. For better or worse, I am the Guardian of the Moondragon."

Silence fell, heavy and absolute, as though the very room absorbed her words. Then the Celtic spiral flared, silver light blazing upward before slowly sinking back into the golden wood. The air hummed with quiet approval, as if The Mother herself had nodded in agreement.

Sera drew a steadying breath, clasped her hands on the table, and let her gaze sweep the council. "Nothing any of us can say— myself included—will change that fact. So, let's move on."

She waited for a beat, then spoke, her voice firm and controlled. "Before we get down to business, there are two members of this council I have not been introduced to. Could you please tell me your names and your business, if you have one?" She nodded to a short man with sharp eyes, a green-yellow hue, with pointed ears sticking out from a head of dark, messy hair. His skin bore a greenish tint.

He stood. "Milo Greenbriar, part owner of Havenwood Arcade & Gaming Lounge. I run it with my brothers, Baxter and Max. We are of the Goblin Tribe." He lifted one bushy eyebrow. He lowered his lean and wiry body back into the chair.

"Thank you, Milo. I'm pleased to meet you." Goblin? Sera kept her features schooled. She nodded to the man next to Milo with a few wood shavings in his hair. He too stood.

"Ethan Hartwood. Whispering Woods Artistry Cottage. My mate is Elysie." He bowed his head.

Rowena added for Sera's benefit, "Ethan belongs to the Woodland Elves Tribe. There are more members of this council, but those in attendance tonight are our festival committee. Each tribe has one representative on the full council."

*Tribes.* The word felt right. Not species, not races, but tribes—woven into the fabric of Havenwood Cove. It was like stepping into a fairytale—except this one came with a council meeting and responsibilities she was still learning to navigate.

Sera adjusted her chair and looked around the table. Sylvie Star didn't meet her eyes while Rowena nodded with approval. Fin gave her a wide grin, and Sam, sitting with his arms crossed, wore a scowl she figured might be his default. The others waited in silence.

Sera drew in a deep breath, feeling a mixture of relief and trepidation. There was no turning back. Whatever came next—whether festival preparations, cursed quilts, or facing a threat she still barely understood—would test them all. And Sera had a sinking feeling that Havenwood Cove's future would depend on her far more than she'd ever imagined. She smiled at the assembled members. Her chair creaked as she leaned forward, resting her arms on the table. "Let's begin."

She picked up the agenda in front of her. "The opening ceremony ritual takes place on the beach." She gulped when she saw that her grandmother was listed as the person in charge of the ritual. Turning to Rowena, she asked, "What exactly does the ritual involve?"

Sylvie tapped one of her long, polished nails on the table. "Normally, a Blackthorn would open the ritual with a spell that lights the bonfire. Perhaps I should do that part this year."

The smirk on the woman's face put Sera's back up. "No, I will do it." How? She wasn't sure, but she would not let the unpleasant woman win. A week ago, she hadn't even believed in magic. Now she sat on a council of Witches and creatures, expected to lead. Sera swallowed hard. *Ready or not,* she told herself, *you're it.*

###

Sleep usually dragged him into ash and ruin, but tonight the dream opened like a flower greeting the new day. No fire. No fear. Just her—gliding along a forest path, runes shimmering on her gown, charms singing at her belt.

Though the woods were cloaked in fog, a break in the canopy let through a single shaft of golden sunlight—just enough to strike her hair. She spun in a circle, her red-gold curls catching like fire as she lifted her arms in wild abandon.

From the shadows, Ryker watched, his breath stolen. His heart hammered, and his blood pulsed hot and heavy through his veins.

Some deep instinct urged him to step forward and claim this magnificent woman for his own. The tattoo on his shoulder burned and throbbed, as though he had two hearts. He slapped a hand over it and pressed hard. But it was too late. The beast within roared and demanded he claim his woman.

"Drakon?" The woman turned in a circle. "Where are you, my love?"

The call was too strong to resist, but before Ryker could go to her, another figure emerged from a stone wall across from him. "I am here, Saoirse."

The woman ran to Drakon, and the couple embraced for a long time, but instead of feeling their joy, Ryker felt their sadness and desperation. The woman stepped back, not relinquishing her grip on the man's hands as her gaze beseeched his. "They refused," she whispered, her voice breaking. Tears turned her bright green eyes into twin pools, deep with pain.

"Yes, my heart," Drakon admitted, anguish contorting his features. "I cannot—will not—give you up. For me, there is no other. I will not take another for mate."

Saoirse slumped against her lover. "What are we going to do? How can we fight them?"

Drakon tangled his fingers in her curls, brought her face to his, and kissed her so gently it brought tears to Ryker's eyes. As he watched, the male lifted his head to the sky. A roar of pain and fury echoed through the forest.

An answering cry ripped from Ryker's throat and jerked him awake. His arm shot out to the side to keep him from falling out of his chair. The stale mug of cold coffee went flying.

"Dammit!"

He'd fallen asleep while writing. Again. He'd closed his eyes— just for a moment—to find and gather the threads of his current scene, but like a thief in the night, the dream carried him off into the past. At this rate, his newest book, *Fury of the Forgotten*, would never get finished.

Blinking against the rays of light spilling into the room, he rotated his left arm. It ached deep inside, and so did his heart. A profound sense of sadness ripped through him.

Drakon and Saoirse. The ill-fated lovers were a legend among his people. He scrubbed a hand over the stubble shadowing his jaw and then brushed his fingers across the burning tattoo that covered his left shoulder. It felt as alive as Drakon had once been.

The knot of dread in his chest grew tighter, each breath heavy and ragged as the air itself seemed to crackle with the tension of an approaching storm. Standing, a current of energy from the floor swept up his legs and spread throughout his body. His body grew hot as the beast eagerly absorbed the heat and demanded to be set free.

"No," he whispered harshly as he struggled for control. "No," he repeated as he changed into a fresh pair of black jeans a black tee shirt and pulled his long, dark hair back and secured it with a leather thong. Shoulders back, he strode out of the bedroom.

He paused in the doorway and studied the living room. He swore it was larger than when he and his group had arrived. Even the walls were a brighter yellow, not the dull beige he'd first seen. A cozy group of couches with bright pillows and throws over the back provided ample seats, along with a few single chairs.

Liana, his younger sister, rose languidly to her feet. She eyed him from deep-set eyes that, in the light, appeared to shift from warm hazel to fiery amber. She tossed her rich, dark hair. "Coffee is ready. I'll grab you a cup." She held her empty cup high. "Need a refill myself."

"Thanks, Li," he told his sister.

"Judging from the noise, you had another dream," Elyn stated from where he lounged next to where Liana had sat. He held a glass of water.

Accepting the cup of strong black coffee from his sister, Ryker sagged onto the couch beside his eldest brother, Eldrak, and lifted his mug to his lips. After nearly burning his mouth, he set his coffee down on the table in front of him and rubbed the back of his neck. "Yeah." He leaned forward, hands dangling between his knees.

"There're coming almost nightly now." Elyn also leaned forward to set his glass down. His hands dangled between his legs as he studied his friend with concern.

"Yeah," Ryker muttered as he swiped a hand across his jaw. "But this one was different." He turned his head toward Eldrak, who was dozing not so quietly in his corner of the couch. He punched him, none too gently, in the arm. "Wake up!"

His brother's dark eyes shot open as he jumped to his feet. After glancing wildly around, he glared at Ryker. "You got a death wish?" His voice rumbled; his eyes blazed.

"Boys, boys, boys," Liana taunted.

Unfazed by Eldrak's furious glare or the hint of red at the center, Ryker shrugged. "Listen up. I saw them."

Frowning, Eldrak glared at his sister's amused glance as she resumed her seat. "Saw who?"

"Drakon and Saoirse."

Eldrak whipped around, his gaze latching onto Ryker's. He let out a low whistle as he reclaimed his spot on the couch. "Council was right. Something is happening, and it's connected to us and our homeland."

Ryker nodded. He felt on edge, off balance, and lost; he did not know what was happening. Or why.

Eldrak jabbed the dragon tattoo on Ryker's arm. "It's changing."

Ryker slapped his brother's hand away. "Tell me something I don't know. Burns like hell." He sent his brother the stink eye and lifted his shoulder. "This should have come to Father. Or you. I wasn't in line to receive it, and I sure as hell never wanted it."

He sucked in a deep breath. Asking why he'd been chosen to become the newest Sentinel was pointless. All males born to the Stormrider line bore small birthmarks in the shape of a dragon scale. Except for the Sentinel, traditionally the eldest male of the line chosen to carry the dragon tattoo.

Eldrak smirked, though his eyes held worry. "And yet it did."

Two months ago, Ryker woke to find himself branded as the new Head Sentinel. No choice. No appeal. Only fire under his skin and a legacy he never wanted. The familiar dread and panic washed through him, as did the fear he lived with daily, fear that he couldn't control his beast. The world was safer with him secluded away deep in their mountain home.

Eldrak yawned. With his long, flowing, dark hair streaked with silver and misty-gray eyes, most thought him the best looking of the three brothers. "You were chosen for a reason, brother." He stood and with a smirk, bowed. "Ryker Stormrider, his mightiness the new High Sentinel."

Ryker glared at his brother, too tired to invite a wrestling match if he retaliated. He rested his elbows on his knees. *Why* was a constant question in his mind. Why him? What was he supposed to do or achieve? The role of Sentinel had always been more of a figurehead, the keeper of knowledge and his family's legacy.

"Drakon was a great warrior," his sister offered from her spot, curled on the couch beside Dreki, the youngest of the brothers. "He was the first Sentinel, and according to legend, he guarded the entrance to the old world—or so the legend goes."

Ryker absently rubbed his tattoo. "Not just a story. Drakon and Saoirse sealed the portal. So why are we here? The location is unknown and not in any of the written accounts, and even if we knew where it was, it's too dangerous to open it." Before he'd set off for Havenwood Cove, he'd read everything the elders had collected over the years.

Long ago, the ill-fated lovers' story became legend, but the lingering power of their tale manifested in his dreams had sent him on a quest for answers far from his home.

"The energy is shifting," Elyn announced, his eyes unfocused, his body tense. "Something dark hovers."

Ryker's dreams supported his friend's statement. Elyndor's Faekin blood gave him a keen sense of not just the physical world, but unseen forces. "Can you find the portal?"

Elyn's eyes cleared. He shook his head. "No, and I don't know how or why I am connected to whatever is happening here, but I am."

Restless, edgy with suppressed energy, Ryker stood and paced from one end of the room to the other. His tattoo continued to pulse as though it had a heart of its own. At the large plate-glass window, he stared out at the view of the ocean.

A golden sheen in the garden in front of the big house caught his eye. Saoirse? No, that was a dream, and he was wide awake. Going to the door, he quietly stepped outside and silently walked to the line of trees that afforded the cottage, and its renters, privacy.

Through the trees, he spotted a woman standing in front of a cauldron. She waved her hands and muttered. The light fell upon her hair and formed a halo of flame. He sucked in his breath, and the blood in his veins grew hot. His gaze sharpened, and his sense of smell heightened as he inhaled her scent even from this distance. Deep inside, as in the dream, the beast stirred, demanding he claim this woman who looked like Saoirse. She was also the woman in danger in all his other dreams. He clenched his jaw. She wasn't his to claim—not in dreams, and not now.

But his dragon tattoo reacted. It pounded hard against his flesh. His breathing grew ragged, and his fingers curled into a tight fist as he fought the urge to sweep the woman into his arms and disappear into the forest. As his ancestor had done.

"Breathe, Ryker." A hand on his shoulder grounded him and stopped the beast from bursting free.

Ryker let out a shaky breath as he continued to watch in silence as the woman consulted a book and then waved her hands toward the cauldron. She peered inside, stepped back, and gave the cauldron a small kick. He smiled despite himself when he realized she was trying to start a fire.

He leaned into the shadows, his body half swallowed by the tree. She tried again, and this time a spark leaped into the cauldron.

"Yes!" she cried, fist thrust skyward, joy ringing like a victory song—until the wind snuffed it out.

Ryker's lips curved despite the pounding in his chest. The world had burned beneath Dragons, yet somehow this stubborn woman's spark mattered more. His dragon tattoo burned hotter, reminding him that wanting her and taking her were two very different things.

# Chapter Twenty

May 23 - Frustrations, Flickers & Flames

Sweaty, irritated, and more than a little frustrated, Sera yanked at her hair. "Shoot! Almost had it," she ground out. She scowled at the closed journal sitting on a small table along with two sheets of paper. "You gave me a fancy pen and a key. Why can't you give me a wand? Everyone knows a witch needs a wand!" She glared at her useless fingers.

Hands jammed on her hips, Sera paced in front of the cauldron. "Okay, so Nonie didn't use a wand, so that means it can be done." She couldn't help thinking about Rowena's instructions from the night before.

*Every witch will add their magical spark to the bonfire, but as head of the council and Guardian, you will go last. Your flame will join all the sparks.*

Huffing out a breath, Sera glanced at a piece of paper with her grandmother's neat script filling the page. She'd found it at her place at the table that morning. Courtesy of Molly? Or Maude? It didn't matter because though the instructions on how to create fire sounded simple enough, after what felt like hours of practice, Sera had only managed one teeny-tiny spark. "I'll be laughed off the council if that's all I can produce," she moaned.

Sera rolled her shoulders to ease the gathered tension and then read her grandmother's instructions once more, skipping past the part about focusing her intent. "Yeah, yeah, yeah." Her finger slid down the paper and tapped on one line: *Channel your core flame.*

"Sounds like something a sarcastic yoga instructor would say," she grumbled. Taking a deep breath, she visualized a roaring fire and held her hand out, one finger pointing into the cauldron filled with dried sage, thyme, and basil.

She envisioned a spark and held her breath when one flew from her finger. Again, it winked out before reaching the cauldron. "Thistlethorn! How am I going to light the bonfire when I can't even magic up a little fire?" Doubts crept in. Maybe Sylvie was right and she wasn't ready to open the ceremony tonight.

"Nope. I will not fail and give that woman the satisfaction. Maybe I need more sparks." This time, she used all her fingers. Closing her eyes, she concentrated on producing a nice, big roaring fire. As she'd done in her apartment when she'd used magic to lift an object, she focused and drew not just a deep breath, but her will. She saw what she wanted, felt the power rising inside her, building. Her fingers tingled.

"Yes, yes," she whispered to herself. Using all her will, she channeled the energy within her into the cauldron. Her eyes went wide as sparks shot into the cauldron. Instantly, flames rose to feed hungrily on the dried herbs. Excited, she focused and lifted her fingers, as though beckoning the flames to follow her direction. Slowly, the flames rose higher than the cauldron.

Before she could lower her hands, and the flames, a voice from behind startled her.

"I come in peace, but if that fire spreads, I reserve the right to run."

Startled, Sera whipped around, her hands flying toward the two men stepping out from the trees separating her home from the cottage rented to the famous author. To her horror, flames shot out and flared toward Ryker. She gasped and dropped her hands to her side. "Good one, Sera. Only you would set fire to a famous author!"

She held out her hands in apology, then clasped them behind her back. "I'm so sorry," she said in a rush. She felt as though she'd been given a sword when she barely knew how to peel a potato. Embarrassed and mildly annoyed, Sera glanced over her shoulder toward the smoldering ashes in the cauldron.

Instead of being furious or berating her, the dark-haired and oh-so-handsome author regarded her calmly, as though she had flicked water at him instead of a wall of flames. She admired his calmness, especially when she'd nearly set him on fire.

"Nice fire," Ryker said as he flicked ash off his shirt.

Sera groaned. "You think? Almost fried you." Her gaze swept over him. "Are you all right? I didn't burn you?"

"Not even a little. I'm fine. And impressed."

Sera rolled her eyes. "Guess I found my core flame after all."

Ryker's eyes, a deep, captivating blue, held hers, their depths pulling at something within her. She felt something—a connection, like a key finding its lock. The sensation left her breathless and lightheaded. And wary. He smiled like a man who hadn't a care in the world, yet his eyes beneath the brilliant blue held a hint of something darker. Studying him, his form wavered, like heat rising off stone. Not magic exactly, but not mundane either. Her gut said, *There's more to him than he's letting on.*

Sera nervously fingered the oathstone beneath her forest-green sweater. Around them, the air grew chill, and a dark shadow blotted out the sun. She glanced skyward. "Okay, that's strange. Not a cloud in sight."

She shoved her fingers into the back pockets of her jeans and took a couple of steps back. Her gaze flicked to the man beside Ryker — good-looking in a too-perfect way. *He reminded her of the elves in Lord of the Rings*: tall, white-blond hair, sharp cheekbones, a pointed chin, and eyes too bright to be ordinary — too sharp, too luminous, almost otherworldly.

Ryker inclined his head. "This is Elyndor."

Elyndor bowed with smooth, deliberate grace. "Most folk call me Elyn, and as you've guessed, we've rented your cottage. The rest of our group — Ryker's brothers and his sister — are inside."

Sera nodded, then cleared her throat. "Welcome. If you need anything, please let me know. Or Molly." Her voice trailed off as she glanced at the cottage. "Or Maude, I guess."

Ryker lifted a brow. "Molly, we have met. Who is Maude?"

Wrinkling her nose, Sera pointed toward her grandmother's house. "Maude is the house, and she's—magical."

Grinning, Ryker nodded. "Ah, that explains a lot. Like rooms that change size and how my broken coffee mug disappeared before I could clean the mess."

Sera nodded. "Well, I've got a lot to do before the opening bonfire ceremony this evening." And banning improper thoughts of the writer was one thing she vowed to do. She had enough on her plate — like finding a portal and saving a town, or the entire world. But first, she needed to get through the festival's opening ceremony. With a quick nod, she walked back to the table, picked up the journal and her notes, and strode toward the house. Behind her, she felt Ryker's eyes on her.

She might have run had she been able to hear his thoughts. She did not know what she'd awakened. Neither did he. The weight of a vow not his own coiled beneath his skin—ancient, insistent—a whisper from another life that refused to fade.

But history wasn't meant to be remade. And she wasn't a ghost of what was lost.

She was the fire.

And the fire was calling back what should have stayed buried.
###

The breeze off the ocean swept across the harbor, rustling sails and setting docked boats creaking. The briny air mingled with the pungent smoke of sage and cedar, creating a heady perfume.

High above, the full moon hung like a luminous pearl, its silvery glow illuminating the beach below. Stars twinkled like diamond dust as she lifted her arms. "It's perfect," Sera breathed, relieved that the earlier clouds had vanished, revealing a brilliant night sky that made the upcoming ritual feel even more special. She stepped out of a shimmering, rose-colored cart. Other pastel carts zipped along the path, playfully tooting. The carts created a bouquet of spring flowers.

Though she was early, dozens of townsfolk were standing in groups or gathered around a wide sandpit, their lit candles casting a soft, magical glow. Another scent caught her attention. She lifted her head and sniffed.

*Peppermint.*

Whirling around, she scanned the beach, her gaze honing in on a large boulder on one side near the water. In the shadows, she spotted the familiar figure of the driver who'd delivered the journal from her grandmother. Her heart seized—a sudden ache so fierce, she staggered back. She blinked furiously, wishing for the impossible to become real, for him to be her father. As soon as she headed his way, he moved, ready to flee.

"No," she called out.

Her breath caught, the peppermint sharp in her throat. The man turned, and his form wavered—like a reflection in rippling water. For a heartbeat she thought she was seeing double, but then her vision sharpened, her veil sight pulling truth from illusion. The disguise fell away.

Silver hair glinted under the moonlight. His green eyes—her eyes, her grandmother's eyes—met hers.

"Da." Her chest cracked open, grief and joy flooding through her all at once. She was looking at her father. "You're alive." Tears coursed down her cheeks. Sensing he was about to flee, she held out her hands. She felt the little girl inside her panic. "Don't go. Please."

With a heavy sigh, Eamon Blackthorn stepped forward and drew his daughter into his arms. He pulled them both back into the shadows. "Ah, my sweet *Eldling*." He buried his face in her hair and sighed, his breath shaky. His body trembled. "Your veil sight has grown strong if you could see through my glamor."

Closing her eyes, Sera breathed in peppermint and an earthy scent that spoke of secrets and forests. "Why?" she asked as she pulled back and opened her eyes. "Why the lie? Why have you stayed away?" Sadness, joy, and anger collided inside her, tangled with betrayal and confusion.

Eamon brushed the hair from her face. "I can't tell you, Sera. Not yet. But promise me you won't tell anyone you've seen me. Not even those you trust. My reasons will become clear in time." He ran his hands down her arms and gripped her hands in his. "*No one.* There is too much at stake."

She didn't understand why, but nodded. "Of course. I promise." She pulled her hands free to swipe tears from her face. Her mother had withheld knowledge of her grandmother, magic, and Havenwood. Did she know Sera's father was alive too? "Does Mom know you're alive?" She held her breath, afraid of the answer. Afraid of more betrayals to come to terms with.

"Let's just say in order to protect my family, I had to disappear. Telling you even that much is dangerous."

Which means she knows, Sera thought as the ache in her heart grew.

"I promise you will know everything in time." He gripped her shoulders with his hands and gave her a gently squeeze. Now, go." He smiled sadly. "You have a big part in tonight's ritual. Make not just me proud, but yourself and your grandmother."

Sera glanced around. "Is she—"

"No, she's not here. She can't be in Havenwood with you."

Nodding, Sera tipped her head. "Will you be watching?"

"I shouldn't, but I will. So proud of my little Eldling." He stepped back, and with a wave, he shimmered and faded from view. Only the scent of his minty candy remained.

"Okay, that is a neat trick." Her heart still ached, her mind whirled with questions, but she felt a little lighter as she returned to the beach. Whatever secrets her father carried, she clung to the fragile hope that they might yet find their way back to each other. And in time, she'd find it within her heart to forgive him. And her mother.

"Sera!"

Glancing up, Sera spotted Lila, holding a candle high, hurrying toward her. Her gaze swept over Sera's face. "Are you all right?

You look like you've seen a ghost," Lila said, her brows drawn together in concern.

"I'm fine," she assured. "In fact, better than fine." Her father was alive. The rest would straighten itself out. Sera focused on her friend. "Wow, Lila, you look wonderful." The rich, purple cloak trimmed in silver brightened Lila's violet eyes.

"Not looking too bad yourself, Sera. You look fabulous in that cloak."

When she'd left the house, Sera had felt conspicuous in the cloak her grandmother had left for her. But seeing everyone else dressed in ritual wear, she grinned. The dark green shimmered black in the moonlight, edged in golden runes—simple, but richer than any gown she'd ever worn.

"Gifts from Nonie," she said. Glancing around, Sera absorbed the cheerful energy of the gathering crowd. "I think most of the town is already here, and I'm early!"

"Here's a candle," Lila said as she handed one to Sera. "Part of the ceremony." She tipped hers so she could light Sera's candle.

Sera held her hand up. "Wait. Let me try." Concentrating, she focused her energy on the wick and then touched it with the tip of her finger.

The familiar flush of warmth rose within, and to her delight and relief, the candle flickered to life.

"Sera, that is very cool! Wish I could do that!"

Laughing, Sera hooked her arm through Lila's. "Well, I wish I could fly!"

Giggling, Lila eyed her friend. "With your Fae blood, Sera, I bet you can shift—move from one place to another."

Sera's jaw dropped. "Like Fin?!"

"Well, Fin is unique, but yes."

"Well—wow!" she exclaimed, her mind blown. "Imagine being able to just go *poof*?" She flicked her fingers.

"Who's poofing?" a cheerful voice demanded.

One moment, it was just her and Lila, and in the blink of an eye—snap of fingers—Fin appeared on her other side.

Sera jumped. "Ugh! Don't do that, Fin. And right now, you are the one shifting."

Fin snapped his fingers. A lit candle appeared in his hand. "Shifting?" He gasped theatrically. "I don't shift. I twindle. Or maybe I skimble."

Raising her brows, Sera shook her head in disbelief. "What's the difference?"

Grinning, Fin twisted and appeared on the other side of Lila. "That was a twindle." He skipped forward and faded in a blur of movement.

Sera blinked and then shook her head. At least he'd taken his mischief with him.

She jumped when he whispered, "Skimble," from behind her. "Fiiin!"

"Oops, need to go," he muttered as he ambled off to avoid the sheriff heading toward them.

Sera leaned closer to Lila and, with her voice low, admitted, "Not sure I'll get used to him."

Lila giggled. "He means well. Sam too." She threaded her arm through Sera's and led the way to the bonfire pit.

"So, the Bloom and Moon Festival is a celebration of spring?" Sera hadn't had time to read about the history of the festival but gathered it celebrated the renewal of life.

Nodding, Lila paused and held out one hand. Pink, gold, and violet glitter appeared. "It's one of our most important traditions. We celebrate magic and the enduring legacy of our magical community." She tossed the glitter high.

Enthralled, Sera watched the sparkling glitter dance in the air, its movements guided by the gentle breeze; a magical, shimmering display. "Okay, that's seriously cool." They paused as they reached the fire pit, where vines and twigs formed a large nest of sorts. "Molly said this festival also marks the historic sealing of the portal between Earth and Thyron, so it's also a celebration of freedom."

"Yes," Lila replied.

Sera nodded her greeting to Daisy and Rowena, who were setting out jars of glowing orbs while two other women placed gleaming, wooden bowls carved with runes just inside the circle.

"I thought bonfires were tall, more like a haystack."

Chuckling, Lila shook her head. "Wait and see. I don't want to spoil it for you."

Sera pressed her fist into her stomach where butterflies didn't just flutter, but zipped and zoomed, making her feel nauseous.

Lila squeezed her arm. "You'll do great, Sera. Trust yourself." She hugged her. "Gotta go take my place."

Sera squared her shoulders as she continued around the circle toward Rowena, who was waving her over. Another cloaked figure crossed her path and bumped her shoulder hard enough that she nearly fell into the pit.

"Watch where you're going." Sylvie's eyes flashed with disdain.

Sera tipped her chin up. "Take your own advice, Sylvie. You bumped into me." She crossed her arms, irritation tightening her voice. "Just what is your problem, anyway?"

Sylvie narrowed her eyes and cocked a hip. "You're not special."

Rowena, in a flowing silver cloak, slipped between them. "Sylvie! Not the time, and not your place. This was settled last night. Go take your spot."

With a look of fury, Sylvie stormed off, disappearing into the gathering crowd.

"Wow." Only been in Havenwood a couple of days, and already she had enemies.

Rowena patted Sera's shoulder. "Don't mind her, dear. Feels the same toward your grandmother. Thinks her family is just as powerful and important. Now, forget her. It is time to begin." She led the way to the eastern quadrant, the gateway of beginnings.

Holding her candle in both hands to hide her nerves, Sera pulled her shoulders back and lifted her head high. She might be shaking like a leaf inside, but no one had to know. She would not let her grandmother down or those who had faith in her.

Rowena clapped her hands sharply. "Gather around. It is time," she called out in a voice that carried across the beach.

People shuffled into position and fell silent. She lifted her candle, and everyone followed suit. Rowena's wand gleamed silver under the moon. Her voice rang out, calm and clear: "By root and river, by The Mother's breath and leaf and sky, rise, little flames, and light the night high."

The candle in Sera's hand trembled—and then rose higher, slipping out of her hand. Around the circle, one by one, the candles floated over the assembled townsfolk, like seeds caught on a soft, rising wind. Hundreds of glowing points rose upward, casting the clearing in a golden, sacred glow.

Sera tilted her face up, awe stealing her breath. "Amazing," she breathed.

"We now welcome the Heartlog." Rowena's voice pulled her back to the ceremony.

Across from Sera, the crowd parted to allow Lady Lillian, dressed in her habitual white, to enter the circle. Her steps were slow and measured, and in her arms, she carried a log carved with runes passed down through generations and burned only during the Bloom and Moon Festival.

The silence was absolute as Lady Lillian gently placed the log in the center of the nest of twigs, vines, and small branches. She pulled a pouch from her belt and sprinkled the log with her herb mixture. With a low bow toward Sera, she moved to Sera's other side.

With two powerful women on either side of her, Sera glanced around at the expectant faces turned toward her. She picked out a few people she knew: her yarn whisperers, council members, including a scowling Sylvie, Molly, Ellie the bookstore owner, and off to one side, she spotted the unfortunate Talia in all black, including her defiant expression. Sheriff Sam, wearing an almost identical expression, stood off to one side.

Rowena sent her a subtle nod. Drawing in a deep breath, Sera reminded herself that she was the Guardian and head of the council. She could do this. She stepped forward, her boots whispering over the sand.

"Welcome to the circle of woven flame." Her voice, soft and hesitant, swept over the assembly. She drew in a breath. Then another. Everyone was watching—some with reverence, others with curiosity, a few with barely concealed suspicion, or worse. But it was thoughts of her father, somewhere out there, watching, that gave her courage the boost she needed. Acting on instinct, she kicked off her boots and immediately felt grounded by the earth beneath her feet. Pretending she presided over a hostile takeover from her accounting days, she steadied her voice.

"Tonight, we gather as one—many threads, one flame. The forest watches, and the magic listens. May each of you speak the truth of your heart, and may the fire weave it into the night."

Murmurs of approval greeted her opening. Molly beamed, Fin gave a dramatic bow, and at her feet, Willow, who'd just appeared, flicked her tail.

"Tonight, we begin not with fire, but with thread. Each of you—each thread—brings your truth. Your strength.

She paused for a beat. "Let the Forest witness. Let The Mother weave our hearts into Her song."

She nodded to Fern, who represented the Verdans and Woodland Elves.

Fern stepped forward, her staff tipped with moss and crystal. "From seed and soil, from whispering roots and old rain, we offer balance and breath." She pressed her palm toward the Heartlog. A spark of deep green light flickered and spiraled down, sinking into the runes like a root finding its home.

Lila stepped forward and bowed to Sera. "I speak for the Fae and elves." Her voice was soft; her presence shimmered with layered glamor. "From memory and moonlight, from the veil between, we offer truth dressed in wonder." Her violet-silver spark glimmered as it drifted like pollen to the waiting log.

Bram approached, one hand on his walking stick. "From craft and cleverness, from deep stone and patient hands, the gnomes offer foundation." His spark emerged with a low hum—copper-blue, heavy and slow, spinning once before nestling into place. The fire pit groaned softly, as if accepting the weight of history.

Milo shuffled forward. In a low, raspy voice, he intoned:

"I speak for the Goblins. From fire and forge, from oath and iron, we offer strength and warning." Molten red light spat outward from his fist, crackling like a coal flung into the pit. Sera flinched. The Heartlog hissed—but held.

Syrus flapped down onto her shoulder. "From feather and fury, from wisdom no one asked for, I offer what I damn well please." He flared his wings. A flicker of electric teal shot from his eyes, zinging into the center with a pop.

Sera groaned. "Thanks, I think."

"You're' welcome, Guardian," he muttered as he disappeared.

Fin approached barefoot, leaving a faint trail of glitter behind him. He bowed low—too low—then rose with a grin that didn't quite meet his eyes. "From chance and charm, from the edge of knowing, I offer change." His spark coiled like smoke—shifting color with no fixed hue—before weaving through all the others, slipping into the fire like a rumor. The air held its breath.

All eyes turned to her.

Sera stepped forward. Her heart thudded like a drum in her chest. Raising her hand, she spoke confidently and firmly.

"Thread unknown, root unspun—I seek the fire. I am the one." Her spark shimmered into being—moon-silver with a ribbon of sea-glass blue—and drifted like a sigh from her palm to the Heartlog.

For a heartbeat, nothing happened. Dread trembled through her. Had she missed something? Then—the fire bloomed, larger than ever before, rising in a blossom of silver-blue at the center, threaded with every other color. The crowd gasped, followed by murmurs of awe.

"The Guardian's fire ..." someone whispered.

Color burst upward like stitched light unraveling into the sky: green, violet, red, gold, copper, silver, and shifting wildly. Threads of magic danced above the flame, twining like ribbons through the air. The vines around the pit tightened, weaving the fire into place.

From the edge of the circle, Fin whispered in awe, "Well ... that's never happened before."

Sera's voice trembled. "Tonight, we don't just light a fire—we weave it. With breath and root, with craft and memory. Let the forest listen. Let magic bind us."

The wind shifted—sharp, cold, and wrong. The ground gave a faint pulse beneath her feet, like a heartbeat from something buried. Sand trembled. A subtle vibration climbed her legs, coiling in her gut. The air around the flame wavered, and for a breathless moment, it felt as if something vast and ancient stirred beneath the earth, stretching in its sleep. *The portal?*

Glancing around, Sera saw that only a few had noticed the tremor—Lady Lillian gasped, Fern stiffened, Syrus tilted his head, and Fin swore under his breath.

She was the Guardian. Was she supposed to do something? Say something? But the moment passed—fleeting, like a ripple in a dream. Unsure what to do, Sera stepped back. Tradition dictated that everyone—magical or not—now send their wish or blessing into the flame. She lifted her hands, and at the signal, sparks flew like fireflies, laughter rising with them.

Spells and sparks from the crowd flew overhead and popped into the growing flame. Where others saw only flickering firelight, Sera glimpsed the tails of the spells, like comets—soft ribbons of color, weaving and curling through the air, woven into the night with invisible hands. Sera blinked, her eyes tracking the trails of magic as they twisted and twirled around each other, the energy lighting up the night in flashes of silver, gold, and green.

Each trail of magic seemed alive, weaving through the air, leaving a glimmering, almost smoky path in its wake. "Wow, beautiful," Sera said to Lila, who'd moved to stand behind her.

"It is a beautiful fire, Sera."

"Not just the fire, but the ribbons of spells falling around it like stars."

Lila frowned. "You can see the spells as they hit?"

"Can't you?"

Shaking her head, Lila grinned. "Nope."

"Huh." Glancing around, no one else seemed to notice either. As the spell-trails converged on the woodpile, she felt a prickle run down her spine. This wasn't just magic—it was something she could see. Something she'd never been able to do before. Her breath caught in her throat, but before she could process it, the pile exploded into flames.

Sera's eyes widened as the bonfire grew, its bright flames licking the sky. Amid the laughter and cheers, a sudden jolt of sharp, burning magic sliced through the rising sparks—too fast, too focused. A rogue spell sped through the air—not wild, but aimed. At her.

She saw the trail clearly—darker than the rest—cutting through the ribbons of spell fire like a knife. Her skin prickled. Her breath caught. Too fast to react.

Before she could move, Fin lunged forward, his form a blur, intercepting the spell mid-air.

A hush fell over the crowd, the festive atmosphere momentarily replaced by a palpable tension.

Fin turned to Sera, his usual mirth absent. "That wasn't wild magic." His grin was gone; his tone was flat. "Someone aimed for you."

Sera stumbled back, breath caught in her throat, heart hammering so hard it hurt. Someone in this crowd wanted to harm her. Maybe even kill her.

Her mind flashed to the porch roof. The shadow outside the window. The glare in Sylvie's eyes. Overhead, the floating candles flickered and dimmed. A hush fell. The air turned colder. Heavier. And beneath her bare feet, the earth pulsed again. Not a tremor this time, but a breath—deep, ancient. A presence stirring.

The fire had listened. But so had the dark. And deep beneath the cliffs, something vast stirred, restless in its slumber. Her flame had touched an echo older than memory—woven once in blood and vow. The earth gave another faint pulse, like a breath through stone. The binding still held ... but it remembered ....

###

Deep beneath the cliffs, where seawater met stone and magic clung like mist, something stirred. Her flame had reached farther than she knew—down into roots, into dark, into memory. A pulse answered, faint as a heartbeat, vast as the sea. The trees listened. The sea pulled back as if afraid.

On the beach below, the Guardian stood in the firelight, heart still pounding.

And high on the cliffs, two birds circled the house where magic slept—a pair of sentinels watching the dark.

# Chapter Twenty-One

May 25 - Portents, Pages & Poisoned Heart

Cool, misty fingers trailed along a slick, moss-covered path that wound down a steep slope. Sera strolled, feeling at peace surrounded by immense trees, their branches forming a shadowy tunnel high above. The air, thick with the scent of damp, composting earth, filled her nostrils, while the rhythmic crashing of distant waves provided a calming backdrop.

The path ended in front of an ancient cave, the dark entrance carved into the base of a shadowed cliff, its mouth yawning wide and dark. The dampness of the air seeped into her very bones. Chilled, she hugged herself and watched waves lap gently at the entrance to the cave as the tide rolled in.

Something drew her to the mouth of the cave. She peered inside. Darkness blacker than the blackest night greeted her. Uneasy, she stepped back from the unknown. Tunneling her fingers through her hair, she laughed nervously. "Who am I kidding?" she muttered, fighting both dread and curiosity. "The minute I became the Guardian, my life went from predictable and boring to crazy and strange." She rubbed her stomach to ease her nerves. Her gaze drifted back to the yawning mouth of the cave. "Spooky and strange? Yep, and I can do this." The silent words *I hope* floated through her mind.

She scanned the sky—cloudless, too perfect. Like the lake dream. Too calm. Too still. She remembered that vivid dream: the lake, the island, the sense that it might be a portal, and how the beauty of that alien world had called to her. The dream had started out so peaceful and beautiful, tempting her with its unearthly beauty.

She shivered when she also recalled how in a heartbeat, everything had changed with the dark, evil beings. In her mind, she still heard the frightening shrieks and the echo of her terrified screams.

This dream—because she knew it was a dream—also left her heart pounding and her mouth dry. Was this the way to the portal? Staring into the darkness, into the unknown, she stepped forward. Something crunched beneath her foot. She froze, blood chilling— until she looked down. Shells. Just shells. Her laugh was thin, brittle, but it steadied her.

Breathing in the cold, stale air coming out of the cave, she froze mid-step, unable to cross the threshold. "Come on, it's a dream, and dreams can't hurt you." But her body refused to enter. She couldn't forget how real her fear had been in that other dream. Her mind was brave, logical. But her body refused to budge.

The stone wall just inside the cave wavered, like heat rising off hot pavement. Or like her father's glamor. A low hum ripped through the air, and the oathstone beneath her shirt pulsed, a heartbeat visible beneath the fabric.

Her knees trembled as she stumbled back, her breath lodging in her throat. Whatever, or whomever, watched, the oathstone was responding to its hidden presence. Hands clasped in front of her and chin tipped bravely, she called out, "Show yourself!"

The stone wall flared to life with a pair of brilliant, blinding, blue eyes that stared out through the rock. Her hand went to her throat. Something about those eyes ... they reminded her of Ryker? The same intensity. The same fire.

Soft as wind through leaves, a voice whispered, "Saoirse."

The name echoed deep into her soul—the name of her ancestor. Her heart seized as the anguished cry came again.

Sera woke, still caught in a strange dream with those eyes burning into her soul. Her heart hammered as the name he'd called echoed in her mind: *Saoirse.* The sound lingered in her chest like a tolling bell. She jolted upright in the window seat, gasping.

Willow tumbled off her lap with a startled yowl of outrage, the mundane noise breaking through the dream's lingering weight.

Saoirse.

She knew who Saoirse was now, knew the woman was one of her ancestors. Sera pressed a hand to her chest, feeling the steady thump of her heart and her pulse beneath the gemstone bracelet. Her fingers found and rubbed her heart-stone. The lovers, Drakon and Saoirse, had somehow sealed the portal, but what role did the ill-fated couple play now? Why dream of them?

Willow jumped back onto Sera, her front paws pressing into Sera's chest as the cat glared at her. "Little Human! Some of us are trying to sleep," the cat's plaintive voice complained.

Groaning, Sera swept the indignant cat into her arms and held her close. "Sorry, Willow. Strange dream." Even wide awake, the dream lingered. Those brilliant eyes, so mysterious, filled her with longing and left a deep sadness in her soul. Why?

Sera glanced out the bay window. Light streamed in; pink-tinged clouds drifted over the sea. Around her, the house was quiet, bathed in soft pink dawn. The embers in the fireplace pulsed to life. A steaming mug of coffee appeared on the windowsill with a soft clink. She didn't remember falling asleep. "The journal!" She found it beside her.

After returning home, she'd taken the time before bed to detail her first ritual—her awe of the floating candles, the power of the sparks, the strange beauty of her own magic, and how the ribbons and trails of spells and sparks had fascinated and amazed her with their beauty. For the first time since arriving in Havenwood, she truly felt like a witch and Guardian.

But with the awe and pleasure came fear. She replayed the moment Fin had stopped the rogue spell aimed at her. Who had tried to attack her? And why? A woman didn't attain her position in the corporate world without making enemies, but no one had ever tried to harm her, and this now made two attempts on her life. Had the spell come from Sylvie? Was she that angry over a council position or the fact that she was in Havenwood?

Sera vowed to be on guard as she turned her attention back to her incredible view. The first blush of light brushed the horizon, painting the ocean in soft strokes of rose and gold. Gentle waves caught the color, turning silver at the crests as they rolled toward shore. The sky, still hushed with the last whispers of night, slowly brightened—its palette shifting from lavender to coral with each heartbeat of the rising sun.

"What a way to start the day." She sighed. No traffic. No shouting. Just wind, waves, and the soft hush of magic. The peaceful setting seemed unreal, like a muted movie. She leaned her head back and smiled, her heart warmed by the sight of Willow on her back, stretched out between her legs.

"I've missed this," she realized. Missed both the sea and her cat. And her father. She sighed, wishing they were together. She didn't commit to paper her reunion with him, though she longed to, just so she could come back to it and find comfort in the discovery that her father was alive.

"He's alive." The words slipped out. She clapped a hand over her mouth, as though speaking them aloud might make him vanish again.

Willow shook her head. "We know, Child."

Brows furrowed, Sera glared at the cat. "You didn't think to tell me?"

"Not our place." She lifted a paw, licked it, and swiped it over her ear.

"All right. I can accept that." Gazing out the window, Sera felt whole again, despite the worry and fear being in Havenwood brought her. Knowing her father was still alive provided a calmness to her life, along with the stability of roots she hadn't known she needed. It didn't matter why the secrecy, just that he was here. The rest could be dealt with later. She decided after her grandmother returned that she was staying. This was home.

She glanced around, enjoying the dark wood of the bed and furniture, the soothing pastel landscapes against cream-colored walls, and accents of colors that reminded her of both the sea and forest. "The only thing missing in this wonderful bedroom is a window that opens so I can hear the birds and smell the ocean."

Immediately, the house groaned and trembled, causing Sera to bolt back upright, her arms around the cat this time. The bay window blurred and shivered. Or was it her vision? She rubbed her eyes and blinked.

"Oh!" It was all she could manage as windows appeared and opened. The blast of cold air knocked the breath from her. A moment later, the window eased partway shut, allowing a gentle breeze filled with birdsong to enter. The rhythmic sounds of crashing waves swirled around her.

"Oh," she whispered again, pressing her palm to the new screen. The wood beneath her fingers thrummed faintly, alive. Was this Maude's gift to her—or the house's own will? A nervous giggle escaped her lips. "Okay, this is my life now. I think I could get used to this!"

She glanced around the room. "Um, thank you, Maude."

Her phone chimed from the windowsill. She glanced at the incoming notification.

Maude: *You are welcome. All you need to do is ask.* ☺

Sera giggled, feeling lighter. And loved. "The impossible is truly possible," she whispered. She knew she should get ready for the parade but reached for the journal instead. She had time. Last night she'd been too tired to do much more than commit the bonfire to the pages, so she opened the cover, intending to reread what she'd written. She bolted upright, her brow lifting and her jaw dropping when she found only a blank page.

She thumbed through the pages in case she hadn't started at the beginning. Nothing. She turned the journal over in her hands, opening and closing it. It wasn't very thick, not for all the entries it supposedly contained. "Odd." She was sure she'd written about the bonfire. Had she dreamed she'd done so?

"Where the heck is my entry?"

The journal vibrated, and a page turned, revealing a list of seven names, including hers at the top of the list. She relaxed her shoulders. "Ah. Magic. Of course." Would she ever get used to a magical life? Flipping back to the blank page at the beginning, she found her blue pen and wrote a single word: *Testing.*

The ink faded, and when she touched her name in the index, she saw her page. Magic. Simple. Absolute. And there was her bonfire entry. "Okay, whoever created this journal was very creative and organized."

She glanced over her account of the bonfire, feeling the awe once more. She'd never been one to journal, always wary of prying eyes—her first diary as a child had ended in humiliation when her mother read and mocked her fanciful words. And Evan? She never would have trusted him with her secret thoughts.

But here, with this journal, her words felt safe. Alive!

She smiled as she reread her description of the spell trails, marveling that she could actually see what others could not. Like her father's glamor. She realized now that she had almost pierced it the day he came to her home as a delivery driver. Even in her dream, she had sensed eyes upon her.

Then another thought sparked. She sat bolt upright. *The quilts.* She had seen through their damage to the beauty hidden beneath. "They aren't destroyed," she breathed. "It's a spell."

A slow grin spread across her face. "Willow, I think I know who cursed the quilts." Her gaze drifted toward the window, thoughts racing. "Too early for the Festival. But if I get there before the crowd, I can see if I'm right."

The answer brought a flicker of relief. One problem she might finally solve. Turning back to the index page, she traced her finger over each name, watching colors shimmer across the edges of the journal like painted ribbons. "Pure magic," she whispered. She tapped her grandmother's name, and Elowen's last entry appeared.

*My dearest Sera, the Guardian's Journal offers its help, for you cannot do this task alone. You must find the pieces of this puzzle. Discover the history, the birth, of our town and those within. So many secrets, so much knowledge has been both hidden and forgotten until such a time as they were needed.*

*The time and need are now, and you, as the Guardian of the Moondragon, hold the key. If desperate, ask Syrus for help or advice, although heaven knows what help you'll get. He is an odd one, that bird.*

"You got that right, Nonie," Sera said with a chuckle as her fingers closed around the hidden oathstone she wore beneath an old, ratty sleep shirt that should have been torn into rags a long time ago. "Odd, but there is more to him than the snark and sass," she said as if her grandmother sat beside her. She returned to her grandmother's entry.

*Here among these pages, you may find answers, or maybe just more questions, but isn't that the way life goes? And remember, this quest is about more than saving Havenwood Cove. It is about saving yourself, my dear child. Chin up, Seraphina Blackthorn. You will not be alone in this quest.*

Sera turned the page, noting another journal entry, this one a week ago and full of worry and fear. Her grandmother penned her worries, wondering if she was doing the right thing by passing such responsibility to her granddaughter.

"So where do I begin?" The page flipped back to the index page, and one name glowed.

*Aisling Blackthorn.*

Tapping the name, the journal opened to the corresponding entry.

Aisling Blackthorn, May 1758

*I am undone. This day, I lament the loss of my twin, my most beloved Saoirse, the very other half of my soul.*

Saoirse. The name resounded in Sera's mind, ancient and known, a part of her very being. Her gaze flew back to the page.

*How shall I bear so grievous a burden? My sister is gone—yielded to a fate I scarce may comprehend—and with her hath fled the light of my spirit. What cruel providence compels me to draw breath whilst she breathes no more? Each moment is torment, each sigh a betrayal.*

*I cast mine eyes heavenward, yet the firmament grants no answer. The world is dimmed, bereft of warmth or cheer. My heart lies riven, and yet I must persist, though I know not by what strength. Cruel is the hand of destiny to sunder us, when once we were united in all things—heart, mind, and spirit. Why was I left to wander this mortal coil alone?*

Saoirse. The name echoed again—this time not from a dream, but from the page. From the past. Woven with the future. Hers? Her chest tightened—not with fear, but with something deeper. With connection.

Heart racing, Sera eased Willow off her lap so she could lean over and reread the short passage. "This is intense." Captivated, she reached to turn the page—music drifted through the window, soft at first, then swelling, unmistakably festival horns and drums, calling her to duty. Her stomach sank. As the Guardian, she was expected to stand at the opening. She was already late.

She had things to do, people to see, and trouble to avoid—hopefully. Jumping to her feet, the cat immediately slipped into the warm spot Sera vacated.

Changing into well-worn jeans and a hip-length sweater, she slipped her feet into a pair of ankle-high boots. Carrying the journal, she set it on the bedside table for later. As much as she needed to learn what happened to Saoirse and the connection with the blue eyes in the cave, she had responsibilities. As Guardian and head of the magical council, she was expected to be there for the opening ceremony.

From outside, she heard the toot of a horn and realized her ride to the festival had arrived. "Chin up, Seraphina Blackthorn," she whispered to herself. "You've got time." Then she wrinkled her nose. "Three moons. Starting now." The pressure of time weighed her down.

She grabbed her sweater and gave Willow's exposed belly a rub. "Come on. We're late."

The cat yawned, rolled over, and curled into a tight ball. "Later."

"Nope. You and me, Cat." Sera scooped her up into her arms.

Willow narrowed her eyes. "Little Human! Seen one festival, seen them all!" She yawned.

"Yeah, but I haven't." Sera gave the cat an affectionate rub. "Please?"

The cat sighed. Loudly. "Fine. But I'll walk."

Setting the cat down, Sera reached out to open the door just as Willow strolled through, head and tail held high. "Ugh. Must you?"

Willow's eyes gleamed with mischief. "Must. I must. So fun to see your reaction, Little Human. Now hurry. We're late."

Rolling her eyes, Sera hurried after Willow. Eager, determined, and hopeful, she set off with her grandmother's words still echoing in her heart and the memory of her father's embrace. She wasn't alone, and she wouldn't turn back.

Magic stirred. The town was waking—and so was she. Whatever waited at that festival, whatever hid behind those eyes in her dream, or within the pages of that journal, she was ready. She would walk into that festival with her head held high and both eyes wide open. Someone had already tried twice to take her out. She didn't plan on giving them a third chance.

###

She watched the house from the shadow of a Hawthorn, shifting her weight, careful to remain hidden and silent. Two chances. Two failures. And still, Sera thrived. She had friends, a home that bent to her whims, and respect she had not deserved. Havenwood embraced Sera as if she belonged, when it had never once cared for her.

The first time, that wretched elf had spoiled everything. The second, clumsy and rushed, was stolen from her hands by that silver-haired trickster. Her nails dug deep crescents into her palms, hot blood welling. Always someone there to save Sera. Always a shield to protect her.

The festival would be different. Crowds. Music. Magic spilling like wine. No one would look for her. And Sera—Sera would not be looking at all.

From the cliff road, she heard the cheerful tooting of a cart and watched as it stopped at the bottom of Sera's steps. The contrast stabbed like glass: her enemy's bright, charming home against the hovel she called her own. Why should Sera have so much? Because she was a Blackthorn? Because fate had chosen her?

The thought curdled. She imagined the cart tumbling over the edge—but the Rootwall would stop it, as it always did. Havenwood itself stood with Sera. With her. *Never with me.*

Her breath shuddered as she turned away. The shadows curled close, gathering at her call, wrapping her like a cloak. When she vanished, the only trace she left was the acrid tang of scorched leaves.

# Chapter Twenty-Two

May 24 - Of Festivals, Foes & Familiars

The cart danced at the bottom of the stairs as if impatient to be on its way to fun and festivities. Enchanted by Havenwood's magical carts, Sera stepped inside her lavender ride with its moon-silver trim.

Willow growled, as though telling the magical cart to settle. Sera chuckled. To her delight, fresh flowers decorated the canopy and doors. Each bloom shifted color as the cart rolled down the driveway. Sera glanced back at the house. The windows gleamed, the front door swung gently shut on its own—as if to say, *go on now*. She exhaled and faced forward. The road ahead sparkled with anticipation.

The song of the sea, the whitecaps of waves, and cries of gulls followed her as the cart zipped along the cliff road. A chill nipped the air, making her glad she'd worn a sweater. Above her, the blue sky remained clear, as though to honor the spring celebration.

The cart turned and scooted up A Street with a cheerful toot, its wheels crunching over a path sprinkled with golden flower petals. The area behind the shops was dotted with tents. Zipping up to her shop, it stopped with an excited wiggle. Willow leaped out and ran to the table in front of the yarn shop where she jumped up and sat, like a queen on her throne. Sera stepped down and smoothed her skirt, her gaze sweeping over the street, which unfolded before her like a sun-drenched painting come to life.

The fountains gracing the center green strip were gone, replaced by booths in a riot of spring colors—lavender and seafoam, ocean blues, pale yellow and greens. The stalls overflowed with glittering trinkets, bundles of herbs, and enchanted kitchenware. Witches in wide-brimmed hats waved wands while explaining the difference between "a harmless sparkle" and "accidental combustion." A sign read: *Wand Etiquette: Always Point Down.*

Children shrieked with delight as they chased unpoppable bubbles that left behind faint trails of rainbows. To her left, a group of out-of-towners tried their hands at the *Try-Your-Magic* booth, their enchanted ladles twirling wildly as a supervising gnome ducked to avoid being pelted with what looked suspiciously like magically animated Jello, wiggling and dancing in bowls and on the table.

From another booth, flying fairy dolls on brooms zipped out and flew in a circle. On the ground, miniature carts tooted and raced to the delight of two small boys while a young girl, dressed like a fairy pointed to the flying dolls.

Mingling with the crowd, jugglers performed, tossing colorful, glowing orbs high. One juggled balls of flame to the delight of the crowd. And like all festivals, there was no shortage of food, including huge delicate flowers made of cotton candy. She grinned. Her teeth hurt just thinking about the sweetness, even as the saliva pooled in her mouth.

A distant chime, soft and clear, rang through the air, as if the very festival had a pulse. Everywhere she looked, magic shimmered at the edges of the ordinary—just enough to make someone doubt their eyes. And yet ... beneath the laughter, the sunshine, booths brimming with joy, something tugged at her senses.

A hush in the Rootcurrent beneath her feet.

A twitch in the air.

As if the land itself held its breath, waiting.

Holding her breath in response, she sent her senses outward, seeking, but was unsure what she sought. She threaded her fingers through her hair and glanced around. Something felt off. She glanced over at Willow, who was also alert and watchful. "You feel that too?"

The cat gave a brief nod. "They watch. And wait."

Willow's voice, so soft Sera barely heard it, sent a tremor through her. "They?"

"They who seek retribution. The seal thins—and they hunger." The cat held her gaze with eyes that glowed a luminous, unnatural blue.

"Who are they, Willow?" Knowing that an enemy race wanted to enslave, or destroy, Havenwood didn't tell her who—or what—they were. She gripped her bag tighter as a chill raced up her spine. "How can I stop a portal from opening unless I know what I'm facing?"

The cat's eyes dimmed with sorrow. "You face a life and death choice, and choices carry weight, Little Human. Some heavier than life itself." With that, Willow leaped down.

Sera nearly dropped her bag at the harsh revelation. "Willow!" Her heart pounded. Whose life? Whose death? Hers? Havenwood's? The world?

At the shop door, Willow glanced back. "You will understand. Soon. Just don't take too long, Little Human." Then she slipped through the wooden door.

Sera stood frozen, Willow's words echoing like a curse. Life or death. The fate of Havenwood—perhaps the world—hung in the balance, and that kind of power terrified her. Another faint tremor rippled beneath her feet. Gripping the oathstone, now warm against her palm, Sera hurried after the cat, who always seemed to know more than she let on.

A sudden burst of children's laughter cut through her unease, pulling her back into the present. The scent of sugared almonds drifted on the breeze, and a ripple of applause and cheering rose as the first notes of parade music started down the street.

The Bloom and Moon Festival was in full swing, bright and alive—even as shadows whispered at the edges. Reaching the shadow of the roof overhang, she paused and glanced upward, remembering how someone had tried to kill her by dislodging the roof. Without both Fin and Sam to magically hold the roof suspended in mid-air, she'd have either been killed or severely injured.

"You're safe, Sera," a voice above her head called out.

Stepping back a few steps, she shaded her eyes and spotted Fin sitting cross-legged on the roof.

"Fin, what are you doing up there?" He looked like part of the festival, but also apart from it—watching, waiting. Was he keeping vigil? Guarding the Guardian?

The elf grinned. "What better way to enjoy the festivities than from up here? The parade starts soon. Best seat in the town."

Sera glanced around.

"They will enter from that way, my dear girl. From the cliff road."

Sure enough, after peering around the corner of her shop, she saw a group of kids leading a herd of Velwynths toward Main Street.

"Good, you're here in time for the parade," Lila said as she hurried up to her. She lifted a whimsical, berry-packed smoothie that sparkled with the magic of pixie dust and held it out to Sera. "Pixie Dust Delight. One of my most popular concoctions."

Sera didn't want to miss the parade. The quilt tent could wait. She accepted the drink with a wide grin. She took a sip and wrinkled her nose as popping bubbles, like champagne, tickled. "Oh," she exclaimed. She lifted an eyebrow. "Mmm, this is heavenly. At this rate, I'll need a spell to fit into my clothes."

Lila chuckled. "Calories don't count if they are magical calories."

Lifting her brows, Sera said, "Really?"

Giggling, her Fae friend took a sip and sighed. "I don't know, but seems that it should be true!"

Laughing, Sera tapped her own purple and silver glass to Lila's. She regarded the mixture of berries and Greek yogurt with just a touch of honey. "Brilliant, Lila," she complimented as she popped the strawberry sitting on top of the foam into her mouth. She closed her eyes and groaned. "I might have to get another one of these later."

She glanced around as the crowd thickened. "There are a lot of people here," she observed. The magical carts were working overtime to bring visitors to the festival from the parking lot.

Lila nodded. "One of our biggest tourist attractions."

Sera frowned. "What about all the magic?" She pointed to a booth with brooms zipping and zooming around the tent.

Lila chuckled. "Non magical folk will assume there are clear threads and motors making the brooms fly. And those who manage to see the magic will forget once they leave." She smiled gently at Sera. "The Mother protects her town and all who call Havenwood home."

Before Sera could ask about The Mother, she heard soft, musical lowing along with tinkling bells. Sera turned her attention to the start of Main Street. "Oh-oh, look it's the Velwynths—a whole lot of them," she exclaimed, her eyes wide as the miniature cow-like creatures rumbled up onto Main Street.

Mesmerized by the colors ranging from pretty pastels to vibrant oranges and reds, Sera clapped in greeting with the crowd as she took in the intricate braids and beads and feathers dangling from the animals' unique turned-out horns. Spotting Ella, Sera waved and sent out a piercing whistle through her fingers.

Lila leaned close. "Tomorrow, they'll crown the Bloom and Moon Queen and King."

Music drowned out the Velwynths as a marching band followed. Group after group showcased their skills to the town of Havenwood Cove: dancers, jugglers, acrobats in swirling cloaks.

"Look!" Sera pointed to a large, wooden ship that appeared to sail down the street. "There's no truck or flatbed!" Her eyes lit with wonder. "Man, I love magic!"

Loud barks drew her eyes to the ship's deck. She laughed and waved at three barking dogs—Lady, Mariner, and Salty—then let loose with another whistle to their owners, each dressed in sailor's gear. They returned her call with smart salutes as they passed.

Sheriff Sam marched alongside the ship. A gust of wind whipped through the street, billowing the sails and sending the sheriff's wide-brimmed hat skittering down the parade route. He jogged after it, trying to look official while dodging a group of twirling                                                                 dancers.

Sera glanced behind her and up to where Fin sat. She smothered a laugh. "This town," she murmured, shaking her head.

Lila leaned close, talking into Sera's ear to be heard over the crowd. She pointed to the floating ship. "That's a nod to your ancestors, Sera. The Blackthorns founded Havenwood Cove with their shipbuilding business."

"Really?" The revelation struck a chord. How little she knew about her own family. She vowed to read every entry in her journal—not just to understand her role as Guardian, but to understand her bloodline as well.

After the last stragglers of the parade went past, Lila stretched. "I better check on my shop—my brother's managing today, and that's always a gamble."

"Thanks for the magical calories," Sera said with a grin.

"Don't mention it—unless they go to your hips." With a final wink, Lila darted across the street.

The parade done, it was time to face the cursed quilts. Glancing up at Fin, she called out, "Hey Fin, if anyone comes, tell them I'll be right back."

He saluted, and she headed behind the shops. Though tempted to stop and browse, she headed straight for the judging tent and stepped inside. Festival attendees wandered from one booth to another to examine the displays.

Reaching the quilt stall, she stepped inside and found it busy but subdued. No ribbons graced the walls. Perrin, wearing another colorful vest over a white cotton shirt, spotted her. "Head witch! Do you know the cause of the damaged quilts?"

The two owners of the quilts rushed over. "Yes, what happened?" They were no longer sniping at one another as both were victims.

Sera nodded. "I believe so. Perrin, I'd like you to clear this stall of all but the entrants."

Perrin immediately cleared the stall. When the last person left, leaving a dozen quilters standing in a tight group, he returned. "Done, Head witch."

"Thank you," she said. Glancing at the quilters, she waved her hand to the quilts and clothing displayed on the walls and smaller items like table runners and placemats on the tables. "I'd like everyone to please stand with your entry."

When everyone was positioned, Sera did a quiet and quick walk around the entire stall before going to Siobhan's quilt. As before, she saw the quilt as it should have been: the colors and quilting before the damage covered it. The same with Deirdre's. Another quilt showed just a hint of the same magic but not enough to distort the work.

"Will everyone please hold out your hands." A quick glance didn't reveal any traces of the cursing spell. Except one person, who quickly put her hands behind her back.

With a heavy sigh, she went to Marla. "You have traces of the spell on your quilt. And hands," she said gently.

Marla's face blanched, her hands trembling as she tried to hide them. "I—I must have touched their quilts ..."

Sera shook her head gently. "No, Marla. You touched your own, after casting the spell."

Siobhan rushed over. "Marla, why?"

The woman's shoulders sagged, tears welling. "I never win. I just wanted someone to like my quilt this year ..."

Staring at her hands, Marla let out a shaky breath. "You two always look down your nose at my work. I know I'm not as good a quilter, but I worked really hard on mine this year." She glanced up. "I didn't harm yours, Siobhan, or Deirdre's. It's temporary."

"Can you remove the spell?" Sera asked.

Nodding, shoulders hunched, Marla walked over and lightly touched each quilt. Immediately, each quilt reverted to its true form.

Perrin pointed his finger at Marla. "You should be disqualified and banned from ever entering another quilt again."

This time it was Deirdre who spoke up. "A bit harsh, Perrin." She glanced at her biggest rival every year. "I think we share blame in this. We've gotten arrogant and even mean-spirited in our desire to win."

Siobhan nodded. "I agree. I guess we've been a boastful couple of bullies, and I daresay we deserved this." She put her arm around Marla's shaking shoulders and glanced at the rest of the quilters. "I propose we gather as quilters, sharing a love of fabric and stitching and share our knowledge. Train up our competition. She met Deidre's eyes. "I'll open our shop to weekly quilt-alongs. Her gaze took in everyone. "And it is open to everyone, no matter your level. Time to pass this craft down to the young."

Deirdre nodded approvingly. "That sounds marvelous. I think the focus on winning has made us not so nice. Or honorable."

A round of applause broke out. Perrin waved at the quilts. "What about this year's awards?" he asked.

Sera glanced at the three women. "I think they are postponed until the next quilt show," she said firmly. She left after admiring everyone's work and even purchased a lovely quilted vest in shades of green with thread that glittered and a row of shimmering gold buttons in the shape of acorns.

She returned to her shop with a happy, satisfied smile. Her veil sight had revealed more than the truth of the quilts—it had shown her that her father was alive and near. If it could do that, perhaps it might also help her find the portal.

A group of women were waiting for her shop to open. A touch of her hand was all it took for Sera to unlock the door. "Welcome, ladies," she said, pleased to have customers. She motioned them inside and took her place behind her desk, where she stashed her bag and sunglasses.

Staring at the dark display screen of her computer, she chewed her lower lip. "Okay, you can do this." She placed her palm on the wooden surface and waited for the runes to appear. Choosing one, she shifted her computer and grinned when it powered up.

"You're catching on, Guardian," Syrus said as he popped onto his perch next to the counter.

"Syrus!" She held a hand over her heart. "Must you do that? Most birds just fly."

"Boring," Syrus cackled.

A low whisper drew Sera's attention.

"Hear that? Told you she was the new Guardian," murmured the rail-thin woman with short, dark hair—just loud enough for Sera to hear.

Her tall, well-dressed companion sniffed, chin tilted high, voice dripping disdain. "Guardian of what? Skeins and stitch markers?"

The third woman, steel-gray hair wound tight in a bun, pretended to admire a ball of glowing yarn. In a pointed undertone, she nudged her friend. "Sylvie's the proper leader, hosting the council's booth, while this one hides behind her little counter. That's what happens when you hand over an important role to an outsider."

The rail-thin woman gave a brittle laugh. "She didn't even grow up in Havenwood. How's she supposed to protect what she doesn't understand?"

Finally, the tall woman's gaze swept Sera from head to toe, unimpressed. "Her grandmother was Guardian, and what did that get us? A crumbling seal and neighbors living in fear. The old woman ran off. And this one will too."

Aghast at the rudeness, Sera straightened. It was clear to Sera that Sylvie had sent her little gang of vipers to undermine her authority as Council Head and Guardian. The women clearly wanted her to falter, to doubt herself—but their scorn only sharpened her resolve. She would protect this town, whether they believed in her or not—even if her own doubts lingered. Beneath her palm, the desk gave a faint, steady hum, as though Havenwood itself lent her strength.

Willow's ears flattened, her tail lashing sparks into the air. "Careful," she warned in a low, dangerous purr. "You trespass on more than a shop when you speak against the Guardian."

Syrus flapped his wings and landed with a thump on the counter. "Besides," he announced, his voice shrill, "jealousy doesn't age as well as wine. And none of you were bottled in Havenwood's best year."

The women gasped. "Well, if that is how you treat customers, it's no wonder this place is empty!"

Hissing, Willow's tail snapped over her back and head, pointing like an arrow at the door. Blue sparks flew over the heads of the women and slammed into the door, which flew open. "Better empty than filled with spiteful hags."

Syrus squawked, his voice harsh. "So polite, our Willow. Gives guests the chance to leave before they're tossed out on their ears."

One of the rude women sniffed. "Well, I never."

"Learned manners? Yes, yes, we can all agree on that score," Syrus agreed.

Biting her inner lip to keep from laughing at the antics of her crazy crew, Sera joined in by waving her hands, envisioning a small puff of air to help the undesirable customers on their way. "I believe you ladies have overstayed your welcome." She released her magic, her intent focused on showing the rude women the door. To her shock, the small puff she imagined turned into a full gust, sending the three women stumbling and flailing out the door.

Her eyebrows shot up. "Wow. Um, oops, didn't mean to do that!"

Syrus stretched out his wings. "Good job," he praised while Willow, with her eyes gleaming, licked one paw. "There is hope for you yet, Little Human."

As the laughter and comments continued, Sera noticed a hesitant figure at the open door, quiet and watchful, as though unsure whether to step inside.

# **Chapter Twenty-Three**

May 24 - Looms, Legends & Other Mental Breakdowns

A hesitant voice drifted through the doorway. "Is it okay to come in? I don't want to intrude." The woman cast a glance over her shoulder at the three women still muttering as they staggered away.

Sera wiped her tears with the heel of her hand. "Oh, my goodness—yes, please come in. Just—" She faltered, not sure how to explain why she'd just kicked out customers.

Syrus beat her to it. "Just tossing out the day's poor decisions."

Willow licked a paw. "Should've used the broom," she muttered.

Sera rolled her eyes. "Thanks, Syrus, and thank you, Willow." She turned toward her visitor. "Let me know if I can help you find anything."

The sun spilled into the shop from the open doorway and fell on the woman's dark glossy hair that shimmered with auburn highlights. She entered with grace and poise and a sheepish grin. "I don't know a thing about whatever one does with yarn. To be honest, I wanted to meet you, Miss Blackthorn." She came forward, slender hand outstretched. "Liana Stormrider, Ryker's sister. I'm staying in your cute cottage with my siblings." Her smile warmed her hazel eyes.

"Please call me Sera, and it's great to meet you." Sera took Liana's hand in her own. A sharp zing of power snapped in the air between them. Both women pulled back abruptly. "Wow, that's some spark," she said as she rubbed her palm with her other hand.

Liana, eyes wide, shook her own palm as if trying to disperse the shock. "And those women thought you weren't powerful? I'd say you have a strong core of power." Her voice was both impressed and incredulous.

Sera regarded her tenant. "I think that goes both ways," she murmured. So, she too carried a sense of being more than she appeared. She waved her hand toward the counter. "The cat is Willow. Be warned, she likes to go through walls. And sometimes people. And the sassy and snarky bird is Syrus. Not sure what he is."

Liana giggled, and the awkward moment passed. "Ryker is out there doing his book signing, and Elyn, a family friend, is with him."

She wrinkled her nose. "My brothers are still sleeping—creatures of the night the lot of them. With nothing to do but enjoy this wonderful town, I thought I'd come see your shop—book signings are a bit boring," she confided with a playful grin.

Fin rushed in, interrupting the exchange. "Is everything all right? He stared out the door where the rude women had regained their feet but not their dignity. They stormed past the shop, their loud mutterings carrying inside.

Rolling her eyes, Sera said, "A bit late, Fin. Sleeping?"

"Uh, went to check out the famous author signing his books."

Sera tipped her head to one side. "You read fantasy?"

He snapped his fingers, and a copy of Ryker's book appeared. "I do now." He grinned. Once again, he glanced out the door.

"Everything is fine here. Just a couple of rude ladies."

"Questioning whether our girl here is a true Guardian," Syrus explained.

"Or even a witch," Willow growled. She glanced at the bird. "We showed them."

Syrus cackled. "That we did, Your Majesty."

Willow narrowed her eyes. She pointed her tail at the bird, and a shower of sparks flew toward him. "Told you not to call me that, you foolish bird."

Sera ignored the bickering. Fin floated up the staircase and lounged on the rail and watched as Liana plucked a midnight-dyed skein of moon-blessed yarn from the shelf, her fingers moving with the grace of someone who might not understand threads but could feel the magic in the yarn.

But it wasn't the yarn that caught Sera's attention—it was the way the edges of the woman's form shimmered faintly, like starlight seen through glass or on a patch of fresh snow. Power cloaked her like frost, not like heat rising off stone as she felt when around Ryker, whose image flickered with something primal, and she didn't have that ghosting effect like her father. Hers was ... different. Rooted. Ancient.

"You're not what you seem," Sera said softly.

Liana brushed the yarn across her cheek and arched a brow. "Perceptive as well," she murmured. "And what do I seem?"

Embarrassed to speak her thoughts aloud, Sera hesitated, but the words came unbidden. "I see what others cannot see. It's not about how you look, or not exactly. It's what I feel. There's more to you. Your power ... it's like Ryker's. Old, not borrowed, not learned. It's ... born." Sera shook her head. The depth of her certainty, her intuition, surprised her, but she added, "Forgive me for being outspoken."

Liana smiled—not amused, not alarmed. Just curious. For just a moment, something flickered behind her eyes. A flash of sorrow or pride. Or both. Then she shrugged and said simply, "One could say the same for you, Guardian. While your power is young yet, your blood is not, and it doesn't forget."

Sera drew her lower lip between her teeth and let out a loud sigh. For reasons she didn't understand, she felt a connection to Liana and a trust she didn't feel with many. "Those women, while nasty and rude, have a point," she whispered. "I am the Guardian, but I don't even know where the portal is or how to destroy it." She turned away and paced the length of the shop, her fingers touching various skeins of yarn as though drawing comfort from the fibers.

"The seal is weakening," Liana offered. She shrugged. "Yes, I feel it. Most who are tied to the land feel it."

"My dreams ..." Sera let her voice drift.

"Dreams?" Liana moved closer.

Sera glanced at each person in her shop: Liana, Fin, Willow, and Syrus. She recalled her grandmother's advice in the journal—to seek help—that she didn't have to do this alone. So, instead of feeling awkward or crazy, she shared her thoughts. Whatever Ryker and Liana were, they were powerful. Especially if the woman could feel the weakening seal.

Sera picked up a ball of yarn, more to steady her hands than out of interest. "I've had several," she admitted slowly. "Dreams. Nightmares. A forest path ... a lake beneath the moon. And an island where I think I saw the portal."

Fin slid down the rail. His eyes sharpened. "You saw the portal?"

Her laugh was thin, uncertain. "Maybe. I don't know. But there was another world beyond it—beautiful, with two pink moons."

Fin closed his eyes, his voice hushed. "You saw Thyron."

When he met her gaze, his eyes shone with something Sera couldn't identify. A combination of pain and hope radiated from his silvery-green eyes.

Sera's throat tightened. "I think so. But the seal—it closed when something evil tried to break through. The shadows screamed." She shuddered, hugging herself.

Fin's eyes were wide, his movements uncharacteristically jerky. "Sera, you must find it. Find the portal."

"It was a dream, Fin. There aren't any lakes in Havenwood. And my latest dream led me to a cave where someone watched me." She hesitated. "From inside the stone as though he was one with the stone. He whispered the name Saoirse. I felt his pain. His anguish."

She tossed the ball of yarn back into its display bin. "She's my ancestor, but how does that help me find the portal?"

Silence stretched, heavy. Liana stepped closer, lowering her voice as though sharing something forbidden. "My people speak of a legend. Lovers whose love was forbidden. To save both realms, they sacrificed themselves to seal the gate." Her gaze flicked to Sera. "Drakon, my ancestor, was Sentinel of that gateway. Ryker now carries that title."

Sera blinked. That fit with what she'd read that morning from Aisling's diary entry, who'd grieved over the loss of her twin. "And I'm a Guardian. That means—" She wasn't sure what it meant.

Syrus shook out his feathers. "The portal was sealed by two. Two hearts joined to seal it. It cannot be done by one."

"So Ryker is here for the same reason I am: to destroy the portal and keep these evil creatures from entering our world." Sera felt a moment of relief that she wasn't alone in this quest. She glanced around, seeking confirmation. Syrus opened his beak to speak, but nothing came out but a few clicks. A glance down at Willow made her heart drop to her toes. The cat sat with its head hung low. She glanced up, her eyes colorless.

"No, Seraphina," she said, using Sera's full name, something she had never done before.

"I don't understand." A clacking and whirling noise in the back of the shop had her whipping around. The back room shimmered, a gentle pulse of magic calling to her like a plucked thread vibrating in the air.

"The loom," she breathed as she hurried to the back of the shop. She stepped into the alcove, her breath catching. Fin and Liana crowded close. Golden threads appeared as the loom wove a new message: *Only ashes end the threat.*

"What does that mean?" Her voice broke off.

A memory stirred—Syrus, the night he had given her the oathstone, telling her that destruction, not containment, was the only way. She'd brushed it off at thinking he meant the portal that connected the two worlds.

She turned to Syrus, who'd flown silently to join them. "Syrus, what does this mean?" Her voice rose as panic set in.

Syrus, his voice sounding old, spoke so softly, she barely heard him. "We thought sealing the portal entrance would be enough. It was not." His gaze sharpened, the violet color darkening to a soulless black as he held Sera's gaze. He shook his head sadly. "Portals can be replaced in time," he said.

Sera reacted with horror. "But that means—I—"

Fin went white. He gripped Sera by the shoulders. "No!" Catching himself, he released her. "I mean—there has to be another way."

Gazing into his stricken and pain-filled eyes, she did not respond. Not yet. Deep down, she knew. She glanced around at the stunned faces of those in the room. Liana turned away, her shoulders hunched as though in great pain. Willow faded until she was nearly transparent, and Syrus's vibrant feathers dulled.

The loom continued to weave; the tapestry shifted like a movie. Two worlds formed, one of earth, forest, and sea, and the other with a pink sky, two moons, and glowing fauna. Then came darkness. It seeped from the world of Thyron and spilled across Earth, a hungry dark fog that devoured all it touched.

The full realization struck hard and lodged in Sera's throat, and the room tilted. She doubled over. Her chest cinched tight, each breath strangled before it reached her lungs. Her thoughts scattered like frightened birds. The room seemed to shrink, walls pressing closer, her own heartbeat pounding in her ears like war drums. She couldn't breathe. Couldn't think. She couldn't bear the truth clawing its way into her heart.

Destroying the portal had sounded like locking a closed door, but now she realized it wasn't just a passage. It was a lifeline that had to be destroyed, and that meant destroying all that lay beyond it.

She dropped her head into her hands and moaned. Her choice wasn't just to protect Havenwood Cove and the rest of the world, but to sacrifice Thyron itself. Liana helped her up. With trembling legs, she watched the ultimate message appear, which confirmed her worst fears.

*SACRIFICE.*

"No! You can't ask that of her!" Fin cried out in anguish. His eyes were wild. "There has to be another way—has to be." He vanished with a shimmer—like slipping away before the truth could take hold.

The loom shuddered, threads snapping like brittle bones. Havenwood's magic seemed to hold its breath, waiting for her answer.

Her gaze locked on the trembling loom. Her knees buckled, and she stumbled, would have fallen had Liana not snagged her arm. How could she sacrifice an entire world to save another world. Her world?

###

Late afternoon found Ryker sitting outside in the cooling afternoon breeze. He sat at an antique golden table polished to a high luster, a piece that looked more suited to a royal dining hall than a festival. Piles of his novels covered the surface, their metallic titles catching the slanting gold of the late afternoon sun. Fairy lights overhead blinked to life, glowing faintly as shadows lengthened across the cobblestone entry that led into the bookstore. Elyn slid another copy across the narrow space.

Ryker glanced at the line of fans, which showed no sign of ending. But he smiled and gave each reader his full attention. He considered signings a necessary evil—something most authors either yearned to do or felt duty-bound. He supposed he landed somewhere between the two.

Without his fans, he wouldn't be a successful author, but he'd rather be pounding his keys or just staring at that blank page on his monitor. Lately, he was stuck rereading old pages, hoping new words would come. Unfortunately, every night when he tried to write, he'd fall into a dream. Or nightmare. He clenched his hand around his pen. It was frankly pissing him off. A not so gentle nudge from Elyn reminded him where he was. He quickly regained control of his emotions. He could not afford to give in to frustration or anger.

"You okay?" Elyn slipped another book in front of him.

"Yeah. Thanks."

He smiled at the dark-haired woman in a heavy cloak. "Who should I make it out to?"

"Talia," she answered in a low voice, barely above a whisper.

He scrawled her name across the title page, adding one of his usual inscriptions. *Enjoy the adventure*, he offered.

Her fingers brushed his as she took it—cold despite the warmth of the day. She gave him a thin smile, then moved into the crowd.

Something about her retreat left him cold. Too careful. Too quiet. As though she carried her own shadow with her.

The fairy lights overhead glowed brighter as the sunlight faded. Shadows stretched long across the cobbled path. The festival was shifting toward evening. The next reader stepped up. Elyn passed another book across the table. Ryker signed it, then another. The line inched forward. Laughter and chatter ebbed and flowed like the tide. But the unsettled feeling remained.

He was halfway through signing his name when it happened. A flare beneath his skin—not sharp, not searing, but undeniable. The dragon tattoo on his shoulder burned like embers stirred by a phantom wind. The pen nearly slipped from his grasp. Heat curled up his spine. Not from the dwindling warmth of the spring day or the press of bodies from the crowd. This came from somewhere deeper. Older. As if something long asleep had shifted in its slumber.

He inhaled sharply. The world tilted—just for a moment. Like the tide pulling sand from beneath his feet. Familiar, yet wrong.

"Ryker?"

Elyn's voice cut through the hush that had settled in his ears. Sound returned. So did motion.

Ryker blinked and forced a smile for the woman waiting for her signed copy of his novel. "Fine," he murmured, more to himself than Elyn. "Just ... something."

Elyn raised an eyebrow. "Magic?"

Ryker nodded slowly. "Maybe." But it didn't feel like magic in the spellbook sense. This wasn't cast. It was *called*.

The tattoo's burn dulled, but the strange pull remained. Not a pain. A presence. A thread tugged at his core. Heat coiled beneath his skin, threads of fire winding through his veins. His breath hitched, his pulse quickened—not from the crowd's noise, but from something older, deeper, pressing awake.

*Seraphina.*

Not a whisper. A summons.

Not just a call. A *need*.

A memory stirred—her laugh, the way her eyes caught starlight. He didn't know why or how—but he knew exactly where he needed to be. He stood, the crowd blurring to shadows. Only one truth burned clear—Sera.

# Chapter Twenty-Four

May 24 - Save One World. Destroy Another. Try Not to Cry

The sun slid from the sky and dipped into the ocean, casting the festival in shades of amber and indigo. Floating lanterns swayed gently above the booths, their soft, golden glow unnoticed by Sera as she wove past booths, blind to laughter and the scent of cinnamon and sugar. She was blind, deaf, and closed off to the celebrations of life.

How could she appreciate the celebration and laughter around her when lives were at stake? If she refused to destroy Thyron, she put her world at risk, yet there had to be innocents in Thyron. After all, many of those here came from that other world. Pausing, she took a good look around her. She found joy, people greeting friends and family and having a good time. But inside, she felt only despair.

Holding the oathstone in her hand, she rubbed the smooth amber. It warmed, felt almost alive. Around her wrist, the gemstone bracelet gleamed and winked as though each stone felt a connection to the stone Syrus had given her.

At a booth selling wood carvings, she spotted Bram with a woman and three children. Another woman with an infant in her arms held the hand of a screaming toddler as they hurried past. Sera's gaze scanned the crowd. Mixed among the humans were witches, gnomes, goblins, Rootlings, Fae, and more. Human and non-human, co-existing.

A terrible knowing weighed her down. If all these tribes had originated from Thyron, whether they came to Earth to find a new life or were forced into slavery, then these people had family—ancestors—living in another world. How could she choose?

Save one world. Destroy another.

Bile rose and burned her throat. She glanced off into the distance where the magical forest created a wall to keep Havenwood Cove safe from the outside world. Golden orbs cast the canopy of trees into a golden glow. The Mother. What of her? Was there a "Mother" in this other world?

Somewhere, the seal on the portal connecting the two worlds weakened. Dark energy demanded entrance. Why? For what purpose? Enslave an entire planet? Destroy Earth? Did the answer lie with the legend and a forbidden love? "I don't know," she moaned.

She forced herself to breathe, to stay present, to pretend the cobbled streets weren't trembling beneath her feet. Children darted past in glittering costumes, wings flapping, faces streaked with paint and joy.

A voice drew her attention. "Dad, look, the lights are floating. There aren't any strings or cords."

The tall man holding the young boy's hand smiled patiently. "Of course there are, son. See, they are there. Lights don't float." He hesitated, glancing at his wife, a small, petite woman with pointed ears.

She smiled knowingly and patted his shoulder. He groaned. "Ah, okay. Magic. I get it," he said, staring hard at the colorful bulbs hanging over the festival like a net of lights.

How many families like that one would vanish if she made the wrong choice? Her heart and mind felt heavy as she continued to move through the crowd like a ghost in her own life, smiling when expected, nodding when needed. The truth sat heavy on her shoulders. To save Havenwood Cove—no, all of life on Earth—she might have to destroy a world she'd only glimpsed in dreams.

*Thyron.* And with dusk bleeding into night, she felt it—magic shifting, rising, warning that something was coming. The countdown had begun, and whatever waited knew it.

Sera inhaled. Something was off. The air tasted wrong. Not just festival magic or stray enchantments in the wind. This was targeted. Tense. Watching. Waiting.

"How can I choose which world deserves to survive?" Most pressing, could she? Her new mantra of where there's a will, there's a way echoed in her mind but this time, it didn't give her courage or confidence. In her heart, she knew she could not destroy innocent life, even if it lived on an enemy world.

"Miss Sera! Miss Sera! Come see!"

Spotting Ella waving madly from a booth, she pasted on a smile and entered the booth selling souvenirs. The girl pointed to the blue ribbon pinned to her shirt. "Look! First place for the best decorated Velwynth."

"Wow, that's great. Congratulations, Ella."

The two boys, Ella's constant companions, rolled their eyes. "No living with her now."

As soon as Ella shot them a fierce look, Liam nudged Nate with his elbow and said, "Her yarn changes color." He grinned. "Seriously cool, Ella."

"Yeah," Nate added. "Our potion worked too," he added.

Ella's dad, Jake, joined them and greeted Sera. "Found out this trio were planning to spike drinks with a potion that would turn people's skin color."

Sera's jaw dropped. "Seriously?" She narrowed her eyes. "I thought you were all up to no good in the shop."

All three bowed their heads, the picture of guilt. Jake laughed. "Pretty good potion too."

Forcing a laugh, she was about to congratulate them on their ingenuity when Sera caught sight of a dark flash slicing through the air from the other side of the street—like an invisible bullet. It twisted like smoke, slithering through the air, leaving behind a trail of reddish glimmering energy. Sera narrowed her eyes, and her heart sped up.

Using her veil sight to keep it in sight, she reflexively lifted a hand. "Not today," she snarled. "You picked the wrong witch. Return to your caster, but do no lasting harm." With that, she focused her intent and sent the spell whipping back through the air—clean, precise, like threading a needle with fury.

It flew toward Sylvie, who was walking among the rude women Sera had ousted from her shop that morning. Their eyes locked. Sera braced for impact. But the spell flew past the woman and her friends.

"Well, okay, she didn't fire that one off. She's just a nasty troublemaker, not the one trying to kill me." So who, she wondered, besides Sylvie, hated her enough to attack not once but three times? There wasn't any reaction from anyone else that Sera could see.

"Nice catch," Ryker said as he suddenly appeared in front of her.

Sera gasped and stumbled back a few steps. "Where did you come from?"

He shrugged, his mesmerizing blue eyes holding hers. "Thought you might need help deflecting that. Don't like sneaks," he said, his voice deepening to a low, rumbling growl.

"You saw the spell?"

He nodded. "Who dares to attack the Guardian?"

She shrugged. "Not sure. Not the person I thought it was." She absently rubbed her Oathstone. She frowned. The stone felt warmer.

Hot, even. She dropped her gaze to the amber. The darkness inside, shaped like half a heart, pulsed. No—beat. As though an actual heart was trapped within. She held it out from her skin. "What the heck?"

Ryker's eyes were wide as he stared at her stone. "Sera. What is that?" He reached out and touched it.

"Something Syrus—" The stone, as though awakened by his touch, flared to life like a lit match. The ground beneath their feet shook, lights in the booth flickered, and the canvas tent rustled then swayed as the ground swelled and bucked as though from an earthquake. The children screamed as the booth swayed violently, the poles giving way and the canopy flapping wildly. Sera tried to protect the children as lanterns flew at them. Jake rushed over and grabbed the kids.

Ryker's arms went around Sera, tucking her against his chest as he pulled her out the back of the tent.

Crushed between them, the stone pulsed like a third heartbeat. It grew hot against her, burning her. She heard a voice in her head.

*I, Drakon, claim Ryker of the Stormriders.*

For a moment, Sera stared into Ryker's shocked gaze. Syrus's Oathstone recognized Ryker. "What?"

With a cry of something more than pain, Ryker wretched free, one hand covering his chest where a burn mark had seared through his black tee shirt.

Sera cried out and pulled his hand away. "Oh my god, Ryker." The hole in his shirt was the exact size and shape of her stone. His flesh beneath the hole in his shirt was red. Raw. Angry and blistering.

His eyes, so dark a blue, blazed fire as they bore into hers. "What did you do to me?" he whispered, his voice barely audible.

"Ryker?"

He stumbled back. One step. Then two. His hands held his head as though in great pain.

"Ryker! I don't know what happened." The confusion and agony on his twisted features tore her apart. Somehow, she'd caused this. Her hand went to her stone, which was warm but no longer hot. She quickly tucked it beneath her shirt.

She reached out to Ryker, but he turned and ran as though the hounds of hell were after him.

Shaken, confused, Sera followed, but he put on a burst of speed, and in the blink of an eye, he was gone.

The burn flared beneath his skin and spread, every cell catching fire. The tattoo on his arm blazed, and deep inside, everything shifted. He heard Elyn shouting, but he didn't stop. Couldn't. And then he couldn't hear his friend over the voice in his head—couldn't hear anything or anyone.

Pain radiated through his body. Something crawled from his shoulder, rippling across to his chest, slithering into his mind. He screamed—raw, guttural, the sound dragged from some place deeper than fear.

*It is time*, a gravelly voice cut through his mind with the precision of a surgical knife.

His insides felt squeezed, as though wrapped in a band of steel. It tightened, forcing him to halt his retreat. "What is happening?" he cried out. He braced his hands on his thighs and fought to regain control of his breath, his mind, his body. He glanced at the tattoo on his shoulder that burned as though it were raw. Instead of the head of a dragon that had replaced the dragon scale tattoo he'd carried since birth, there was an image of a complete dragon. As he watched in horror, the tail coiled around his forearm.

Elyn appeared out of nowhere, having shifted to follow Ryker. "Ryker, what the hell is going on?"

He could only shake his head.

*We are one. Two into one*, the voice chanted.

Ryker's vision blurred as his tattoo moved across his chest, growing larger. The tail wrapped around his waist. It pulsed, not like ink, but like a living legacy. A binding.

*You carry my blood. My shape. My vow.*

"No," Ryker groaned. "I carry my fate." He struck his fist into the dirt, trying to hold onto the earth, to the now.

But the ground did not hold him. And the past did not loosen its grip.

*You are the last Sentinel. The fire-forged end of our line. We sealed the gateway. Now you must unmake it. Or burn with it.*

Ryker shook his head violently. "No," he shouted again. "I didn't ask for any of this!"

A ghost of laughter echoed across his thoughts.

*That is why you were chosen.*

Elyn shook his shoulders. "Ryker, what the hell is happening to you?"

"Go away," Ryker demanded.

"Ryker," Elyn began.

Ryker turned his tormented gaze onto his best friend. "Not you." Ryker's voice cracked. "*Him.*"

Elyn frowned. "Who?"

Ryker ripped off his burned t-shirt, revealing the living tattoo on his chest.

"What in the hell?" Elyn's jaw dropped. "A full dragon—and it moves!" He jumped back when the head with blazing blue eyes turned toward him.

Ryker dropped his head back. "It was bad enough when Grandfather died and I inherited his tattoo. But this? How did *she* do this?"

"Who, Ryker? Who did this?"

"Sera."

Ryker fisted the shirt, revealed the burned fabric, and covered the healing burn on his chest. "The stone she wears. It did this."

Something coiled inside him—scales of heat and memory rising like smoke. His limbs felt wrong, too small for what stirred beneath his skin.

*The past and the present have become one.*

"Who the hell are you?" Ryker demanded, pressing his hand hard over the dragon.

The tattoo shifted, moving to his arm. *I am Drakon. The first sentinel. And you, Ryker of the Stormriders, are the last.*

Ryker straightened and smacked his fist into the palm of his other hand. "No! I. Refuse."

A low chuckle rumbled through his mind. *To be so young and foolish. Choices are illusions.*

Ryker felt it crawling inside him—his body, his mind. His emotions, nearly out of control, awakened the beast within, which demanded freedom, while the voice in his head demanded obedience. Unable to do either, Ryker ran for the cliff.

"I am not yours," he shouted to the voice in his head.

The cliffs loomed ahead, the sea raging below, the air strangely still—as though the world itself held its breath, waiting for him to fall or be claimed by the sea.

# Chapter Twenty-Five

May 24 - The Weight of What Comes Next and My Renter is a What?

*What did you do to me?*

Ryker's anguished cry echoed in her head. What had she done? Her fingers closed over the stone—it was warm, though it had blistered his skin.

Why? How? She needed answers. Driven by the desperate need to see Ryker, Sera ran down Main Street, but when she left the lights and gaiety behind, she paused, her gaze searching, seeking him with her veil sight.

A faint bluish-green blur halfway up the hillside caught her attention. She ran in that direction but didn't get far before she tripped over a hidden stone and fell, landing on her hands and knees. Jumping up, she cursed under her breath. How could he move so fast? She'd never catch up with him, especially in the dark.

Recalling the way his image always appeared distorted, and the speed at which he ran, she grabbed her head, her fingers tangling in her wind-blown curls. "What are you, Ryker? *Fae?*"

She thought of Fin and sucked in a breath. *Shifting.* Lila had told her Fae could shift—could she? Desperation roared through her, and magic answered. The world snapped sideways as though she'd been hooked and yanked from her own skin.

Keeping her eyes on the hillside, she spoke firmly. "Take me to him. Take me to Ryker."

As though caught on a fishing lure, magic yanked her off her feet. The world blurred—her stomach lurched, and before she could draw in a breath to cry out, she tumbled across the ground, stopped by one of the stone benches overlooking the cliff. Staggering, she held onto the back of the bench as she fought a wave of sickness.

"Ryker," she gasped, spotting him at the edge of the cliff. His outline shimmered, as though there were two of him.

Ryker whirled around, his eyes a wild stormy blue and his long, dark hair a halo around his head, though there was no wind. His eyes blazed. Burned. Not with fear, but with fury. For one heartbeat, their gazes locked. "Stay. Away," he gasped.

"Please, Ryker!" she cried as she crawled and stumbled forward. "I'm sorry. For whatever I did. Please, come back."

"Too late," he shouted as his outline fractured—one form overlapping another. Shadows twisted around him, not cast by any light. "Not supposed to be me!" He turned his back on her, and with a loud roar of pain, he leaped.

"No!" She lunged forward. Strong arms grabbed her from behind, jerking her back from the edge of the cliff where Ryker had stood. She fought to get free, wild with panic.

"Let me go! Ryker!" she screamed, struggling to get free. The world tilted and spun. Her stomach lurched, and to her horror, she doubled over, violently sick.

"Breathe, Guardian. You're not used to this. First shift always hits hardest." Elyn's arms tightened around her as if bracing them both against the unbearable.

Sera closed her eyes and leaned back in Elyn's arms and waited for her world to steady. Shifting? Her last memory was of the festival—the pain in Ryker's eyes, his voice, and her desperate need to reach him. And then the wild surge of magic tearing her loose from everything.

"I—shifted?" Her magic obeyed—not because she knew how, but because she needed it too. Urgency had become her spell. Later, she'd reflect on that ability and what it meant.

But right now, all she cared about was Ryker. "Elyn," she gasped. "I—did something—to hurt him—don't know what—" She struggled to get free.

"Let me go." She tore free and stumbled toward the hedge. It grew a foot taller, letting her know she was safe, that it wouldn't let her follow Ryker. Yet it had allowed Ryker to jump. "Why?"

The ground beneath her trembled with pounding footsteps. Ryker's siblings rushed around both her and Elyn, who stood behind Sera. Tears streamed down her cheeks as she met Liana's gaze. "He—he jumped," she whispered. "He just—" Her voice broke. "He jumped!"

Before she could say anything more, offer an apology, anything, Ryker's brothers and sister all shimmered, their outlines growing as they dived headfirst after Ryker.

Shocked speechless, Sera sagged against Elyn, unable to breathe. The world tilted, and she pressed her fist into her stomach. "I'm going crazy. I've passed out, and this is a nightmare." She leaned her head back and closed her eyes.

"Sera! Look!" Elyn gently cupped her face and turned her head. "There, Sera. They are safe."

The air shimmered, thrumming deep in her bones. Within the glow, something massive ripped free of shadow and sky. Wings, vast and gleaming, carved the night. The cliff shook with the downbeat of power. A roar tore through the heavens—anguished, triumphant, undeniable.

Ryker.

She shook uncontrollably. "What?" she whispered. "Can't be? Can it?" Glancing at Elyn, who'd moved to stand beside her, one arm across her shoulders, she asked, "Dragons? Dragons are real?"

Elyn smiled grimly, pride mingled with pain flickering in his eyes as he pointed skyward where, one by one, other Dragons rose to soar into the stars. Two midnight-dark, one pure white, their powerful forms circled Ryker like a flock guarding their own.

The air crackled with magic, and below her, the cliff pulsed in reaction. But was it fear, recognition, or welcome? The barrier hummed, its energy vibrating up her spine.

Sera gripped one of the thick vines. Her chest ached, and she drew in a deep breath. The down sweep of massive wings stirring the air stole her breath. "By the moon's last breath," she whispered, wonder and terror mingling in her throat.

"There be *Dragons* in Havenwood."

Elyn nodded. "Indeed. There are dragons."

Her entire world shifted yet again as she struggled to accept another impossibility. Ryker was a Dragon. The dragons vanished into cloud and starlight, their roars echoing like thunder over the sea.

Still reeling, Sera stumbled back to the stone seating circle and dropped onto one of the curved benches. Around her, the twilight deepened, casting the garden in shadows and silver. Deep down, she'd always known Ryker wasn't just a man. He was more. And now, the truth had wings.

What she'd just seen rewrote everything she knew or believed. The myths were real. And Ryker—he wasn't just part of this story: He was the story.

The last echoes of Ryker's roar rolled out over the sea. A beat later, thunder answered from the heavens, and the wind whipped her curls into her face. The skies darkened, heavy with a storm too perfectly timed to be coincidence.

Elyn's arm tightened around her shoulders as he nodded toward the horizon. "Storm's coming, and they'll be out all night. We should go inside."

Sera hugged herself tighter. As if she needed more chaos tonight. "Creatures of the night," she murmured, recalling Liana's words about her brothers. Her world still spun out of control, but the storm's fury echoed the tempest in her chest.

Lightning split the sky over the sea. She straightened, her voice cutting through the thunder. "No. The storm is here." She jabbed a finger into her chest. "And I've got a few things to say to that man."

She tipped her head back and stared at the sky—where dragons were now apparently a thing. Her mental to-do list was getting out of hand.

Save one world.

Destroy another.

Confront her renter about the "No Pets" clause.

And maybe most importantly—figure out if falling for said renter was the worst idea she'd ever had.

Stars pierced the dusky sky, and somewhere out there, Ryker flew above them—no longer hiding what he was. And neither would she. She was the Guardian. And with Ryker in the skies, her story was no longer just hers—it was theirs.

The End

Turn the Page for a Special Bonus Scene

# Bonus Scene: Ryker's Flight

The world split open inside him as he jumped off the cliff. Fire in his veins, thunder in his bones. Wings—impossible, searing wings—ripped free as he plunged from the cliffs into the storm.

When his wings unfurled, the heavens answered. Lightning slashed the clouds, thunder cracked like the roar of another beast, and the air smelled of ozone and salt. The storm rose with him, wild and furious, as though the sky itself rebelled at the truth unleashed.

The ocean rose to claim him, black waves clawing upward, the salt stinging his eyes, but the dragon carried him higher, higher, until the wind screamed through his chest. Pain lanced through every muscle. His skin throbbed where Sera's stone had burned its mark into him, the brand searing as though her mark was carved into his soul. He tried to fight it. Tried to cling to the man he had been.

*What did you do to me?* But no answer came. Only the voice that was not his own, ancient and relentless.

*We are one. You cannot escape what you are.*

He roared, the sound tearing across the coastline, half-human anguish, half-dragon fury. He banked against the storm winds, desperate to outfly the agony, desperate to silence the voice that whispered destiny into his bones. He flew into the storm, became the storm, adding flames of fire to the cracking bolts of lightning spider-webbing across the clouds.

Surrounding him, his brothers and sister gave him the space he desperately needed. Time blurred—minutes, hours, he couldn't tell—as the storm raged and the night bled deeper around him. When the faint glow of dawn lightened the clouds, exhaustion dragged at his wings, muscles trembling, every beat a battle. He'd pushed too far—both man and dragon fraying at the edges. He reluctantly circled back toward Havenwood, heart heavy as the tide.

Below, the town slept, unaware of the monster above their rooftops. Unaware of the man unraveling in the sky. And then he saw her. On the bench next to the cliff, a small figure curled beside Elyn, a shield above them to protect her from the elements. The brightness of her red-gold hair called to him. Waiting. As if she had believed he would return.

His chest tightened until it nearly shattered. He wanted to land. To tell her everything. To let her chase away the darkness.

*Saoirse.* The anguish and longing of the voice in his head tightened his gut.

*No, she is not yours,* he responded silently. Though exhausted, the Dragon shifted restlessly within him, warning, not yet. Not safe—for her, for me. And so he circled once, a shadow stirring the air above her, before the clouds swallowed him again. He left her waiting, and the emptiness of that choice hollowed him more than the night.


The story of Havenwood Cove continues in **Book Two, SECRETS, SPELLS & SHADOWS.**

# Dawn's Embrace Shawl

Crochet Pattern

The **Dawn's Embrace Shawl** reflects the triangular shape of the shawl, much like the rays of the rising sun, symbolizing new beginnings. Dawn represents the start of Sera's new life, one full of promise and possibility. The "Embrace" captures the comforting, protective nature of the shawl as it wraps around her, offering warmth and renewal, just as she is learning to embrace her journey of self-discovery and healing.

This shawl is based on the timeless **Granny Stitch**, reimagined into a graceful triangular shape.

Materials

**Yarn**: DK Weight (suggested: Wendy's Wonders—Croma Hue). Gradient yarns create a nice flow of colors, but any yarn will work. You can also change colors at intervals if desired (note: this will create more ends to weave in).

Hook: 4mm (G) or size that complements your yarn for desired drape.

Abbreviations (US Terms)

Ch = Chain

DC = Double Crochet

SL ST = Slip Stitch

Turn = Turn work

[ ] = Work all stitches within brackets into the same ch-space

Repeat * *** instructions as indicated

Project Notes

DK weight yarn–ch-2 between 3-dc clusters works well.

Worsted or bulky yarn, use a ch-3 between clusters to maintain an open, airy structure.

**Foundation Ring:** Magic Ring (search online for video tutorials). OR ch5, join with sl st in first chain to make a circle.

Row 1

Ch 4 (counts as dc + ch-1 throughout).

Work 3 dc, ch 2, 3 dc, ch 1, dc all into the ring.

Row 2

Ch 4 (equals dc + ch-1), turn.

3 dc in the first ch-1 space, ch 1.

[3 dc, ch 2, 3 dc] in the ch-2 space, ch 1.

3 dc in the next ch-1 space, ch 1.

Dc in the last stitch (3rd ch of starting ch-4 from the previous row).

Row 3

Ch 4 (equals dc + ch-1), turn.

*3 dc in next ch-1 space, ch 1; repeat from * to ch-2 space.

In the ch-2 space, work [3 dc, ch 2, 3 dc], ch 1.

*3 dc in next ch-1 space, ch 1; repeat from * across, ending with a dc in the last stitch (as in Row 2).

Repeat Row 3

Continue repeating Row 3 until the shawl reaches your desired size.

"Magic's like yarn; it entangles those who pull too hard"

# Coming Soon

Secrets, Spells & Shadows (Book 2)

Charms, Curses & Clues (Book 3)


Secrets, Spells & Shadows
A Guardian who can't walk away. A Sentinel who can't let go.
Havenwood Cove's fate depends on both.

Sera thought surviving the Bloom & Moon Festival was the hardest test she would face. But Havenwood Cove has other plans.
Ryker's secret is out, the fragile magic sealing the portal is beginning to unravel, and someone clearly doesn't want Sera in Havenwood Cove. Shadows and danger stalk her every step, and Sera must uncover the mysteries buried in the town's past before they consume its future.
With the town depending on her—and a reluctant Sentinel Dragon shifter at her side—Sera has to decide who she can trust and what she's willing to risk. Because being Guardian isn't just about protecting magic. It's about protecting the people she loves most.

Don't miss the next magical chapter in the Havenwood Cove series. Sign up for Susie's newsletter for early news and access to the Secret Library filled with extra content.

# Dear Reader

Thank you for spending time in Havenwood Cove with Sera, Willow, Syrus, and the rest of the crew. I hope their story brought you a little magic, laughter, and heart along the way. Writing this book has been such a joy for me, and knowing it found its way into your hands means the world.

If you enjoyed this story, I'd be so grateful if you left a review. Your words help other readers discover Havenwood Cove—and they truly make a difference for authors like me.

Want to keep the magic going? You can join my newsletter for behind-the-scenes peeks, updates on upcoming books, and a touch of cozy fun.

You can also connect with me and fellow readers on my Facebook page and in the reader group Whiskers, Brews & Books, where we chat about life, books, cats, and of course, Havenwood Cove. From the bottom of my heart—thank you for reading. I can't wait to share the next chapter of this adventure with you.

With gratitude and magic,

Susie Swenson

P.S. If you'd like to linger a little longer, I've tucked away something special for you—**The Lost Chapters of Havenwood Cove.** These are the unedited, unrevised, uncorrected opening scenes that didn't make it into the final book … but still carry a bit of Havenwood Cove's heart.

You can download them (along with free crochet patterns) in my **Secret Library** here: susieswenson.com/secretlibrary (need to subscribe to the newsletter for the password)

**Let's stay connected!**

https://susieswenson.com/

https://www.facebook.com/susieswenson2/

https://www.facebook.com/groups/whiskersbrewsbooks

https://susieswenson.com/subscribe-to-my-newsletter-2/

# Praise For Susie Swenson

## MAGIC, MIRTH & MAYHEM

"Whimsical and charming — sprinkled with light and shadow, and filled with a deep wave of relatability. A magical, heartfelt read that wraps you in warmth." *~Annmarie, Best Books* (https://bestbooks89.blogspot.com)

"Sera's newly discovered life at Havenwood Cove is filled with intrigue, laughter, friendship, mystery and magic. Lots of Magic.

Magic, Mirth & Mayhem had me hooked from the first page and kept me smiling, intrigued, and thoroughly engaged! Joining Sera on her journey and witnessing her magical adventures along with moments of self-discovery was an absolute joy. Loved it!" *~Pam, early reader*.

# About the Author

**Susie Swenson** writes cozy fantasy mysteries where magic weaves through everyday life, seaside towns hide ancient secrets, and courage is found in unexpected places. Her Havenwood Cove series blends heart, humor, and a sense of wonder, inviting readers into a world where talking cats, enchanted houses, and second chances are part of the adventure.

Beyond writing, Susie is a lifelong crafter who knits, crochets, quilts, does machine embroidery, and her newest passion: 3D printing. She finds joy in creating with her hands. She also keeps a planted aquarium—a mini underwater world she calls her "living art."

Susie lives in California with her husband, three dogs, and five cats (all of whom believe they run the household). Whether she's writing, crafting, or watching the magic of an aquarium, she's always dreaming up the next story.

**Connect with Susie on the web**
Email: susie@susieswenson.com
Goodreads:
https://www.goodreads.com/author/show/58646125.Susie_Swenso
n
Instagram: https://www.instagram.com/susieswensonauthor/
Amazon Author Page:
https://www.amazon.com/author/susieswenson
Pinterest: https://www.pinterest.com/susieswensonauthor/

Susie Swenson, author of the Havenwood Cove Cozy Mysteries

www.ingramcontent.com/pod-product-compliance
Lightning Source LLC
Chambersburg PA
CBHW071526110726
47908CB00003B/954